STARFOLK RISING

ALSO BY MARTHA DUNLOP

The Starfolk Trilogy

The Starfolk Arcana

Starfolk Falling

Wild Shadow

Subscribe at www.marthadunlop.com
to hear about new releases first,
and receive a free copy of

STARFOLK ILLUSIONS

A Starfolk prequel.

STARFOLK RISING

BOOK 3 OF THE STARFOLK TRILOGY

MARTHA DUNLOP

Produced and published in November 2023 by
TanLea Books, www.tanleabooks.com.

ISBN 978-1-913788-09-4 (paperback)
ISBN 978-1-913788-10-0 (ebook)

Cover design by Ravven, www.ravven.com
Edited by Kathryn Cottam,
Copy edited by Eleanor Leese, www.eleanorleese.com

www.marthadunlop.com

For Helen

PREVIOUSLY IN THE STARFOLK TRILOGY

CONTAINS SPOILERS FOR BOOKS 1 & 2

The Fear began in a TV Studio in St Albans, England.

Event planner and psychic, Beth Meyer, was in the audience as the celebrity guest, Amelia Faustus, told a bizarre tale of paranormal attack by mysterious entities called Soul Snatchers. Beth couldn't understand why people fell for Amelia's obvious scare stories or why she, herself, was immune. Only Jonan, the man with the violet eyes, didn't buy into the illusion.

How could a man she had never seen before feel so familiar? Beth's instant connection to Jonan began to make sense as she got to know him and discovered they had loved each other throughout multiple lifetimes and across dimensions. But in each life, someone always came between them: Amelia.

In this life, a young Jonan walked away from an affair with Amelia, one of his mother's best friends. But Amelia never truly let him go. Her love for him warped into something sinister, leaving her determined to stop Jonan and Beth finding true happiness. But Jonan wasn't Beth's only soul connection: she discovered a brother, and a mother, in another dimension - Salu and Lunea, who offered her strength and guidance.

Amelia came to Earth as a member of the Triad, one of three women – Amelia, Doriel and Miranda – with a big destiny. But she never recovered from being rejected by Jonan and losing his mother, Miranda's, friendship as a result. Amelia walked away from the Triad and her destiny. As an act of revenge, she started a relationship with Jonan's brother, Roland. But Roland's relationship with Amelia faltered as he started to realise how dangerous she was. He finally left her and found his way back to his family, as well as developing feelings for Layla.

When Amelia hired Beth to arrange a high-profile launch event in a haunted hotel for her protection racket, Amelia's Haven, Beth, Jonan and Amelia were thrown together. Amelia accused Jonan of leading the Soul Snatchers and of kidnapping Doriel, his aunt, and Bill, the caretaker at the hotel. Jonan and Beth rescued the captives, pulling them from Amelia's basement prison cell. But her violence was more than physical and neither Doriel nor Bill bounced back. As Beth and Jonan did their best to protect them from her onslaught, they were forced to recognise that they couldn't fix everything themselves.

Beth and Jonan hired Layla to help them provide a safe space for people targeted by Amelia. But Layla turned out to be more than a contractor. Along with her daughter, Abi, Layla quickly became part of the family. But when Abi was attacked by the children at school and ended up in hospital, Layla's loyalty to the group fractured. Swamped by fear and fury she left to protect her daughter, leaving Roland heartbroken.

Amelia's support was waning too: Beth's old flatmate, Laura, one of Amelia's first followers began to question her idol. Another follower, Steve, had enough of doing Amelia's dirty work. When they started to develop feelings for one another, and decided to work together against their guru, Amelia realised she had made a tactical error.

Jonan and Beth knew that they and their soul family were the only ones who could stop Amelia. Only by disarming her for good could they bring their loved ones back and be together at last.

But as we meet them, fate is pulling them in different directions. Beth has to go to Layla and Abi to help them heal. Meanwhile, Jonan and Roland have to find a way to get through to Amelia by giving her what she wants: Beth out of Jonan's life.

Will it work, or are they simply playing into her agenda?

1

BETH

THE LAST THING SHE WANTED TO DO WAS SAY GOODBYE.

The platform at the City Station was packed with rush hour traffic, commuters staring at their phones, coffee clutched in cold hands. The ground shook as a train whizzed past. People swayed back on their heels but didn't look up.

Beth closed her eyes for a moment, wishing she were anywhere but here. Jonan squeezed her hand and she took in a deep, shuddering breath. Meeting his gaze, she lost herself in the deep purple of his eyes. How could she walk away and leave him to face Amelia alone?

Strong as he was, Jonan's history with Amelia made him particularly susceptible to her psychic manipulations, and she had got to him more than once. Beth had been able to help him throw off her influence, but could he do that if she weren't here?

'I'll be fine.' He smiled. 'I've spent a lifetime dealing with Amelia. Focus on Layla. Help her. Then come back to me as soon as you can.'

'I hope she's receptive to me turning up like this.' Beth sighed. 'It could take a long time to get anywhere if she won't talk to me.'

'It's not you she's angry with. She ran away to escape Amelia. Don't forget that.'

'But won't I just remind her of Amelia, and of how much damage that woman did to Abi?'

Jonan smiled. 'Abi won't let her keep you at arm's length for long. Just be yourself. Be her friend.'

A wave of muttering engulfed the platform. Beth looked up at the monitor. Train delayed. She let out her breath in a rush. 'A reprieve, for a moment at least. What will you do while I'm gone?'

Jonan rubbed his forehead. 'God knows. Roland knows her better than I do now, and he's good at reading people. We'll put our heads together and figure something out. But, Beth, one way or another we *will* sort this.'

'I know.' She took his hand in hers and squeezed. 'So will I. We will each play our parts, and then I will come home to you.'

The train pulled up and Beth swallowed. People surged forwards, only reluctantly allowing passengers to disembark. Beth hung back, grateful for the excuse to delay, but she had barely taken a breath before the doors beeped a warning that they were about to close.

Jonan picked up her case, put it inside the carriage, and then pulled her into a tight hug. 'Call me. And don't fall in love with Bournemouth,' he said, his eyes bright as she stepped into the carriage.

She smiled. 'I won't. Don't let Amelia get to you.'

He blew her a kiss as the doors closed between them.

Jonan disappeared from view. She turned on the spot, but the train was crammed full of people and there was nowhere to go. This was going to be a long journey.

2

BETH

Beth climbed out of the taxi and stood on the pavement. It was a busy Thursday lunchtime and Southbourne Grove was bustling with cafes full to bursting, people spilling onto pavement tables, sipping coffee and eating sandwiches while tapping on their phones. Beth had expected a tourist spot, but this was real life, shot through with sunshine and the tang of sea air.

The bookshop looked warm and inviting. Beth took a deep breath, opened the door and walked inside. Layla was serving a customer at the till, but she looked up when Beth walked in, her eyes widening. She rummaged in a cupboard for something, but her gaze kept flickering to Beth.

Walking further into the shop and dragging her suitcase behind her, Beth pretended to focus on a stack of books, giving the woman time to gather herself.

She scanned the shelves. Maps, books of local walks and notebooks. She wished her impulse had led her to a fiction aisle, but she took down a book of walks and started flicking through. There were glossy, colourful photographs of the beach, the New Forest and a gorgeous river. If she was going to spend time here without her own home to retreat to, maybe this book would be worth getting after all.

'Can I help you?'

Beth turned.

Layla was pale, her hands clenched into fists at her sides. 'Would you like that?' She gestured to the book in Beth's hands.

Beth nodded. 'Are you okay? Is Abi okay?'

Layla let out a long, slow exhale. 'I found a nice local school for Abi. She's happy. It's better than the other place, at least.' Layla's lips pinched at the memory of the school where Abi had been bullied so badly by Amelia's followers that she took a fall onto concrete from a high climbing frame. Abi had recovered, but Beth's friendship with Layla was still on the rocks because Layla blamed Beth and Jonan for bringing Abi to the attention of Amelia's Haven.

'And you?' Beth reached for her hand, but Layla jerked it back.

'That doesn't matter. Abi is safe. That's all that counts.'

Beth nodded. 'You said you were going to stay with your parents.'

Layla shrugged. We started out there, but I found a flat. It's lovely being near them and Abi enjoys seeing so much of her grandparents. I'm not sure how I'd manage without them, to be honest. I need the childcare so I can work enough hours to keep us.'

They wandered back to the till and Layla rang up the book.

Beth paid and then waited while Layla got a paper bag and slid it inside.

'What about your branding career?' she asked, trying to make herself sound casual, but knowing she fell way short.

Layla shrugged. 'Obviously I'm keeping an eye out for branding work, but in the meantime, Abi and I need to eat. This place has been great for me. We're making nice friends.' She handed Beth the bag. 'Look, Beth, it's nice catching up, but what are you doing here? I can't believe you came all this way for a book on Dorset walks.'

Beth sighed. 'Could we talk properly? Do you have a break coming up?'

'You came because of me, didn't you?'

'Of course I did. We've been worried about you. You weren't okay when you left, and we didn't want you to be isolated. I've come to offer support.'

Layla glared at her. 'Look. I know you're not letting go of things with Amelia, and I know you think Abi and I play into your big destiny somehow. But I'm not going back just to fill a spot in your personal crusade. Amelia harmed my child. Nothing you or Jonan can say will change that. I don't believe in gurus. I know that's what you're trying to become, but we all have to make our own decisions and take responsibility for our choices.'

'I don't want to become a guru.' Beth shrugged. 'That's Amelia's game plan, not mine. I don't want followers or an audience. I just want to stop Amelia from hurting anyone else. I want to show people they can find wisdom within themselves rather than having to follow some celebrity who pretends to know it all. Anyway, my visit isn't about destiny. It's about making sure my friend is okay. It's about me missing you and Abi and, if I'm entirely honest, it's also because Roland is in love with you, and he's been a mess since you left. You asked him not to follow you and he's respecting that. So I'm here instead.'

Layla's eyes narrowed and she clutched the edge of the reception desk, her shoulders hunched. 'You're here because of Roland? Not because you want my help to get in Amelia's face?'

Beth stepped backwards. 'Yes, but I can see I've upset you. That wasn't my intention. I'm going to leave now, but I'll be around for a couple of days. If you'd like to chat, get a drink or do something fun together, let me know. It would be lovely to spend time with you and Abi. I've missed you. My phone number hasn't changed. If I don't hear from you, I'll leave you alone. I promise.' She walked out the door and down the road to her B&B, not letting herself turn to look back.

3

JONAN

JONAN'S KNEES HURT. HE HAD SWEPT A PATCH OF FLOOR FREE of glass and crystal, but he'd obviously not done a good enough job and sharp fragments were forcing their way through his jeans into his skin.

He wanted to ditch, throw a tantrum and storm out of the shop, or just vac the lot up with an industrial sized machine. But there were still some intact crystals amongst the mess, so he was going to have to fish them out one by one.

Doriel wasn't helping. She was trying, in her own way, but getting down on her hands and knees and fishing through shards of glass and stone definitely wasn't her thing. Instead, she was making endless cups of tea, reorganising the shelves and alphabetising the books. He was pretty sure she was only here to keep him company, but all he really wanted was to be by himself so he could wallow.

Doriel padded over, crouched down and put a hand on his arm. 'She'll come back to you. I know she will.'

Jonan sighed and stood up. 'I know she will too, but it may not be soon. My shop has been trashed. Again. I have to deal with an ex-girlfriend who's tried to have me arrested, has illegally imprisoned my girlfriend and my aunt on two separate occasions, and has kicked my brother out of his home onto the street. I reserve the right to be annoyed.'

Doriel walked over to the desk, sat on the stool behind it and started shuffling a tarot deck.

'Oh for goodness sake, Doriel. Tarot isn't the answer to everything. Sometimes real life is just too much.'

'What can I do, Jonan?' Doriel spread her arms. 'You're not okay. I can see it. I may not have birthed you, but in every other way I am your mother, and I want to make the pain stop. What can I do?'

He shrugged. 'Make Amelia back off. When she stops, Beth and Layla will come home. Amelia used to be your best friend. You were virtually sisters. But when Mum walked away, you gave up. I'm putting everything on the line to sort this mess, but neither you nor Mum are doing anything to help. What are you going to do to fix this so Beth, Layla and Abi can come home? What are you going to do to bring us all back together again?'

'I wish I could do this for you, but ...'

'For *me*?' Jonan stood up, putting his hands on his hips and squaring up to her. 'Do this for me? You used to tell me the Triad was your destiny, your purpose. What's happened to that?'

'It ended when the Triad broke apart. My destiny has changed irrevocably.'

'It doesn't have to be this way,' he said from between gritted teeth. 'Mum blamed me; she said I had smashed our lives to pieces. But there was no need for you to fracture everything because of Amelia and me. That incident could have been a small, embarrassing blip in my history rather than a life-defining crisis. But you and Mum chose to let a teenage boy's stupid fling change the course of all our lives. You allowed pride and irritation to derail us all and blamed me for it. I've lived with that guilt for far too long. It's time for you and Mum to shoulder your share of what went wrong.'

Doriel swallowed. 'I understand you're angry.'

'Do you? Do you really? Because you're allowing Roland and I to make the sacrifices all over again.'

'Have you forgotten who was abducted and locked in a cellar?' Doriel's voice was brittle. 'Have you forgotten who gave up the life she had chosen when the Triad broke apart? Miranda chose to go into seclusion, but I was happy being the Oracle. I never dreamed of being a mother, but I stepped into that role when I was needed. For you. What makes you so sure you're the only one who has made sacrifices? I know you're upset Beth has gone, but it's temporary. She's coming back. I bet Roland envies you that. Stop moping and start putting all that brain power into figuring out how to get Amelia to back off. I will help you, of course I will. But if you choose to focus on being broken, that is how you will stay. If you want your life to mend, fix it.'

Jonan swallowed. He closed his eyes for a moment and took in a deep breath. 'You're right. I'm sorry. We've all had a rough time. I'll be okay. I just need to get my head together and figure out what to do.'

Doriel picked her way through the glass and reached up on her tiptoes to kiss his forehead. 'You take as long as you need, my darling. I will always be here for you, whenever you need me. And I promise not to get the tarot cards out unless you ask.' She winked, put the deck next to the till and went upstairs.

4

JONAN

Jonan started sweeping up the mess. Any crystals left on the floor would have to fend for themselves. He had to persuade Amelia to abandon this ridiculous feud and leave him alone. What had possessed him to agree to solving this before Beth came home? The only way to get her to back off would be for Beth to stay away forever and that was definitely not an option.

But perhaps he could concede defeat in another way and allow Amelia to save face? Maybe if he agreed to ignore Amelia's Haven, she would leave them alone? He stared out the window at the streams of people walking past. Many looked furtively in at the window, flushing as they met his gaze. The riot Amelia caused in the shop had been covered by the national media. For a while, Amelia's attention had brought them extra custom. But could his business survive if she kept attacking it like this? Goodness knows how long they would be out of action while they got the shop back on track.

'So that's it then,' he murmured to himself. 'Leave her be, on the promise that we get our lives back?'

If only it were that simple, a voice said into his mind.

Jonan slumped and then turned slowly.

Salu, Beth's guide and brother from another dimension, had manifested fully and was sitting on the stool behind the desk. *You know I can't let you give up now.*

'You can't stop me either.'

Salu sighed. *We both know that's true. The choice is yours. And Beth's. What would Beth say if she were here? Would she give up on the destiny you've so enthusiastically sold her?*

'But she's not here, is she?' Jonan sat down and crossed his arms over his chest. 'That's the point. She's coming home when I've persuaded Amelia to back off, but I have no hope of doing that. This destiny is too heavy. I can't do it anymore.'

You have more hope of getting through to Amelia than anyone else. Salu shrugged. *She loves you. She wants your approval and affection. You have been denying her that and for good reason, but maybe if you gave her friendship she would respond in kind?*

'Friendship? You think that's what Amelia wants from me?' Jonan chuckled, but even he could hear how flat the sound was.

Salu sighed again. *Maybe not. But my question still stands. What would Beth do?*

Jonan rolled his eyes. He didn't have the energy for this. 'She would stick to the plan. She'd tell me Amelia wouldn't give up, even if I did. And the only way to make ourselves safe is to tackle this head-on.'

Salu said nothing.

'So of course that's what I'll have to do, because otherwise Amelia might target Beth to get at me.'

Salu nodded.

'But that doesn't move me forward; it puts me back to step one. I do not know how to stop Amelia.'

'And do you know anyone who does? Anyone who's spent the last few years with her?'

'You think Roland has the answer? You don't think he would have mentioned it by now?'

Salu shrugged. *Why don't you give him another chance?*

'You don't let up, do you?' Jonan stood up and grabbed the keys from the hook behind the desk. He opened the door at the bottom of the stairs. 'Doriel, I'm going to see Roland.'

'Have fun!' she shouted, and then he heard her singing. Pulling the door shut, he waved to Salu, before realising he had disappeared already. 'So now you've got what you wanted, you've left me to handle it all by myself,' he muttered. 'Thanks a lot.' Pulling his collar up, he headed out into the street, slamming the door behind him.

5

ROLAND

ROLAND HUMMED AS HE UNPACKED, SLOWLY TAKING ONE SHIRT out of the case, putting it on a hanger, and placing it carefully in the scruffy, built-in wardrobe. He went back for another, playing for time, stretching out each action to maintain the sense of feeling busy.

He'd lived with Amelia his entire adult life. She had everything, so he'd never needed much. Now, unpacking his meagre possessions in this old Victorian house, he was beginning to realise how little impact he had made on his own life.

He took out the white suit she loved so much. He had always hated it. He only wore it to please her. Now it just reminded him of that first time he'd seen Beth and Jonan at the Monk's Inn. He winced, remembering how obnoxious he'd been. He'd been so angry on his own behalf and Amelia's. Even then he had known something wasn't right with her, but loyalty and duty had such a strong grip he couldn't see past his outrage.

He put the suit in the charity shop pile.

Picking up a box of kitchenware, he went downstairs and put it on the worktop. He lifted out a saucepan, looked at it, and then put it back down. Turning his back on the kitchen, he went through to the living room and slumped on the sofa. Leaning back, he closed his eyes. He could almost hear them here. Layla calling up the stairs telling Abi to get ready for school. Abi giggling, hiding behind the curtain during a game of hide and seek, not realising her feet were sticking out at the bottom. Abi and Layla laughing and singing. Behind the threads of memory embedded in the building itself was profound silence. The occasional roar of a car was a welcome release from the oppression of emptiness. How was he going to fill this space on his own? There wasn't enough of him left to turn this into a home.

Feeling a lump digging into his back, he reached around and pulled a cuddly leopard from between the cushions, its fur deep and thick, face friendly. 'Ah, Abi,' he murmured. 'I really miss you too.'

He put the leopard on the back of the sofa and went upstairs. He had claimed the master bedroom for himself, but there was another good-sized double bedroom and a generous single room with a gorgeous view over the garden. He put his hand flat on the wall. 'Maybe I should turn this into a bedroom for Abi. Surely they'll come back soon? One day, maybe?' The walls were immaculately decorated. This can't have been her bedroom. She would have made more of an impact on the paintwork.

He went into the second double bedroom. That was also beautifully done out, but there was a small leopard drawn in a child's hand on the skirting board by the door.

Roland crouched down and traced the cat with a finger. A series of images flickered through his mind. A huge white tiger and a sleek leopard running through a nearby forest. A shiver shot down his spine. *I wonder if my paints have any life left in them?* He thought as he stood up. *It's so long since I've used them, but I can see it on that wall ...* He stood back and eyed the space. Excitement shot through him and he all but ran to his bedroom, pulling down a case from above the wardrobe and taking out his large and well-loved set of oil paints. Once upon a time he had lived to paint. But when everything fell apart, his energy went into pretending to be an adult for Amelia. He'd forgotten what made him happy.

Shutting the suitcase, he carried it into the hall. He paused for a moment outside the small room and then shook his head. If he really wanted to manifest Layla and Abi in his life, he should put them first. Abi would need room to play.

Going back into the big room, he took out a graphite pencil and started to sketch the line of the cats on the wall. He drew the head of the tiger, and then shivered. He saw something move out of the corner of his eye and turned to look. For a moment, he saw a white tiger, but then it was gone. *My imagination is getting the better of me.* He rubbed out the line without thinking. *Now, why did I do that?* He started again, drawing the head in one fluid motion. It was nothing like his usual style, but as he sketched, the cat took on a life and fluidity of its own.

The drawing lulled him into a trance state. Images flickered through his mind and movements caught in his peripheral vision, but he didn't stop. Even when something soft settled by his feet, he kept going.

It was dark when he woke from dreams of tigers and leopards. He yawned and stretched, reaching up to turn on the light.

As his eyes focused on the images on the wall, he gasped. The cats were huge and so life-like they seemed about to leap off the wall. As proud as he had always been of his art, he knew this was beyond his talent. Would Abi be frightened of them? No. He thought about the leopard on the skirting board. He had an unshakable certainty that Abi would understand. He would say they were her guardians, there to protect her while she slept and played.

He cleared up his paints and shut the door carefully behind him, as though something was sleeping in there. He had no idea what had just happened, but he couldn't wait to see whether it would take hold again tomorrow.

THE NEXT MORNING, ROLAND PUT OFF GOING INTO THE bedroom. The evening before had merged into the strange dreamscape that had dominated his sleeping hours and he couldn't put his finger on what had been real. Would the pictures of the cats be there when he opened the door? And if they were, could he do them justice? He drank his coffee and ate his breakfast, wishing he had someone to talk to, to laugh over the strange experience and help him settle into the harsh reality of morning. He thought about Jonan. They'd never had an adult relationship, but maybe now was their moment.

With a sigh, he pushed his plate away and picked up his mug. He would need fortification to face whatever damage he had done to that poor room. Going upstairs, his legs were heavy with exhaustion. He paused at the door, his heart pounding. Then he pushed the door open and stepped inside.

The room had a lightness that flushed through him, wiping away any dread. He turned to look at the cats and gasped. They were beautiful. He hadn't known he could create something so powerful. This was the beginning of a special room for Abi, and by the time he'd finished it would be even better.

6

BETH

BETH PULLED ON HER COAT AS SHE STEPPED OUT OF THE crystal supplier's warehouse and walked through the carpark towards the town centre. She didn't know much about crystals, but that place had been a treasure trove. Pulling her phone out of her pocket, she scrolled through the images and sent some to Jonan. She'd got pictures of all the main pieces she had bought based on his instructions. It had been like running up a tab at a toyshop. Reaching into her pocket, she took out the one thing she had bought for herself. A small, quartz tiger, stripes carved into its back, tiny teeth bared in a snarl. She had always loved tigers, but this particular one had screamed at her to take it home.

She smiled as she slipped it back into her pocket, buckled the belt on her coat and strode towards the centre of Bournemouth.

It was a Friday afternoon, but the town centre felt flat. The shoppers seemed used up, as though the life had already been wrung out of them. She wandered past shops, cafes and restaurants, but was too restless to go inside. Something was tugging her forwards. She fiddled with the crystal tiger in her pocket as the sense of urgency increased.

Turning down a side street, she stopped in front of a gift shop. There was a print of a white tiger in the window, and she reached up, touching the glass with her fingertips. Taking the crystal out of her pocket, she looked from one to the other. 'What is it with big cats today?'

On impulse, she went inside. There was a woman behind the counter, pouring over an account book. Otherwise, the place was empty.

'Could I find out about the picture of the tiger in the window please?' Beth smiled as the woman looked up.

'What do you want to know? It's a print of a painting by Tara McLaughlin. Do you know her? She's famous for painting tigers. She's with that singer. What's his name ...'

'Dylan McKenzie,' Beth said, her voice rough, the sense of synchronicity building. 'I was listening to him this morning.'

'Yes, well. That's one of hers. Would you like it? It's only a print, obviously. The originals are worth tens of thousands.'

'How much is it?'

'Fifty pounds. More if you want it framed.'

'I'll take it as is, please.' Beth felt a stab of excitement.

The woman took the print from the window, went back behind the desk and started wrapping it. Beth wandered around the shop as she waited, looking at the delicate, silver jewellery, mugs painted with seabirds, and a display of ornaments. On one of the shelves, she found a tiny set of filigree silver scales. Picking them up, she turned them over, admiring the fine latticed metalwork. They were so light, but sturdier than she had expected.

'Your picture is ready. Would you like anything else?' The

woman raised one eyebrow and the reminder of Jonan sent a shiver down Beth's spine. God, she missed him.

Beth strode over to the desk and put the tiny scales next to the wrapped picture. 'Just these please.'

The woman's smile was smug as she wrapped the scales and rang up Beth's purchases. 'Thank you for coming in,' she said as Beth picked up the bag and made her way through the narrow walkway to the door. 'I hope you come back soon.'

'I bet you do,' Beth muttered under her breath. She was just heading towards the coffee shop on the other side of the street when her phone rang. Pulling it out of her pocket she looked at the screen and grinned.

'Is that you, Beth?' Layla's voice was bright.

'It is. I was hoping you might call.'

'Look.' Layla took a deep breath. 'I'm sorry. I overreacted. Would you like to come over? I'm at home all afternoon and Abi would love to see you.'

'I'm on my way now.' Beth picked up her pace. 'I'm in town. Do you need anything?'

'Hey!' A woman on the street grabbed Beth's arm and spun her around. 'Amelia warned us about you.' Putting her fingers in her mouth, she let off a shrill whistle. A hush descended as people stopped to watch. The traffic was suddenly loud and intrusive. 'This woman is a *Soul Snatcher*!'

Beth stepped back.

'Oh God,' Layla said on the other end of the phone. 'Is that aimed at you? Are you anywhere near a taxi rank? Make a run for it.'

'I'll be fine.' Beth forced herself to smile. 'I'll be with you soon.' Hanging up, she slid her phone into her pocket. Small and wiry, the woman's angular face was drawn into a scowl.

'You shouldn't be here.' The woman said, projecting her

voice out to the growing crowd. 'We don't need your type. You bring trouble.'

'I'm not causing any trouble.' Beth held up her shopping bag. 'I've been spending money in the local shops and now I'm going to visit my friend. Don't look for problems where there aren't any.'

The woman leaned in, puffing herself up to appear as big as possible. 'You think *I'm* causing trouble?'

Beth veered back as the stench of stale beer and garlic hit her in the face. 'I just want to go about my business. My friend is waiting for me. She'll be worried if I don't turn up.'

'Your friend is right to worry.' The woman crowded Beth, her words harsh and gravelly through gritted teeth. 'You are not welcome here.'

'Then let me leave.' Beth willed her to move backwards, pushing out her energy in an attempt to expel the woman from her space.

The woman swayed on her feet. She stumbled, the movement exaggerated as she lurched backwards. 'What are you doing?' She turned around and stretched her arms wide. 'Do you see? She's manipulating my soul, trying to get in where she's not wanted.' Spinning around, she slapped Beth, hard.

'Urgh.' Beth reeled backwards. 'What was that for?'

'You are not welcome.'

There was a crowd gathering. 'You are not welcome,' a voice repeated from the centre of the throng. 'With me,' it called and then again, 'you are not welcome,' over and over, each repetition louder than the last. They leered, laughing at Beth's obvious anxiety.

'Soul Snatcher!' Someone yelled over the noise. More voices joined. Beth wanted to clutch her hands over her ears. Instead, she drew herself up taller and stood her ground.

Her heart was pounding. The woman kept coming, trying to force her towards the road. It was rush hour and the street was fast and busy. She stepped to the right, but the woman followed, trying to force her back towards the traffic.

Beth planted her feet and imagined roots growing into the concrete, grounding herself into the earth below her. *I will not give in*, she told herself as she saw her energy expand and steadied herself. *Salu*, she called in her mind, recognising the boost as he lent her his energy.

The woman faltered and looked around her, suddenly uncertain. 'What are you doing?'

Beth let out a long breath, steady again. 'I'm standing still.'

Someone in the crowd sniggered.

'Do you see what she's doing? She is trying to get into our heads,' the woman shouted, her voice shrill. She turned to the people behind her. 'She wants to steal our souls. But we will not let her.' She launched herself at Beth, roaring at the top of her voice.

Beth stood firm, holding her ground as the woman barrelled into her, arms and legs flailing. She felt Salu's strength at her back and sent out thanks.

The woman collapsed to the ground and started crying in big, strangled sobs, but there were no tears on her cheeks. 'She hit me.' She pointed at Beth. 'Look at me. I'm hurt.'

'No she didn't.' A woman with blue hair pushed her way through the crowd, her phone pointed at Beth and the woman on the floor. 'She didn't touch you and you know it. We all know it.'

'Prove it,' the woman on the ground snarled. 'Prove it when the police come.' She got out her phone and dialled 999.

Panic shot through Beth. She had done nothing wrong, but that might not matter if Amelia had influence here.

'Happy to,' the woman with blue hair nodded at her phone. 'I have the whole thing on video. I'll just wait until they arrive.'

The woman on the ground paled. She tried to hang up the phone.

'Caller, you can't hang up,' a voice came out of the device. 'Caller, please confirm you are okay.'

'I'm fine,' she snapped into the phone, her face blazing. 'It was a mistake.' She hit the screen again, stood up and slid the phone into her pocket.

'You shouldn't be here.' She spat on Beth's feet.

'I'm still filming.' The woman with blue hair stepped closer, her phone held high.

The woman rolled her shoulders, stuck two fingers up and walked away. The rest of the crowd followed, leaving Beth and the woman with blue hair alone.

7

BETH

'Thank you.' Beth let out her breath in a rush. 'Did you really video all that?'

'Yup,' the woman said. 'I'm Rita, by the way. I've had a run in with her before. I know to take precautions. You have to see this video. You're glowing. She bounced up against your glow and fell over! I've never seen anything like it. Do you have similar powers to Amelia?'

'No,' Beth snapped, and then drew in a long breath. 'I'm sorry. You hit a nerve. Amelia deliberately manipulates people's energy to control them. I clear her out of people's energies so they can come from their own truth.'

'You get rid of Amelia's web? I wouldn't mind help with that. A friend persuaded me to go to an Amelia's Haven meeting and they inducted me. Amelia wasn't even there, but I've not been right since. Can you get her out of my system?'

Beth looked at Rita, narrowing her eyes. She could see the grey cords looping around her, but they were faint. 'You've fought it well. I wouldn't have spotted it in you, particularly with the way you stood up to that woman. But what makes you think you can trust me? You've already been messed with once.'

'I've been following you online. I saw that interview on *Deep and Dark*. You've been standing up to Amelia from the start.'

Beth looked around. 'Could you meet me at the bookshop on Southbourne Grove tomorrow at 4 p.m.? I'll find a safe place for us to work.'

'Thank you,' Rita blew her a kiss and waved as she walked off down the street.

Beth watched her go, breathing deeply in an attempt to get her heart rate back to normal. She hadn't expected anyone to know who she was here, but apparently notoriety had followed her. She was going to have to make sure she kept any negativity away from Layla and Abi.

She tried to hail a taxi, but it drove right past. Pulling out her phone, she searched for taxi companies and called the first one that came up. Moments later, a yellow cab pulled up at the side of the road. She opened the door.

'Beth?' the taxi driver said.

She climbed in. 'Southbourne Grove please.'

The man nodded as she did up her seatbelt. Leaning her head back, she closed her eyes for a moment. She wished Jonan was here. Facing that crowd had brought back a lot of memories from Amelia's attacks. She was getting so tired of it all.

She stared out the window as they travelled back along the sea front, watching the sun go down. It started to rain and she shivered, wishing she had her own home to go back to. She wondered what kind of reception she would get from

Layla. Had things really changed that much? An image of Abi flashed into her mind and she smiled. If Abi wanted them to make up, she was pretty sure Layla wouldn't have the heart to say no.

8

AMELIA

'THEY'LL LAP US UP.' ROBSON FALL KNOCKED BACK HIS VODKA and slammed his shot glass down on the huge table, before refilling it. '*Deep and Dark* is the perfect show for us. With my following, and yours, they'll be begging us to go back over and over. It's the perfect way to get into people's heads.'

'Are you struggling to reach people?' Amelia smirked, reaching for the monks with her mind and calling them to the ballroom. Immediately, the cold crept towards them from the edges of the room. 'I wouldn't have thought you'd be so reliant on a show to get into people's heads. I can't say I've ever found it that hard myself.'

'Don't underestimate the importance of the media.' Robson's glare was steely and his smile as fake as the colour of his black hair.

Amelia rolled her eyes. 'Don't lecture me on the media. They can't get enough of me.'

'Amelia?' Rose said from the door to the ballroom, her face pale. Her gaze darted around the room and she reached out, closing her fingers over the back of a wooden chair, knuckles whitening.

'What is it?' Amelia knocked back her own drink.

'I called *Deep and Dark*. They're not interested.'

Amelia swallowed.

Rob was frowning at Rose. He stood up and walked over to her, standing too close and leering down at her. 'What did they say, Rose, darling? Why did they not want us? Was there any way we could incentivise them?'

Rose inched backwards. 'They didn't give me enough time to find out. I only got through to an admin assistant. She had strict instructions not to talk to anyone from your office.'

Rob frowned and stepped closer, putting one hand on her shoulder. 'Whose office, darling? Who are they angry with? Me, or Amelia?'

A single tear trailed down her cheek. She swallowed again, her face pale even in the artificial light. 'Amelia. Katherine Haversham has blacklisted you,' she said staring at the floor.

'Blacklisted? Me?' Amelia knew her voice was shrill, but she was too angry to care. 'Why would she blacklist me? My last visit was a triumph!'

'I spoke to my friend on the set,' Rose said, her voice so quiet Amelia could barely hear. 'Katherine hasn't been herself since you went on the show. She has banned anyone from mentioning you in her presence.'

'Is that so?' A thrill shot through Amelia and the fury calmed. She had got to Katherine. It shouldn't be too hard to turn this around if she was already that deep under the woman's skin. 'In that case, keep working on them. They'll let me in eventually. Tell them I will run a special Amelia's

Haven event here, just for them. They can broadcast it live. They'll love that. They won't be able to resist.'

'I wouldn't be so sure, darling.' Rob sauntered back to the table, sat down and trailed his fingertips over the back of her hand.

Amelia shuddered.

Rob grinned. 'If you're out of favour you'll need more than a little exclusive to get their attention. I'll talk to them about you. Big you up. I can sort it out. Don't you worry yourself about it.'

Amelia raised one eyebrow. 'Don't worry myself about it? Do you work hard to be that patronising, or does it come naturally, Rob?'

He flushed, the skin on his neck turning bright pink and the colour seeping up to his face. 'There's no need for that.' He picked up his phone, dialled a number and put it on loudspeaker.

'*Deep and Dark*,' an irritated voice said on the other end of the phone.

'Stephanie, darling. It's Robson Fall. I'd love to chat to you about coming on the show. It's been far too long.'

'You were on two weeks ago.' The voice was deadpan.

Rob flushed again. 'Well ... I connect so well with your audience. And these are tough times. I can give people the support they need.'

'Not interested. As long as you're allied with Amelia, you won't be coming on *Deep and Dark*.' She slammed the phone down.

Amelia held Rob's gaze. His face was dark purple now, his eyes blazing fire. His lower jaw protruded and he hung on to the edge of the table with a death grip.

'You were supposed to help me get more coverage,' he

said from between gritted teeth. 'This was supposed to be a strategic alliance for both of us. Fix this, or I will be calling my lawyers and telling them to limit the damage. You won't like what they send your way.'

Fear shot through Amelia, but she painted a smile on her face. 'Honestly, why so dramatic? We've got into Katherine's head. Before you know it, she'll be reliant on me. You have nothing to worry about.'

'You'd better be right.' All traces of Rob's usual cloying desperation were gone. In its place was a meanness that shocked even Amelia. She thought she was the tough one. But Robson Fall would be a pain in her backside if she didn't manage her way out of this mess, and soon.

9

BETH

Beth stood outside Layla's flat and smoothed down her clothes. If she couldn't get through to Layla now, there wasn't much point in staying in Bournemouth.

She knocked on the door, her adrenaline spiking as Layla's footsteps approached. Then the door opened and Layla stood there, her face pale, brown hair tucked behind her ears.

Beth tried to smile. 'It's good to see you.'

'I'm so sorry about earlier.' Layla pulled Beth into a hug. 'Come in. Make yourself at home.'

Relief washed through Beth. 'Thank you. I've missed you. Both of you. How's Abi?'

'Beth!' Abi ran through the flat and threw herself into Beth's arms. 'I've missed you so much. Is Doriel here?'

Beth stroked the hair out of Abi's eyes. 'No, honey, she didn't want to crowd you after what happened. But she did give me something for you.' Beth reached into her handbag and pulled out the greetings card and wrapped gift covered in ribbons and bows.

'Wow, aren't you lucky!' Layla said, 'What do you say, darling?'

'Thank you.' Abi was breathless. 'Can I open it in my room please?'

Layla nodded and the little girl ran off, clutching the gift to her chest.

Layla led Beth into a small, cosy living room with an open-plan kitchen on one side and a soft, deep red sofa in front of a TV. There was a huge window on one side, looking out over a small but mature garden, deep in trees and large shrubs.

'Is that your space?' Beth nodded towards the window. 'It's lovely.'

Layla smiled and put the kettle on. 'No, the woman who owns this building lives on the ground floor. That's her garden. She does occasionally let Abi play out there, but it's not the same as being able to go out whenever we want. Still, we have the beach nearby and there's a park in the sand that Abi loves. It's a good place for us to heal.'

Beth took the cup of tea Layla handed her and sat on the sofa. 'And are you? Healing that is? Is this far enough from Amelia to escape her influence?'

'Sadly no,' Layla sighed. 'Every time I turn on the TV she's there. Every time I go to work I see her calendar for sale. Did you know she's writing a book? It's her story about the Soul Snatchers interspersed with pictures of her, and nuggets of her supposed wisdom. It's going to be dreadful, but I will have to sell it to legions of Amelia's Haven devotees. I might resign before it comes out.'

'I don't blame you.'

Abi skipped in clutching something to her chest. 'Is that

what Doriel gave you, sweetie?' Beth asked, smiling at the obvious pleasure on the girl's face.

She nodded, grinning wide, and held out her hand. A tiny crystal carving of a cat sat in her palm, its face locked in a snarl. 'Look! I wish I could see Doriel.'

Layla flushed. 'One day.' She stood up and gathered the cups. 'Would you like something stronger, Beth?'

Beth nodded. 'I know Doriel would like to see you too, Abi, but we're going to get the bullies to back off before you visit St Albans again.'

'I can look after myself now.' Abi smirked. 'I understand it all. I make things happen when they're in my head. When the bullies pulled me off the climbing frame, I thought something bad was going to happen and it did. But if I think about good things, I will have those instead.'

Beth smiled and patted the sofa next to her. 'That's a lovely idea. We could all do with a bit of that in our lives.'

'You don't understand.' Abi sat down. 'I *actually* make things happen. My friend has been wishing her parents would get back together for ages, but they kept fighting. When she told me, I imagined them as a family and they got back together. Charlotte is so happy.'

'I bet she is.' Beth smiled. 'But you know, it's not your job to fix grown-up problems. Charlotte's parents got back together all by themselves.'

Abi shook her head. 'It wasn't just them. Samina always wanted to win a competition, but she couldn't do it until she told me about it. I pictured her winning an art competition and she did. She was given an actual trophy and money to spend in an art shop.'

'But don't you think maybe Samina was good enough to

win that art competition by herself? If you take the credit, doesn't that mean you don't believe in her?'

'Of course I believe in her.' She pouted. 'That's why I imagined her winning a prize. But it's not just her. Timothy was scared of being chased by a dog, even though it had never happened. But when he told me, I imagined it by accident. I tried so hard to take it back. I pictured it going away over and over again, but I think I made it worse because every time I tried to fix it, I saw it happening again. Then he was chased by a big growly dog and it bit him too. So you see, I make things happen, but I also can't be trusted. I have to force my mind to imagine the right things. If I'm not careful it will be awful for everyone.'

Beth swallowed. 'Abi, darling, I understand what you're saying. And I see that you're scared. But you're not responsible for other people's lives. We all have to be aware of what we create with our minds. Maybe you are particularly good at that, but it doesn't make you all-powerful. And it doesn't make you responsible for things that happen to other people. Never let anyone put that on you. You're a strong girl, sweetie, but you don't hold everything.'

'That's not what Doriel said.' Abi's voice was quiet.

'What was that?' Layla sat on the sofa and took Abi's hands in her own.

'That's not what Doriel said.' Abi spoke loudly this time, looking her mum in the eye. 'She said I make things happen and I have to be careful what I think about. She's right. I know she is.'

'And this is why we're not going back,' Layla snapped.

Abi's eyes opened wide. 'You think it's Doriel's fault?'

'I didn't mean that.' Layla dropped her head into her hands. 'Honestly, pumpkin, I know you're scared, but I don't think this is real. I wish Doriel had never put the idea into your head. Beth's right. You can't control what adults do. You're a child. You should be playing and enjoying life.'

'But I might make something bad happen to you.' Abi knelt on the floor in front of Layla, wrapped her arms around her legs and lay her head in her lap. 'Nothing bad can happen to you. Ever.'

A tear sliding down her cheek, Layla took Abi's arms, untangled them from her legs and pulled the girl up onto her lap, folding her into a big hug. 'Nothing is going to happen to me, darling. You're safe here. We both are.'

10

BETH

THE SUN WAS SETTING OVER THE TREES IN THE GARDEN, painting the sky a vibrant gold. Abi was watching TV, her thumb firmly in her mouth, a white bear clutched under one arm. Layla seemed calm, but the dark circles under her eyes testified to her lack of sleep. She used to be so vibrant, but her colour had faded and it broke Beth's heart to see.

'I could help.' Beth kept her voice soft so Abi wouldn't hear. 'If I cleared Amelia's influence from you, you would still do the right thing by Abi. You would keep her safe just as you always have. But you would feel better, and Abi would be happier knowing you were okay.'

Layla swallowed. 'But I didn't do the right thing by Abi, did I? You warned me Amelia would put her in danger and I didn't listen. I told you I could handle Amelia, and maybe I could have if Abi had been targeted when I was there. But they got to her at school, Beth, the place I can't protect her. I trusted those teachers with her safety and they let us both down. If I can't put my trust in a school, I have to manage her risk level from outside. And that means minimising the dangers as much as possible.'

'It must be exhausting, trying to protect her when you're not even there, when you can't control what's happening.'

'You have no idea.' A tear slid down Layla's cheek. 'I am tired, Beth, so tired.'

'Then let me help you. Trust yourself. Amelia's Fear makes people lesser versions of themselves. Hanging on to that won't do you any favours, and it won't help Abi either. She needs you, Layla, the whole you.'

Layla took a deep breath and then exhaled slowly. She nodded. 'Okay, you can clear my energy. But not Abi's. Not yet. We could go through to my bedroom to give Abi some space?' She stood up and Beth followed her. The bedroom was almost empty, with just a double bed in the middle of the room, and two suitcases standing propped up against the wardrobe. Layla shrugged. 'I guess I haven't settled here.'

'Maybe you will once we get you back to normal. There's no danger in putting down roots.'

'I can't imagine rooting anywhere at the moment.'

'What's holding you back?'

Layla looked out the window, wrapping her arms tightly around her middle. 'It's been a tough time. Shall I lie down?'

Beth nodded. 'Bring your cushions to this end of the bed so I can stand behind you.' She took out her new scales and her tarot deck, and put them on the box at the foot of the bed. 'Just relax and close your eyes. Don't worry if your stomach rumbles or you go to sleep. Being relaxed is good.'

Layla settled on the bed, clasping her hands loosely over her stomach. Closing her eyes, she slowed her breathing. A moment later she was asleep.

Beth positioned herself behind Layla's head and took a

deep breath, imagining a beam of light surrounding her. She saw a bubble forming around herself, and then a second one around Layla. Finally, she added a big bubble around them both. Layla jerked for a moment, and then sank deeper into the bed. Her eyelids fluttered and then lay still.

In her mind's eye, Beth could see Amelia's cords wrapped around Layla, choking her and tightening around her stomach. There was another looped around her forehead, blocking the third-eye chakra in the middle of her brow. *Help me clear away Amelia's cords.* She sent out the thought, and smiled as first Salu appeared, and then Lunea. They linked hands over Layla and a low hum filled the air. Beth sank into the vibration, as the energy lifted and carried her. She sent her awareness out, seeking each loop of the cords, each undulation as they wove in and out, over, under and around her friend.

Lunea stepped out of the circle and lifted a layer of sludgy energy from Layla. The woman's aura brightened, and Beth felt the change in her own vibration. Lunea took Layla's hands, sending waves of energy from her heart, down her arms and into Layla's palms.

Beth kept working at the cords but as Lunea's energy flowed through Layla, they started to crumble. Then they were gone.

Layla moaned in her sleep and turned onto her side. Her face relaxed, her eyelids fluttered, and she was quiet.

Thank you. Beth sent out the thought to Salu and Lunea. *Thank you for helping her.*

Any time, sister. Salu's voice was deep and lulled Beth, making her eyelids heavy. *This is part of our journey.*

Beth released the bubbles that surrounded them, clearing away any vestiges of energy that had been released. She imagined Layla growing roots into the bed, grounding her even in sleep. Layla shifted and started snoring.

Beth smiled. Picking up her scales and tarot deck she let herself out of the bedroom and closed the door softly behind her. 'What are you watching?' She settled onto the sofa next to Abi, letting out her breath as the deep cushions took her weight.

'It's my favourite film.' Abi snuggled into Beth. 'Watch with me?'

'Of course.' Beth put her arm around Abi, pulling her close. Her eyelids were heavy and she allowed them to close.

11

BETH

'COME ON, DARLING.'

Beth heard the words through a thick fog of sleep, but it was receding. A weight lifted from her side, and she felt a shot of cool air as Abi was spirited away. Beth yawned, stretched and sat up. Nodding towards the kitchen, Layla carried Abi through to her bedroom.

Beth stood up and turned to look where Layla had pointed. There was a bottle of red wine, two empty glasses, and a bowl of crisps sitting on the work surface. Beth poured the wine and carried the crisps to the coffee table. She flicked through the channels on TV, but there was nothing that could hold her attention. She was still high on the buzz from the energy work and could sense Salu nearby.

Layla came back into the room and walked over to the worktop. She filled her glass almost to the brim and then sat on the sofa next to Beth.

'That was interesting.' She took a gulp of wine and slumped back into the sofa.

'What did you feel?'

'I dreamed there was a rush of energy, and then I felt beings nearby. There was a woman who lifted something heavy from me, and then took my hands. Energy flowed into me from her, lighting me up. It was incredible.'

Beth smiled. 'That was Lunea.'

'In that case, I see why Jonan named the shop after her. She's spectacular.' Layla swallowed. 'How is Roland?' Her voice was small now.

'He was beside himself when you left. He's lost so much, but when you were there he had hope for the future. Now that's gone.'

Layla paled. 'You don't pull your punches.'

'Because I love you both, and I can see you're miserable. If you had been happy, I would have kept my mouth shut.'

Layla sighed and took another gulp of wine.

Beth reached for her hand. 'If you ever did want to come back, there would always be a job for you at Lunea. You're one of us, Layla, Abi too. We may not be able to pay the wage you deserve as a designer, but if you just need a job, and a family, we're there for you. Always.'

Layla smiled. 'Thank you. That means more than you can possibly know. I remember what it felt like to be a part of that family before Abi was attacked. But she *was* attacked. I've learned I'm not the kick-arse goddess I thought I was. I am vulnerable. And right now, Abi is young enough to be even more vulnerable than me. There is nothing I wouldn't give up to protect my daughter. It doesn't matter how I feel about Roland. Abi comes first.'

Beth leaned back on the sofa, crossing her legs in front of her. 'Of course she does. And I totally understand. But you *are* that kick-arse goddess, one way or another.'

A tear slid down Layla's cheek. 'Thank you.'

'How is Abi doing here?'

'She's struggling. I knew she was attached to Doriel, but I hadn't realised how much. She has friends here, but they're not helping her settle. I don't know what to do.'

'Are you making this feel like home?' Beth looked pointedly at the pile of unpacked boxes in one corner of the room.

'You can see I'm not. This move was a big change neither of us wanted. Damn Amelia for putting us in this position.'

Beth smiled. 'Do you feel any better after the energy work?'

Layla nodded. 'Will you help Abi too?'

'I'd love to. Maybe we can get her settled enough to put down roots. I'm sure that would be good for both of you.'

Layla yawned. 'Do you mind if I go to bed? That energy work knocked me out, and I have to get up early tomorrow. I'm sorry I don't have a bedroom for you. Will you be okay on the sofa?'

Beth pulled her into a hug. 'I'm just grateful we've made up.'

Layla drew back, stood up and stretched. 'See you in the morning?'

'See you tomorrow.' Beth watched her go, relieved that her shoulders were relaxed and her energy was clearer. There was no sign now of Amelia's grey cords and for that she was grateful.

Picking up the tiny set of silver filigree scales and the tarot cards she put them on the coffee table. Then she walked to the other side of the room, took the mounted print out of the carrier bag and admired it as she went back to the sofa. Propping it up against the TV, she got out the tarot cards and started shuffling. A single card fell out of the deck. Reaching down, she picked it up and turned it over. Justice.

Her heart sped as she looked at the picture, a woman sitting on a throne, a pair of silver filigree scales in her hands. She leaned on the back of the sofa, looking from the card to the scales that sat on the coffee table.

What am I supposed to make of this? She sent out the thought.

What do you think? Salu materialised next to her on the sofa, his body angled towards hers.

I think there's something significant about scales, and you're trying to get me to figure it out for myself.

Salu suppressed a smile and raised one eyebrow. *And? Have you? Figured it out, I mean?*

Beth sighed. *Not really. This card is about justice, legal matters and balance. You get out what you put in. Am I on the right path?*

Salu tilted his head. *Only on the most basic level. Yes, you are explaining what the card can mean, but not what it means to you.*

And that is?

When you first met Jonan, you discovered you had a connection with a tarot card called Potential, or The Fool. That is a card of beginnings, of innocence. You can't remain at the beginning forever.

Beth stared at the wall, allowing the images of the cards to settle in her mind. *So, I'm changing to Justice just like Doriel changed from The Oracle to Mother?*

Just like? Not really. I'd say it was very different: A growth process rather than an uprooting. What does Justice mean to you?

I hope it means I can regain my balance. I've been swinging from extreme to extreme for too long. I want that to change. Beth sighed, pressing her palms into the sofa.

What does balance mean to you?

It means peace of mind, being neutral and calm enough to do the right thing, rather than being reactive. It means being me.

Salu smiled. *Are there any other ways Justice resonates?*

Of course. I want to bring Amelia to justice. I want to bring balance to the people she has hurt. And I want to show the world that they can keep themselves strong and safe by being discerning, not by following blindly.

Salu's smile broadened. *Then you understand.*

12

AMELIA

Amelia opened a packet of crisps and propped her feet up on the desk beside the screen. She could see Laura and the Sheep on the CCTV monitor. They were standing in the cellar on the other side of the damp wall, staring around in confusion as they looked back and forth between the damp, bleak room and the scribbled drawings on the piece of paper she'd given them. They had no idea she was watching and that in itself was a thrill.

Expecting them to turn the creepy underground cellar into a romantic hideaway was a tall order, but she was going to enjoy watching them try. And its unexpectedness was the real genius. When Roland obeyed her summons, he would remember falling in love with her. He would come back, and he would be grateful. If there was one thing she'd always been able to rely on, it was her magnetic charm and Roland had never been able to resist it.

'Why has she chosen this as her romantic spot?' the Sheep said, securing fairy lights to the ceiling with masking tape. 'She's got this whole hotel. There must be a better room than this.'

Laura added fairy lights to a vase of flowers on a table that had been put up on one side of the room. 'She must have a good reason. Maybe we could learn from her? If we could find the romance in this place, we'd really be creating our own reality.'

The Sheep frowned. 'You think that? You don't think there's something off about this weird set-up? I mean, is she just inviting him for dinner, or does she have something else planned? That iron ring on the floor has been used before. It's not that long ago she had me tie an old man to it.'

Laura paled. She stepped back. 'You tied an old man to that ring? Then what?'

The Sheep shrugged. 'I left him there for Beth to find. Luckily, it didn't take long. He didn't take well to being tied up in the van beforehand. And he was pretty ill by the time Amelia had me leave him here. I didn't question her. I didn't question her when she had me abduct him with that woman, Doriel, either. But then he died. He died because of me. I've been going over and over it in my mind ever since, but I haven't come up with a single answer that makes sense.'

'That story was true? Amelia really did abduct those people?'

He nodded.

'But why?'

'She told me they were evil. She said they were Soul Snatchers out to hurt people. But the woman just wanted to take care of the old man. Amelia claims to be looking after us all, but she hurts me every day even though I've devoted my life to her. I don't understand it. I don't like it either.'

'Damn,' Amelia said through gritted teeth as she watched

the CCTV feed. 'This is not how this was supposed to pan out.'

Laura swallowed. 'She hurts you?'

'Doesn't she hurt you?' The Sheep frowned.

'Of course not. I didn't think she would hurt anyone. I thought she was here to protect us.' Laura stepped closer and put a hand on his arm.

The Sheep gazed into her eyes. He swallowed. 'Why do you follow her if she doesn't hurt you? How does she scare you?'

'She doesn't scare me,' Laura said, her voice soft. 'I follow her because she inspires me. Because she's trying to save us.'

'Are you still inspired, knowing what she made me do to that man?'

Amelia kicked the bin across the room. 'Damn you Sheep,' she said. 'I programmed you not to think.'

Laura closed her eyes and let out a slow breath. When she opened them again, she stepped back, letting her hand drop from his arm. 'I don't know how to reconcile what you're saying with the Amelia I know. Maybe you got the wrong end of the stick? Maybe you misunderstood? I can't believe Amelia hurt an old man.'

'You think I did it for myself?' The Sheep stepped back, his eyes wide. He started cracking the knuckles on his right hand. 'Why would I do that? I knew nothing about him.'

'I didn't say that.' Laura's gaze darted around the room, and then landed on the small camera in the corner to the left of the door. She stared right at Amelia. 'I don't believe Amelia would hurt anyone. But I don't believe you would either. I'm sure this whole thing has been a huge misunderstanding.'

'Good girl.' Amelia nodded. 'At least someone has learned

their lesson. Now, what lessons can I teach the Sheep this time? What will it take to keep his mouth shut?'

'I'll prove to you that it's a misunderstanding,' Laura said, and then turned back to the Sheep.

Amelia frowned and sat forward in her seat.

'If she's the person you think she is, you'll be punished for what you've just told me. But if I'm right, nothing bad will happen.'

'Why would she punish me? She's not here.' He frowned, his gaze darting around the room as hers had done moments earlier. Then he stared straight into the camera and paled. 'Shit,' he said, stepping backwards. 'I didn't mean it, Amelia, it's not real. I was joking. Laura knew I was joking, didn't you Laura?'

'Of course I did.' She threaded her fingers through his.

Amelia snorted.

'We've finished here. See how romantic it looks?' Laura spread her arms wide and spun around. 'Amelia and Roland will have a wonderful time.'

The Sheep looked forlorn; Amelia would have laughed if she wasn't so angry. He couldn't get anything right. She wondered if Laura could see how smitten he really was with her. Maybe she could use Laura to get him to keep his mouth shut from now on, before he became even more of a liability.

13

BETH

'BETH!' ABI RAN INTO HER ARMS. 'YOU'RE STILL HERE!'

Layla hung up her daughter's coat and tidied away the shoes and bag Abi had strewn across the hall.

'I invited her to stay with us, honey. Is that okay with you?'

'Yes!' Abi squeezed Beth tight and then ran into the kitchen. 'Do we have any biscuits?'

'They're in the usual cupboard.' Layla grinned. 'You can have two.'

'So we'll clear her energy tonight?' Beth asked as they walked through to the living room and sat on the sofa.

Layla sighed. 'The sooner the better. She's been sleeping badly and we're both exhausted.'

Abi came back from the kitchen, two biscuits in her hand. She looked from her mother to Beth. 'Are you talking about me?'

Layla laughed. 'We are.'

Abi sat between them and Layla put a hand on her shoulder. 'Beth can help you feel better. All you have to do is lie on your bed and hold my hand for a little bit. Beth will use energy to clear away the sadness other people have given you.'

'Energy? Like the colour around the crystals?' Abby tilted her head.

'Just like that. Did Doriel ever show you any energy work?' Layla asked.

'Oh yes!' Abi brightened. 'She taught me how to ask my angels for the bright light. Is that what you mean, Mummy?'

'Is Doriel always one step ahead of me?' Layla turned to Beth, suppressing a smile.

Beth laughed. 'Pretty much. You get used to it after a while. Abi, have you been calling in the bright light regularly?'

'I think I forgot after the climbing frame.'

Beth nodded. 'Shall we do it here?'

'How about her bedroom?' Layla said. 'I think she'll be more comfortable.' Abi jumped up and ran down the hallway, leading Beth and Layla to her room.

There was virtually no furniture in Abi's room, only a single bed with its head flanked by a window on either side. Abi had arranged her toys into groups around the edge of the room, with a little family of dolls in one corner, a farmyard of animals along one wall, and a drawing area on the other side. Clothes were stacked into piles that had once been neat, but were now ragged at the edges, with colourful fabric spilling over where Abi had hunted through. The effect was surprisingly neat and cosy.

Abi reached for her mum's hand and lay down on the bed. Layla knelt on the floor next to her, stroking her hair.

Abi's energy was a lot clearer than Layla's had been, but there were traces of stress. Beth called in the light, watching as it cleared the threads that didn't belong. As she watched, Abi's energy brightened, surrounding Beth and lifting her. In that moment, she felt she could do anything, could be anything she wanted. She took a deep breath and pulled back, allowing Abi's energy to settle into her own vibration. As she opened her eyes, she heard a growl.

'Did you hear that?' she asked Layla, looking around the room.

'I don't know what you mean.' Layla didn't meet Beth's eye.

'Abi?' Beth put a hand on the girl's arm. Abi muttered something incomprehensible, turned over and stuffed her thumb in her mouth.

'She's asleep!' Layla bent down and kissed the girl on the cheek. 'I knew she was tired, but I didn't expect that. She can snooze for half an hour before dinner.'

They got up and went into the lounge, shutting the door carefully behind them. 'What did you think?' Layla asked.

'I think she's doing amazingly under the circumstances. Her energy is incredible, particularly now the interference has gone. It's no wonder she's drawn to Doriel. I think you can stop worrying about her and start looking after yourself.'

'I'm okay.'

'I can see you're not. Something's missing.'

Layla swallowed. 'Don't, please.'

'Layla, I'm your friend. You don't need to hide from me. Is it Roland?'

Layla shook her head. 'It can't be Roland. I won't let it.'

Beth reached out and took her hand. 'It's okay to miss him.'

'No, it's not. How am I supposed to function, pining after the man I had to walk away from? I can't take Abi back there.

I can't put her in danger just because I've fallen in love with the wrong man.'

'In love?' Beth squeezed her hand. 'What makes you think he's the wrong man? He adores you. I know I warned you off him at first, but I didn't know him then. I think he'd be wonderful for you.'

'And how has it worked out for you, being with Jonan? Has he made your life better? Or has he just brought you under Amelia's glare and put you in danger?'

Beth let out a sharp breath.

'Look.' Layla shook her head. 'I'm not judging you. I'd do the same if it wasn't for Abi, but I have to put her first. I have to keep her safe. And I have to keep myself safe for her too. She needs me.'

'Of course she does. And Roland would never ask you to put yourself or Abi at risk. He'd love to know you have feelings for him though. Maybe he could visit you here? I'm sure it would do you both a lot of good to spend time together. And we will sort things out with Amelia. You will be able to come back if you want to. Or he would come here in a heartbeat if you asked him.'

Layla shook her head. 'If Amelia is still on this mission, he'll bring the danger with him.'

'Can I tell him that you miss him, at least?'

Layla shrugged. 'What's the point? We need to move on with our lives. He's always going to be connected to Amelia and that is never going to be safe.'

'I have to believe you're wrong about that,' Beth said, her voice soft. 'And I will do everything I can to make it safe for you to come home.'

Layla gave a tight smile.

14

JONAN

JONAN COULD HEAR THE DOORBELL ECHOING AROUND THE Victorian terraced house.

The door swung open. Roland stood there, pale under his tan, his hair sticking up in peaks.

'Did I wake you?' Jonan raised one eyebrow.

Roland stood back and ushered him in. 'I dozed off on the sofa. I've been unpacking for a lifetime, but this place is still empty. I haven't got a hope of filling it. Can I get you a beer?'

'Thanks.' Jonan followed Roland through to the kitchen and sat down at the pine dining table.

'Have you heard from Beth?' Roland handed Jonan a bottle.

He nodded. 'Layla was hostile at first, but they've reconnected.'

Roland's mouth looked pinched, and his eyes were over-bright. He cleared his throat. 'You must be missing Beth.'

'Like you wouldn't believe.' Jonan slouched back in his chair. 'If Amelia's aim is to get under my skin, she's doing a great job.'

'She always does.' Roland grinned. 'She's an expert. But we're not so shabby ourselves. What are we going to do about her? I'm sick of reacting to her games. We need to take the initiative.'

'I like your thinking.' Jonan took a swig of beer. 'What are her biggest weaknesses? Her desire for power? Or publicity?'

'Her weakness?' Roland laughed. 'That's easy! You are her biggest weakness. You, Doriel, Miranda and the Inn.'

Jonan shrugged. 'Maybe once upon a time. But what are her weaknesses now?'

Roland rocked onto the back legs of his chair. 'You are the reason Amelia and I split up. I have never been more than a power play to her, and I've known it for a long time. But you are her Achilles heel, with Doriel and Miranda not far behind. She wants to belong; to be respected for the woman she has become, not the woman she was born to be.'

'It would be a lot easier if the woman she'd become wasn't intent on hurting people.'

'And our weakness is that we won't hurt her in return,' Roland said with a sigh. 'And she knows it. She's relying on us staying the same. I don't think she has any idea how much of a change our breakup was, though, because she was never as invested as I was. For me, everything is different now. *I* am different now.'

Jonan frowned. 'So she will assume you're still loyal to her, and she'll expect us to be estranged.' Jonan leaned forwards, resting his elbows on the table. 'She won't worry about us working together or sharing information.'

'And she will never suspect I might be more loyal to Layla than to her. She will believe I have too much to lose by antagonising her.'

Jonan sighed and leaned back in his chair. 'That's really helpful, but we still need a proper plan.'

The doorbell rang. Roland frowned, and then disappeared into the hall.

Miranda walked into the kitchen and gave Jonan a tight smile. She put a small wooden box on the table. 'This was on the doorstep. There wasn't a note.'

'Did you see who left it?' Roland leaned his hands on the table, bending to look at the box.

Miranda shook her head. 'No.'

'It smells of Amelia's perfume.' Roland picked up the box. He turned it over, looking at it from every angle, and then opened it. Inside was a large brass key.

Miranda took the key from Roland and turned it over in her hand. She shut her eyes and closed her fist around it as her breathing levelled out. 'Do you recognise it?'

Roland nodded. 'It's the key to the basement at the Monk's Inn.'

'Why would she give you that?'

'And why would she leave it in a box on your doorstep?' Jonan said. 'Anyone could have stolen it.'

Roland shook his head. 'There will have been someone watching the box to make sure it reached me and nobody else, probably Rose, or Steve.'

'Which means she'll know I'm here,' Jonan said. He got up and peered out the window. The street was empty. 'Unless I arrived too early to be spotted.'

Miranda opened her eyes and put the key back on the table. 'There's not a shred of unintentional energy on that.' She sat down. 'She's programmed it full of love for you, sadness that you've left, that kind of thing. I'm sorry, Roland, but none of it's real. She's trying to manipulate you.'

'No change there then!' Roland said. 'I think it's pretty obvious what she wants.'

Jonan raised one eyebrow.

'She'll be waiting for me to turn up,' Roland's lips quirked up on one side. 'She'll assume I won't be able to resist her siren call. That I will be hoping she'll take me back. She'll have planned some elaborate reunion where she either punishes me or wins me back. Maybe even both. It will be so real in her mind by now that it won't have occurred to her I might ignore it.'

'And will you?' Miranda raised one eyebrow.

'Ignore it?' Roland put the key back in the box and shut it. Then he stood up and put the box in the drawer of a dresser. 'Absolutely. I have no interest in taking part in any more of her dramas. She's got this far by being unpredictable. It's about time we did the same.'

'Come now,' Miranda said, folding her hands in her lap. 'You know Amelia. If you ignore her, she'll escalate the situation.'

'I won't ignore her forever. She's probably down in that basement waiting for me now with some elaborate scene. I will turn up early tomorrow morning instead.'

Jonan frowned. 'You really think that's enough to get under her skin?'

'Amelia does everything for effect. If she wants me to turn up to the basement now, she's ready for me. She'll be dressed for it, and so will the room. If I don't turn up she'll be furious. She'll stay up late, rage drinking. Imagine the state she'll be in tomorrow. That's when I'll ring the doorbell.'

Jonan grinned. 'I'll be there for that. What about you, Mother?'

'Amelia has no desire to see me.'

'You're wrong.' Roland held her gaze. 'You might have no desire to see her. I get that. But to her, you're the one that got away. You're her biggest failure and she hates that. She had your love and respect, and now she doesn't. You left her for dust, and became something new, something whole without her. You still have Doriel and Jonan, and to make matters worse, you now have me as well. If anyone has the power to turn things around right now, it might just be you.'

Miranda pressed her lips together. 'I don't want a chance. Amelia is the most destructive and infuriating person I've met. I don't want anything to do with her.'

'Even if that means she ruins all our lives?' Jonan held her gaze, not turning away.

She swallowed. 'How is that anything to do with me?'

'She's broken, Mother,' Roland said, his voice hoarse. 'We're all broken because you left. Now you have a chance to help us rebuild. We need Amelia to be happy so she leaves Beth and Layla alone. You can do that for us, surely.'

'I can't.' Miranda's voice cracked. 'I can't be anywhere near her.'

'Please, Mum?' Jonan said. 'We need you.'

Miranda slammed her hand down on the table. 'I said no.' She shoved her chair back and stood up. 'Accept it.'

'Mother,' Roland said, but Miranda put her hand up between them, shaking her head. 'If you want her to be happy, turn up in that basement as she asked. I made my decision many years ago when I walked away. Since then, your choices have been your own. I cannot fix this for you.' She turned and walked out the room, down the hall and through the front door. It slammed behind her.

'Well, that went well.' Jonan rolled his eyes. 'They're cut

from the same cloth, those two. Neither of them can bear to concede the upper hand.'

'And they're both content to leave us in the middle.' Roland sighed. 'We don't have to dance to Miranda's tune any more than Amelia's. I'll meet you at the shop tomorrow morning, and we can walk to the Inn together. We will force Amelia to face us both in the cold light of day after a night of angry drinking.'

Jonan frowned. 'Is this really what life's been like for you, brother?'

Roland chuckled. 'This barely scratches the surface. But Miranda's right about one thing: it was always my decision to stay. My sense of loyalty and duty are stupidly strong. I couldn't bear to let her down.'

'Those are wonderful traits, Roland, and not everyone will take advantage. Layla is lucky to have you.'

'Even if she doesn't know it yet?'

Jonan smiled. 'Even then.'

15

JONAN

THE MOON WAS ALMOST FULL AND HUNG HIGH IN A WARM, INKY-black sky. Jonan looked up, wondering whether Beth could see it too. Jonan couldn't face going back to the shop, seeing his mum after the row, so he skirted past Lunea and towards the abbey.

An owl hooted as he ducked down the alleyway, and his phone rang, jolting him out of his thoughts.

'Jonan, is that you?'

Beth. Warmth filled his chest and the scent of lavender surrounded him. 'How are you? I miss you.' He let out his breath in a rush. The feeling of rightness when they made contact was staggering. 'Any luck with Layla?'

'Yes,' she said, and he could hear the smile in her voice.

He listened as she filled him in, describing the energy work and the crowd she had encountered in the street.

'It was awful.' Her voice caught. 'But then I met Rita, the woman who recorded it all. She's been talking about me online. I now have a whole list of people who want help to clear Amelia's interference. Layla has even arranged for me to use space at the bookshop to do the appointments. I think there could be a future in this, for now at least. People are starting to see through her, Jonan. We couldn't get anyone interested in healing before, but now they're flocking to me for help. We can finally make a difference.'

Jonan swallowed. 'I want to believe that's right.'

'It will filter through. I know it will. You're on her doorstep. She's bound to get to people more in St Albans. But something has shifted. My purpose has changed. Jonan, I'm not potential anymore.'

Adrenaline shot through him. 'You're not? What makes you think that?'

'So many little signs, but then Salu told me. I'm Justice now, and I will help restore balance, even if I have to do it one person at a time.'

'That's amazing.' Jonan walked past the abbey and stood on the grass at the top of the hill. He looked out over the trees, and the clear night sky. 'If you've got any of that energy and balance to spare, I'd love you to send some of it my way. I love Doriel and Miranda, you know I do, but living with them is driving me to distraction. I wish you were here with me.'

'I wish that too,' Beth whispered. 'You could come and visit? I'd love to see you and it sounds like you need some space.'

Jonan swallowed. 'Do you think Layla would mind?'

'She'd be delighted. We've come a long way since I arrived.'

'Could you find out whether Roland would be welcome?'

There was silence for a moment. 'I'll ask. How's he coping?'

A heavy weight settled in Jonan's middle. He walked over to a bench and sat down, not caring that the wooden slats were cold and damp. 'He's devastated and living in her house isn't helping. But he's throwing his energies into dealing with Amelia and I'm grateful. Talking to him makes me realise how little I know her these days. I'm not sure we would have had a hope without him. He understands her motivations in a way I never have. I had no idea how much I wounded her when I walked away. I didn't think she was any more invested than I was.'

Beth sighed. 'Does that change anything?'

'Absolutely. It means I've been messing up over and over. I should have been far more careful not to offend her. Mum and Doriel were right. I was too young and naive to deal with a woman as complex as Amelia.'

Beth let out a breath. 'Don't be hard on yourself. She was the adult. Nobody expected you to be mature and considered. That was her job.'

Jonan swallowed. 'It's how I've been since that's bothering me. Roland is convinced she's still holding a torch for me even now, and that he's been some kind of stand-in. I'm gutted I've done that to him. I've been rubbing her nose in our breakup for years.'

'You haven't done that to him, she has.' Beth's voice was thick. She paused and when she spoke again, it was more controlled. 'But it's not too late to change the way you interact with her.'

There was a rustling to Jonan's left. He turned. A fox trotted across the grass in front of him, stopping to look him right in the eye. They stared at each other for a moment, the cold wind whipping around them, the damp seeping through their skin. Then the fox turned and disappeared. Jonan took his first free breath all day. 'I will be free of Amelia, Beth. We all will be.'

16

JONAN

DORIEL AND MIRANDA WERE SHARING A BOTTLE OF WINE WHEN Jonan got back to the flat. Doriel was curled up on the sofa, her knees pulled up to her chest, long hair flowing around her shoulders. Miranda sat, straight-backed and grim-faced, staring into the fire.

'Jonan,' Doriel said, smiling as he let himself in. 'Grab a glass and join us.'

Miranda didn't look away from the flames, but he saw her shoulders tense further.

He got a glass from the kitchen and leaned back against the worktop, taking deep breaths, trying to hold on to the peace he had felt before he walked in the door. The heaviness in the flat was new. It had always been his sanctuary; the place where life made sense. Now it dragged him down no matter how many times he cleared the energy. Was Amelia messing with it? Or was one of them pumping out something toxic?

Going back into the living room, he sat in one of the

chairs and poured some wine, before topping up Doriel's drink. Miranda held her hand over the top of her glass.

There were no visual clues as to where the heaviness was coming from. Despite all the time she was spending there, Miranda had made virtually no impact on the place; her ascetic lifestyle was so ingrained. The room still looked warm and inviting. The fire roared in the grate, the sofas were comfortable, and the room was tidy. But there was a layer of coldness beneath the warmth that left him constantly looking over one shoulder.

'Is everything okay?' He sipped his wine, wondering whether the ground was about to drop away from under him.

'It's fine,' Doriel said with a tight smile. 'But your mother is resisting the concept of change. She is determined to hold on to her anger and she is uncomfortable with your suggestion that she may need to build bridges with Amelia.'

'Don't soften it.' Miranda glared at Doriel, her hands clenched into fists. 'I'm not uncomfortable with the idea. I hate it. That woman does not deserve our friendship. She is destructive and her judgement is disastrous. Look at what she did to you, Doriel. She had you locked in a prison. And Bill would still be alive if she'd left him alone. Plus, she has been shouting about Salu in the most unforgiveable way and making it impossible for us to do our work. Why would I want to be reunited with her?'

'Because her wound is driving her.' Doriel put a hand on Miranda's leg. 'She needs us, Miranda. She needs to heal. Jonan can't give her what she wants, but we can. That could change everything.'

'You're too soft.' Miranda shifted her leg and Doriel's hand slid onto the sofa. 'You're being taken in by her stories.'

'Or maybe you need to let go of *your* stories.' Doriel's

voice was sharp. You teach non-attachment, but you're so damn attached to your grudge that you're holding us all hostage. Give us a break and practice some of your own high spiritual ideals; let go and move forwards.

Miranda paled, and then her face flushed with colour. Her jaw tensed and a vein throbbed in her forehead. She said nothing, instead glaring deep into the fire.

Doriel picked up a tarot deck and started to shuffle. She cut it, and laid down three cards, the Queen of Cups, the Six of Coins and the Ace of Swords. 'Interesting.' She lapsed into silence.

'For goodness sake,' Miranda snapped. 'Spit it out. We all know you won't be happy until you've given us your interpretation. I do know you're convinced you're the real Oracle and I'm only an imposter.'

'I will always be an Oracle, whatever decision you shove down my throat.' Doriel's voice was harder than Jonan had ever heard it before. 'I have allowed myself to flow around the rocks of our lives. I have adapted to everything you and Amelia have thrown at me. But if you think I have become less than I was because of your tantrums, you are wrong. The only person you are limiting is yourself. Each time I flowed around the jagged edges, I became stronger and wiser. Do not ever challenge my role as Oracle.'

Miranda pursed her lips.

'Do you have a reading for us?' Jonan said, his voice soft.

'Of course.' Doriel stared at the cards, her eyes glassy. 'Miranda is holding herself in an elevated position, trying to keep a moral high ground. But she is acting from repressed emotion and pushing everyone away.'

'I am here, you know.' Miranda's voice was rough.

Doriel nodded. 'This is causing you to be manipulative.

The very thing you detest in Amelia. You are in denial about the role you are currently playing in our little drama.'

Miranda ground her teeth, sending shivers down Jonan's spine.

'It's time to get ourselves out there,' Doriel carried on. 'We need an exchange of energy rather than constant division and separation. We need to get in amongst things and be part of the narrative. It's time to stop giving Amelia the spotlight. We have been falling into the old patterns that created this mess. We need to rise into new ideas and inspiration. We *can* become more than our history.'

'And this is all down to me, I suppose?' Miranda said.

'Of course not.' Doriel held her gaze. 'We've all played into this mess, and we all need to join together to get ourselves out of it. But we also need to recognise that Amelia is one of the group. If we see her as our enemy, we won't ever be able to take that step.'

'You don't want us to see her as our enemy?' Jonan frowned. 'She kidnapped you, caused Bill's death and left Beth in an abandoned theatre to rot. She's manipulating everyone through the mass media, creating panic so she can control people through a fear she knows is unfounded. I know Mum can be stubborn and pig headed—'

'Excuse me,' Miranda said, her voice clipped. 'I am still here, and I am still your mother.'

'—but I'm inclined to believe she's right on this occasion.'

'Thank you,' Miranda muttered.

Jonan suppressed a smile. 'We need to figure out how to manage Amelia and disable her threats. But I'm not sure about welcoming her back into the family.'

Doriel shrugged. 'I'm not saying it will be easy.'

'Are you sure it's not you who's hankering after the past,

sister?' Miranda raised one eyebrow. 'You appear to be in a state of denial. Amelia has travelled a long way from our contracted life path. It is time to let her go.'

'She hasn't let us go.' Doriel sighed. 'She is focusing on us to a dangerous extent, and it is leaking into the wellbeing of the collective. The damage she can do is monumental. You know it, because you are capable of the same.'

'Do not lump us together, sister. You are walking a delusional path.'

'As are you.'

They glared at each other, bodies rigid with anger, faces flushed.

'There's plenty of delusion to go around.' Jonan leaned back into the sofa. 'But we need to find a way to cut through it, to figure out what is destiny and what is delusion. Things used to be clear, but now the water is muddy and it's hard to see through the murk. But destiny and delusion are poles apart. We have to be able to tell the difference.'

'Good luck with that.' Miranda stood up and brushed her clothes down. 'It's late. I'm going home.'

Doriel took her sister's hands. 'Miranda, don't go. Let's not end tonight this way. In fact, don't go at all. Move in with me. It will be like old times.'

'Move in with you?' Miranda frowned. 'I have been on my own a long time, Doriel. I would not be an easy living companion and the space here is limited. Where would I even sleep.'

'You can have Jonan's room. He can sleep on the sofa.' Doriel shot him a grin. 'He'll be moving out soon anyway to live with Beth.'

Jonan raised one eyebrow. 'We haven't even thought

about getting our own place. Why on earth you would you give away my room?'

'Oh, Jonan.' Doriel reached up to cup his cheek. 'It's time you stepped into your own future. I appreciate all the care you've given me, but I don't need a babysitter. This was always a temporary arrangement, and it was inevitable you would meet Beth and need your own space. You know I'm right.'

He dropped his head into his hands. 'That's a lot to throw at me while Beth is away and I'm trying to protect the family.'

'I know. But I also know you need Miranda and I to do our bit. For that, we need to be together. We were the Triad: Miranda, Amelia and I. Wherever this strange life takes us, it takes us together. Until we can get back in sync nothing is going to work.'

'But I promised to walk through the depths with you,' Jonan said, his voice cracking.

'You did, and I appreciate it. But I'd like to come up for air now, thank you very much. I don't need your pity weighing me down.' She picked up the tarot deck, shuffled, cut it and laid down two cards. The Chariot and Justice.

'Justice,' Jonan whispered, a shiver running down his spine. 'Beth.'

'She told you?' Doriel smiled. 'The Fool is only the first step, Jonan. You can't walk the path without moving forwards. Beth is taking that step. Can you?'

'What the hell is that supposed to mean?'

'Think about it.' Doriel shrugged.

Jonan shook his head. 'Roland suggested we use you and Miranda to draw Amelia in. He thinks she wants you nearly as much as she wants me.'

'Oh, at least as much. Probably more.' Doriel put the

cards back in the deck. 'It's just harder for her to acknowledge that.'

'So how do we help her realise?'

'I'll start running classes in tarot and psychic protection.' Doriel put the cards on the table and leaned back on the sofa. 'Miranda can help and we'll advertise for a third person: to take Amelia's place, essentially. That might push her to reconsider.'

'Mum?' Jonan asked, barely daring to hope. 'Will you do it?'

Miranda rolled her eyes. 'If I must. But she won't fall for it. I can't believe you're still underestimating her. Amelia will not play along with your games.'

17

BETH

Beth jogged down the zigzag path towards the sea. The wind whipped her hair around her face and she reached up, twisting it into a knot at the back of her head.

The sky was darkening, but the orange glow of the street-lights warmed the hard grey light. Running her hand along the rail of the path she allowed the rough wood to ground her.

She reached the bottom, crossed the walkway and bent down to pull off her shoes before stepping onto the cold, damp sand. It squelched through her toes, but the immediacy of the sensation held her in the moment, making her a part of the land that was consuming her, filling her up and lifting her above the minutia that usually threatened to drown her.

Taking off her waterproof coat, she lay it on the sand and sat down, just beyond the reach of the frothing waves. She stared out to sea. A single man walked by the surf, a black labrador at his heels. He threw a ball into the sea and the dog dove into the waves after it, its strong muscles bunching as it swam out, grasped the ball in its mouth and turned back to the beach. At the edge of the water, it shook. Beth tasted salt as some of the droplets reached her. The dog looked at her, and then turned and bounded after the man.

Seeing the animal's devotion made her think. She had been hoping Amelia would simply concede defeat. It was obvious Jonan had moved on, and she couldn't imagine why Amelia would hang around when she wasn't wanted.

The sky was on fire now, red streaking the clouds and reflecting on the stormy water. A seagull shrieked overhead, and a particularly big wave crashed a few metres away. Beth leapt up, grabbing her coat and launching backwards, only just in time to avoid being caught by the wave. She laughed as her breathing settled back to normal. That was a close call. Moving further back, she lay her coat out again and sat back down, wrapping her chunky cardigan more tightly around her, and hugging her arms around her middle.

She squinted into the fading light. A small pod of dolphins played in the waves. She held her breath for a moment, and then let it out slowly as they swam away. One single dolphin jumped high in the air, and then dove back into the water and disappeared.

A gust of wind hit her in the face, along with the scent of lavender.

Salu?

Here, sister. The voice shivered through the air before he solidified in front of her.

Beth sighed. *Do I have to explain myself, or do you already know what I'm thinking?'*

Salu sat on the sand next to her. *I know you think Amelia is all-powerful. But Jonan was never hers. This path was always yours to share. She's far too competitive to walk away, but that doesn't make your place in this less valid. As much as you dislike her, she does genuinely love Jonan in her own way.*

So where do we go from here? I don't want to walk away either.

Good! Salu chuckled. *We're banking on that. And you don't have to beat Amelia at her own game. She is falling into old patterns, trying to be a guru. Now is the moment to help people think for themselves, not to lead through brainwashing.*

Beth stared out across the water. *I'm not trying to be a guru.*

I know you're not. But Amelia thinks you are. She sees you as her competition in every sense, and doesn't understand the place you come from. If you grasp that, you have an enormous advantage in figuring out how to move forward.

Beth shifted and leaned on Salu's shoulder. He put his arm around her and pulled her into his warmth, shielding her from the cold and the wind.

How can you feel so real?

Salu chuckled. *I am real. And in this moment, I choose to feel human.*

Beth swallowed. *I wouldn't mind a break from feeling human, even for a few moments.*

A laugh rumbled through Salu's chest. *You have eternity for that, sister. This is your earth moment. You're here to do something wonderful.*

What is that though? Beth sat up and turned to face him. *I keep being told I have this big destiny, but all I'm doing is reacting to Amelia. How am I supposed to change the world like this?*

By showing other people how to look into their hearts to find out what is right. Show them they have the strength and insight within them, and that being kind is more potent than trying to overpower people. Help them discover themselves.

Beth sighed. *Well, that's marginally clearer, but not a lot. You don't make it easy.*

He shrugged. *We're here to support you, not do it for you. If you want help, all you need to do is ask.*

And you'll do whatever I want?

He grinned. *We'll do whatever you need. The two don't always align.*

She rolled her eyes. *Ain't that the truth.* She lay back on the sand with her hands behind her head. *It's hard when I'm always playing catch-up. They all remember everything.*

Salu turned to look at her, a smirk on his face. *Not everything. Would you like to see something they have forgotten?*

She sat bolt upright and grinned. *I can do that?*

I think it would be helpful.

She lay back down. 'Hit me with it.'

Salu nodded, reached out and hovered his hand over her forehead. Close your eyes.

Beth walked along the street, a basket slung over her arm. A man watched her from the front garden of his house, and her heart leapt. She smiled, her chest warming as his face lit up.

'Hey,' he called, opening the gate, jogging through and leaving it open behind him. 'Don't go.'

Beth smiled, but she nodded towards the woman who walked stiffly past him, over to the gate and slammed it shut, her mouth pressed into a thin line. She said nothing but scooped up the twins who clung onto her skirts.

'Come,' the woman said, her voice sharp. 'Leave Daddy to it. He won't want you hanging around now.' She strode back up the garden path and slammed the door of the cottage behind her. A few moments later, Beth saw her peering through the window.

'Go back to your wife,' she said, putting the basket firmly between them.

'But don't you feel it? Don't you sense what's between us? I don't even know how to describe it. I think I've been waiting for you my whole life.' He reached for her hand.

She stepped backwards. 'Of course I feel it. But you have a family, and my father will beat me if I let you have your way.'

'I won't let him.' He took a step closer. 'I will protect you.'

She shook her head, turned away and walked down the path, pausing a moment to meet the gaze of the woman staring out through the window. 'Go back to your wife,' she said, not looking back at him. Nodding at the woman, she turned the corner.

BETH OPENED HER EYES. THE SKY WAS INKY BLACK AND DOTTED with stars. *Was the woman in the garden Amelia?* she sent out the thought.

Salu smiled. *You recognised her.*

But she was nothing like Amelia.

Not in this life, but her energetic signature was the same.

She was married to Jonan, and I was the other woman. Did he leave her for me?

Salu shook his head. *He offered, but you turned him down. You were never the other woman. You didn't want to break up his family, but they were miserable. She never forgave you.*

And did we know all of this when we decided to come into this strange destiny?

He nodded. *Would you like to see?*

She lay down again and closed her eyes.

. . .

She was in the throne room, the white pillars soaring above her. Jonan paced in front of her.

'We can do this,' she said, standing up and stepping into his way. She took his hands and looked into his eyes. 'We can do this. We will all be on the same side this time.'

Amelia smiled. 'I know it feels like that now, but we know how different things are on earth. I'm not sure we'll be able to hold onto that harmony when we're in the middle of challenge.'

Beth dropped Jonan's hands and turned to face the other woman. 'We've been here before, Amelia. We've done the work and come through. We can do this. I know we can. I have faith in you.'

Jonan made a noise that could have been a laugh or a cough. 'Amelia's right. The patterns are strong. It's easy to think we've done it all when we're up here, but the loops will pull us back in if we're not careful. We need a plan; a way out if things go wrong.'

'I am the way out.' Beth's energy flared. 'It is my job to step in when things are falling apart. It is my job to teach people to follow their own light.'

'And it's my job to show them why it is dangerous to follow blindly. I would rather take your role, sister.' Amelia took Betalia's hand in her own. 'We may end as enemies yet. Can we pledge to reunite here as friends? I would not lose you. Either of you.'

Betalia pulled her into a hug. 'We will do this, and one way or another, we will return here as sisters and friends.'

Beth sat up. Her face was wet with tears. *I loved her. I still love her. I had no idea. Are they up there, somewhere?*

Salu smiled. *That's a nice way to picture it. But I am here, yes? Amelia and Jonan are here too, as are you. There is no up there or down here. There just is.*

I promised her we would end as friends. I don't know whether we can do that. Why would I make a promise I had so little control over? Did I not know what she would be like?

Nobody knew for definite, but you had a good idea. You didn't promise to end here as friends, merely to leave your anger at the grave.

So we could fail.

Of course. He shrugged. *Free will is paramount. You made a plan. You set intentions. That doesn't mean you will succeed. We can only guide you. Just as you cannot clear the energy of Amelia's supporters without their permission, we cannot interfere in your journey unless invited.*

Beth wriggled, getting more comfortable in the sand, and allowed her awareness to drift. She saw the stars above her merging with the bright, white pillars and through it all, she saw the face of Lunea, her Starfolk mother.

You can do this, Beth. The words shimmered on the wind. *Believe in your own potential.*

An owl hooted and the waves crashed beyond Beth's toes. She should have been cold, but a warmth spread over her, cocooning her in a blanket of safety.

Sleep, sister. The words filled her mind. *I will watch over you.*

'ARE YOU OKAY, MISS?' A ROUGH VOICE CUT THROUGH HER dreams. A strong hand grasped her arm and shook. 'Wake up. Are you alright?'

Beth opened her eyes and yawned. She pushed herself up to sitting and looked around.

'You must be freezing,' the man said, taking off his coat and holding it out to her. 'This is no time of year to be sleeping on the beach.'

'I'm fine.' She pushed the coat away, stood up and brushed the sand from her clothes. 'I didn't mean to fall asleep, but I was warm enough.'

'There's frost on the grass,' he said, shaking his head. 'How could anyone be warm in a getup like that.'

'I'm sorry?' she raised her eyebrows. 'What did you say your name was?'

'I don't see why that matters,' he grumbled. 'If you're okay, I'll be off.'

She nodded, wrapping her cardigan tightly around her middle as a gust of wind caught her in the face. He was right. It was freezing. How had she stayed warm out here all night? The scent of lavender wafted on the breeze.

Thank you! She sent out the thought and heard a chuckle in her mind.

You've got this, sister.

Digging her phone out of her pocket, she dialled Jonan's number as she walked back up the zigzag slope to the clifftop.

'Beth,' Jonan said, with a yawn. 'It's early. Is everything okay?'

'I just wanted to hear your voice.'

'Has something happened? You sound different.'

'I spent time with Salu and Lunea last night.'

'Do I want to know more?' Jonan sounded more alert now.

'Probably, but I'm going to need coffee and time to process first. How are things at your end?'

'Doriel suggested I move out.'

Beth froze, gripping the hand railing. 'What? Why? Have you upset her?'

Jonan sighed. 'No. She wants to live with Mum. There's

more to this than I've understood, but I do know I need to find somewhere else to live. We haven't talked about our living arrangements in a while, but would you like to find somewhere together?'

'Somewhere that would be ours?'

'That's right.'

Beth let out a breath. 'I'd love that.' A wave of emotion prickled her eyes and tightened her chest. 'We will be okay, Jonan, we have to be.'

'I love you, Beth, don't ever forget that.' His voice cracked. A bell rang on the other end of the line. 'I'm sorry, I have to go. There's someone at the door.'

'Of course,' she said, her voice hoarse. 'Speak soon.' The line went dead.

She was at the top of the zigzag now. The wind was even colder up here, but she had just enough warmth from the walk up the steep hill. She would go back to Layla's flat to change, and then she would figure out what to do next.

18

JONAN

SHE DIDN'T HAVE MUCH STUFF, HE HAD TO GIVE HER THAT. BUT Miranda's presence in the tiny flat was somehow huge and imposing. The bedroom that had been his for years, and had become his shared haven with Beth, was now an empty, ascetic cell with just a mattress on the floor and a small pile of nondescript clothes in the corner. He would have found it sad that she took so little joy in life, except that it was clear she loved the feeling of superiority it gave her. She had transcended the need for stuff. Good for her.

Miranda had woken him up before daybreak, taking over the lounge for her morning rituals, keeping him awake with her chanting and pacing. Miranda and Doriel had been sitting in front of the fire, talking, ever since. He had nowhere to retreat to. Instead he had slumped at the table, his head bleary from lack of sleep, reading the same paragraph of his book over and over again. Their conversation was just interesting enough to catch his attention repeatedly, but nowhere near engaging enough to hold it. This new arrangement was not going to work.

He pushed his chair back with a tooth-grinding screech of wood on wood, and stood up. The women went silent, turning to look at him as though they'd forgotten he was there.

Jonan sighed. 'What's in the cards?'

Doriel shrugged. 'We're making plans for our new tarot workshop. Is there anything you'd like us to include?'

'Readings on how and when a house move might be imminent?'

Miranda glared at him.

Doriel chuckled. 'We have rather taken over. Why don't you go and see Roland. He's rattling around in that big old house, missing Layla and Abi. I'm sure he'd appreciate company.'

'So that's it?' Jonan shrugged. 'Mum comes back and it's time for me to move on?'

Doriel got up, walked over, and took both of his hands in hers. 'I know it must feel like that,' she said, her voice too low for Miranda to hear. 'But we both know that from here, your path lies with Beth and Roland, not with me. I'm not pushing you away, Jonan, I'm setting you free.'

'Right.' Jonan pulled away and grabbed his jacket from the back of the sofa. 'But if this is how Amelia felt when we all walked away from her, I can see why she's angry. It's pretty cold outside the warmth of the family light.'

'Oh Jonan, don't say that. Please. You're not outside the family light at all. You're the centre of it. But there are different parts to this destiny and ours lie in different directions right now. That doesn't mean I don't love you.'

'Of course.' He pulled her in for a tight hug. 'Don't wait up. I may not come home tonight.'

'Send my love to Roland. Remind him I love him too.'

Jonan stood his collar up against the cold as he walked to Roland's house. The damp, early-morning streets seemed somehow unwelcoming and the few people out and about were all staring at the ground, avoiding eye contact. Other people were fast becoming seen as a threat.

Jonan rang the doorbell and sighed in relief as Roland opened it, letting a warm slice of light out onto the doorstep.

'Jonan, I wasn't expecting you this early. Come in. We can have a coffee and go to Amelia's a bit later.' Roland stepped back, giving Jonan the space to enter the empty hall. 'Stick your coat over the banister and come on in. It'll be nice to have company.'

'Would you like overnight company by any chance?' Jonan said, with what he hoped was a smile. 'I'm sick of sleeping on the sofa and being woken up at the crack of dawn by Mum's rituals.'

Roland laughed, a deep belly laugh, and the tension in Jonan's shoulders eased.

'It's your turn to be pushed out now then?'

'Yup.' Jonan walked into the lounge and sat on the sofa. He picked up the toy leopard from the arm of the chair and turned it over in his hands. 'I guess it's time for a new tribe.'

'The tribe of the lost, fallen and lonely,' Roland said with a chuckle. 'Powerful stuff.'

'It will be, believe me. It will be.' A shiver shot down Jonan's spine.

'Why don't you move in here properly?' Roland slumped on the sofa. You're all crammed into that tiny flat, and I'm rattling around this place. I could do with the company if I'm honest. And you could get Mum out of your hair.'

'You wouldn't mind having your big brother cluttering up your space?'

Roland shrugged. 'It's about time we put the past behind us and got to know each other better. Plus, this place haunts me. I hear Layla and Abi in the creak of every old floorboard. There's plenty of room for both of us, and for Beth when she comes back too. Of course, if Layla and Abi move back ...'

'We will get out of your hair, sharpish.' Jonan grinned. 'Beth and I are looking to get a place for the longer term anyway. You're a lifesaver, brother. When can I move in?'

'Immediately!' Roland grinned. 'But let me show you something.' He stood up, beckoning Jonan to follow him. He led him upstairs and to the door of one of the bedrooms. 'I decided to paint this room for Abi. I wanted to put my attention, my *intention*, on them coming back.' He pushed the door open.

Jonan walked in, looked around and then gasped.

'You did this?' he croaked.

Roland nodded.

'Wow. I mean, you were always good at art, but this? This is something else. I had no idea you'd kept it up.'

'That's the thing. I haven't.' Roland came into the room and leaned on the windowsill. 'I haven't touched my paints since I joined Amelia. But the night I got them out again, the night I began this, it was almost as though I was possessed.'

'Possessed? Or Channelling?'

Roland shrugged. 'How would I know the difference?'

'Was it uplifting or frightening?'

'Uplifting, certainly. Inspiring even. I keep hoping it will happen again. I have enough skill to finish what I started that night, but I'm pretty sure I could never have done this without help.'

'Maybe it was Salu and Lunea? Your gifts might be re-emerging now you're out from under Amelia's influence?'

'Maybe. I always thought art was one of my gifts. Amelia pushed me away from it, but after last night ...'

'I think now is the moment you have to choose.' Jonan turned to face him. 'Carry on with the person you became under Amelia, or explore who you were born to be.' He looked back at the mural. 'I can't wait to see what this looks like when it's finished! Abi is one lucky girl.'

'Thanks, Jonan. Would you mind having the smaller room? I'd like to keep this one for Abi.'

'Of course. And I'm sure Layla and Abi will be back soon. I know things are tough right now, but I'm convinced we're heading towards something better.'

19

BETH

Beth yawned as she arrived at the bookshop. She would have liked to have spent the morning sitting around the flat, mooching and drinking coffee, but the number of people wanting help to clear Amelia's interference was growing fast. She already had a full day today with more appointments booking up through the week. She wasn't sure how she would have managed if Layla hadn't offered her a booth at the bookshop to work from.

'What happened to you last night?' Layla handed her a cup of coffee.

Beth yawned again. 'I fell asleep on the beach. I'm lucky a wave didn't get me!'

'You slept all night at the beach in this weather?' Layla raised her eyebrows. 'On your own?'

'Of course on my own.' Beth heard the sharpness in her voice and forced herself to relax.

Layla studied her. 'You must miss Jonan.'

'Like you wouldn't believe. But I have so many people booked in to see me here that I have no idea when I'll be able to get home. Did I tell you he asked me to move in with him? To find a new place together?'

Layla's face lit up. 'That's amazing news. Let's wrap things up here. You can offer to help people remotely, can't you? Everyone's working over video calls now anyway.'

'You wouldn't mind?'

'Mind?' Layla frowned. 'Why would I mind? I didn't expect you to run after me when I moved, and I certainly don't expect you to settle here just because I did.'

Beth let out a slow breath. She hadn't realised how trapped she had felt by Layla's determination to stay in Bournemouth. 'I said I would make it alright for you to come back.'

'That was never going to happen with you here though, was it?' Layla's smile was kind, but Beth could see the pity in her eyes. 'I may have needed a bit of help to settle, but I'm not the problem. Amelia is. If you want to help me move back, go home and sort things out with her.'

'Hello?' A woman came up to the desk. She was dressed in black and had dark smudges under her eyes. 'I'm looking for Beth Meyer.'

Beth ushered her over to the booth, shooting Layla a smile.

The woman sat down and patted her hair into place. 'What are you going to do? Should I be scared.'

'Not at all.' Beth smiled, trying to make herself look as approachable as possible. 'I'm not going to hurt you or give any bad news. I'm just going to help you feel better. Do you have any questions?'

The woman's eyes flittered around the booth. 'Will you touch me?'

'Not at all. I'll just stand behind you. You won't feel a

thing. If you're comfortable enough, close your eyes and try to relax.'

The woman's eyelids fluttered closed, but they sprang open again when Beth stood up. Beth smiled, and then took her place behind the woman, slowing her breathing and sinking into trance.

The energy was muddy, filled with the tangle of Amelia's grey cords. Beth called in a bright white light to burn them up and instantly felt the release. The woman slumped a little in her chair, and her breathing slowed. Beth continued to clear the energy, seeing the muddiness gradually drain away until the woman's aura shone a weak orange. 'Do you feel any better?' Beth asked, half an hour later. The woman opened her eyes and blinked a few times. 'I do. Have you finished? Was that it? I was sure it was going to hurt, but I was so relaxed I think I drifted off.'

Beth sighed. 'Did Amelia say we hurt people?'

The woman flushed. 'For what it's worth, she's clearly lying about you. I'll tell all my friends to come and see you. Nobody's been right since she spoke out. It's like she's holding a thunder cloud over everyone. I thought she was inspiring at first. Now I think she's just poison. But people are too scared to acknowledge it. Have you heard the rumours about bad things happening to people who don't follow her? Like that little girl who fell off the climbing frame? Apparently she's in a psychiatric hospital now.'

'That's not true at all,' Beth snapped. Seeing the shock on the woman's face, she took a deep breath and let it out slowly. 'I'm sorry. You hit a nerve. The little girl is absolutely fine and living at home with her mum. I have no idea how that story came about, but it isn't true.'

'Thank you for telling me that. I've worried about her

often. I have a girl the same age and I know what kids can be like.'

Beth forced a smile. 'If your friends want to see me in person, ask them to book in soon. I won't be here for much longer.'

'You're not going back, are you? Back to St Albans?'

Beth nodded. 'My life is there.'

'But we need you. If you get tangled up with Amelia, you won't be able to help anyone. Then we'll all be stuck with whatever poison she's feeding us. We need to keep you clean.'

Beth leaned forwards, resting her forearms on her knees. 'I can keep myself clean. And I have support. Please don't worry about me. Just look after yourself and don't get drawn back in. I've been there. I know how easy it is to fall for her manipulation. But when she ensnares someone, she connects to them. Each and every person then sends her their strength without realising it. That's why you feel depleted when you're linked to her. She's taking your vitality for herself.'

The woman swallowed. 'She can really do that?'

'And more. But you can keep yourself separate. If you need me, drop me a message. Even if I've gone, I can help you remotely. But whatever you do, don't give her your strength.'

The woman took the card Beth held out, stood up and pulled on her coat.

'Thank you. I can't begin to explain how much this means. I feel like myself again.'

Beth let out a sigh as the woman walked out the door, a spring in her step that hadn't been there before.

'Are you Beth Meyer?' a voice said from behind her. She turned to see another woman in black. 'I have an appointment.'

20

AMELIA

Bang, bang, bang. The noise cut through the fog and Amelia's head started to pound in time with the sound. She groaned, turned over and fell off the narrow sofa onto the floor. 'Urgh.' She pushed up onto her hands and knees. The room spun and she collapsed back down, rolling onto her back and watching the ceiling circle above her.

She had waited in the basement for three hours, but Roland hadn't come. Laura and the Sheep had sat and watched her, their respect draining away, replaced by pity. She couldn't remember precisely what time she had snapped and trashed the room, throwing lit candles at Laura, dragging down the fairy lights and smashing the antique wooden table against the damp stone wall. 'Clear it up!' she had yelled as she stormed up the slick steps to the pitch-black garden.

She leapt up as a wave of sickness swept over her, and threw up in the crystal bowl on the bureau.

The hammering increased.

'Wait,' she croaked. 'Rose?'

'Coming, Amelia,' Rose's voice was full of forced perkiness that made Amelia want to throw up again. Seeing the contents of the crystal bowl, she winced and then eyed herself in the mirror on the wall. It wasn't a pretty sight. Anger drinking was one of her less desirable habits and she always regretted it horribly the next day. She'd been furious with Roland and had punished herself. Now she would have to pay for her temper, not him.

'I'm sorry.' Rose's voice was sharp. Amelia isn't taking visitors right now.'

'I bet she isn't.' Roland's voice held the hint of a smile. 'We won't stay long. I just want to return something.'

'No!' Rose squealed, but Amelia heard two solid sets of footsteps coming towards her. Her eyes darted around the room in alarm, taking in the vomit in the crystal bowl, empty bottles, food remains and goodness knows what else spread across the room. Never mind her stained clothes, dishevelled hair and panda eyes from last night's make-up. She groaned.

The door swung open. Roland and Jonan stood there, looking at her with identically raised right eyebrows.

'You were invited last night, not this morning.' She wished her voice didn't sound so gravelly.

'I wasn't invited. I was summoned. And I don't take your orders anymore.' Roland's voice was cheery but had a backbone she hadn't heard before.

'I came to return this.' He threw the key onto the chair. 'Come on, Jonan. Let's let Amelia suffer in peace.' With identical smiles, they turned. Roland slammed the door behind him so hard her teeth rattled.

She stared after them, numb for a moment before the rage hit, crashing over her with the force of a tsunami. 'Ahhhh,' she yelled, picking up the crystal bowl of vomit and throwing it at the wall. She gritted her teeth and squeezed her eyes shut as she was showered with liquid and broken glass, trying to not to throw up again from the stench.

'I will not let them humiliate me like that.' Slamming the door open, she enjoyed the crack as it ricocheted against the wall. Storming into reception, she glared at Rose's shocked expression, and then ran out onto the street. Roland and Jonan were halfway up the hill already, deep in conversation.

'Stop!' she yelled, running towards them on bare feet, swearing every time the soft skin of her arches hit a sharp stone. 'Don't walk away from me!'

She was shouting loud enough to set the neighbours twitching their curtains, but neither Roland nor Jonan turned around. And they were out of sight and long gone by the time she reached the top of the hill.

21

BETH

BETH GASPED AS SHE WALKED INTO THE FLAT AFTER A LONG DAY of seeing clients. The worktop was covered in plates of nibbles and vases of flowers. And a bottle of sparkling wine sat in a cooler, next to two champagne flutes. 'This is incredible. What's the occasion?'

'You.' Layla winked at Beth as she put out the last plate of nibbles. 'I thought it was time we celebrated your success. I can't believe you've made such a huge impact in such a short space of time. You were still seeing people for two hours after the shop had closed!'

'I'm sorry about that.' Beth grimaced. 'I didn't mean to keep you stuck at work.'

'Please don't apologise.' Layla laughed. 'My boss is ecstatic. Everyone is on a high after your energy work, and most of them buy a pile of books before they leave. Her takings are up by a huge margin and she's giving me the credit since I brought you to the shop.'

Beth poured two glasses of bubbles and held one out to Layla. 'In that case, here's to us!' She grinned.

Her phone rang and Jonan's picture flashed up on the screen.

'Take it.' Layla smiled. 'We have all evening to celebrate.'

Beth ducked down the hall and out the front door. 'Hi.' She turned towards the sea. 'It's good to speak to you. You won't believe the day I've had. There are so many people here who have been damaged by Amelia and they all want help, Jonan. I have a constant stream of people coming for energy work. It must be reducing the power she can draw on.'

'It sounds as though things are going really well.' Jonan's voice was flat. 'Does that mean you can come home soon?'

'Maybe. I need to figure out how to keep this moving in St Albans. Are things not going well at your end? Has Amelia done something?'

Jonan sighed. 'She's far more focused on us than the outside world right now. But that comes with its own pitfalls. Doriel and Miranda are closing ranks and it's cold out here on the edges of the Triad.'

'I think that's good,' Beth said, her voice quiet. 'Maybe Amelia will focus more on Doriel and Miranda and leave us alone.'

'That's what Roland says. And he thinks she will hate me moving in with him. She won't be able to get between us anymore.'

'You're moving in with Roland?' Beth felt a stab of something. Was it excitement or anxiety? 'I thought we were moving in together?'

'I need to get out now. You can live here too until we find a place of our own. There's space for us here unless Layla and Abi come back.'

'*Until* Layla and Abi come back.' Roland's voice came from a distance.

Jonan laughed. 'Until Layla and Abi come back.'

'Thank you, Roland!' Beth called down the phone. A shiver ran down her spine. 'This is one of those moments, Jonan, a point where things start to come together and move in the right direction. I just know it.'

'I hope you're right. And maybe I can fix things properly with Roland,' Jonan said, his voice low. 'That would be a dream come true.'

'Perhaps I shouldn't rush home.' Beth sighed. 'It might do you good to have some time alone.'

'Honestly, it would do us both good to get away from Amelia. Is there any chance Layla might welcome us? How open to seeing Roland is she?'

'*I'd* love that. Let me speak to her. I'm sure she'd be delighted if you came, but Roland is a bit of a sore point. I'll get back to you as soon as I can. And in the meantime, take care of yourself, Jonan. I'm worried about you. It sounds as though Amelia is getting to you.'

'I'll be alright. And hopefully I'll be with you soon, catching a bit of your enthusiasm. Speak soon?'

'Really soon. I love you, Jonan.'

The line went dead.

Beth went back inside to find Layla stretched out on the sofa, channel surfing.

'How is he?' She grabbed a huge crisp from a bowl on the table.

'He's happier now Roland has invited him to move in.'

'He's living with Roland? In my house?' Layla's voice was wistful.

'Do you miss Roland?'

Layla swallowed. 'Like you wouldn't believe. I thought everything was finally coming together for me. I'd found a great job with lovely people, a man Abi loved, and who was great with her, and a fabulous house. Then Amelia happened. She ruined my life. She's *stolen* my life. If anyone is snatching people's souls, it's her.'

'You don't have to let her.' Beth sat next to Layla. 'She's trying to get to people, but you don't have to give her what she wants.'

'That's easy to say, but if she targets Abi again, I'm toast. She is everything to me and as much as I love Roland, being with him isn't worth the risk to my baby.'

'Of course not!' Beth drew back. But what if Roland and Jonan came here, for a visit? Amelia is far away in St Albans, her gaze fixed firmly on Doriel and Miranda. Apparently she hates them living together and closing ranks. I'm not sure she's ever really cared about Roland, but it doesn't sound like she's particularly bothered about Jonan now either. I think they could get away for a bit without drawing her attention.'

Layla's face brightened. She sat up, wrapping her arms around her knees. 'You think so?'

'I know they would leave immediately if there was any evidence she was watching them. They wouldn't let anything happen to Abi.'

'I would love to see Roland. You really think he would come?'

Beth laughed. 'He'd be on the next train if you invited him.'

Layla flushed, but her eyes shone and a smile spread across her face. 'Then yes. He can visit. I have no idea how we'll fit them both in this pokey flat, but they can come, and we'll figure it out.'

Excitement shot through Beth. 'I'll message Jonan now.'

'No,' Layla said, her voice sharp.

Beth looked up from her phone.

'I'll call Roland myself.'

22

LAYLA

The ring tone sent a thrill of excitement through Layla. Pressing those numbers had taken a monumental amount of strength, but not pressing them for so long had taken more. She'd set up the room as though for a romantic dinner, with candles lit and the lights dimmed. Beth had gone for a run and Abi was in bed. For a while, at least, she had the space and silence to breathe, think and settle into herself.

'Layla?' Roland's voice was hesitant. 'Is it really you?'

She swallowed. 'I'm sorry it's taken me so long to get in touch.'

'It's okay,' he rushed to fill the gap. 'I understand.'

'No,' she said, 'you don't. You can't. Seeing Abi in that hospital bed broke my heart and it's mended in a different way. I was naive back then. I thought Beth and Jonan were overreacting to Amelia. I couldn't see why anyone would believe her ridiculous stories. But they do. I was wrong. She's dangerous. Dangerous to Abi.'

'I know.' Roland's voice cracked. 'I know this better than anyone. I've seen what she's like. Seen it from the inside.

She's even more unstable than you think. You were right to take Abi away. It breaks my heart to say it, but you were right.'

'I don't know if I can ever go back. But ... you could come here? You could come for a visit, at least?'

There was silence. She could hear Roland breathing. Heard the catch as he realised what she was saying. She heard the wail of a siren through the phone, so many miles away, and her heart clenched when she thought about all she had left behind. All the loved ones she had walked away from.

'Do you mean that?' His voice was so quiet she nearly didn't hear it.

'Yes. Come. Come now before I change my mind. Come here where the air is clean and full of salt. We can breathe, and think, and figure out whether we have a chance.'

He let out his breath in a rush. 'I'll get a train tomorrow. I'll let you know what time I'll be in. And I'll bring Abi's cuddly leopard with me. I found it down the side of the sofa. It's been looking at me ever since and I swear I hear it roar sometimes.'

Layla laughed. 'You found her leopard? That's what she meant.'

'What who meant?'

'Abi told me her leopard would look after you.'

'She said that? Wow. A shiver just shot down my spine. There's something about Abi, isn't there?'

A warm glow filled Layla's chest. 'Much more than you realise. Maybe you'll find out one day. I hope you will. I hope that's where we're heading.'

'I want you to know how happy I am that you've called. You've made my year. I will stand by you and Abi all the way.'

A wave of relief flowed through Layla. Tears sprang to her

eyes and her breath caught in her throat. 'You mean that? You'll stand by Abi too?'

'Of course!' Roland sounded so affronted she smiled. 'Who wouldn't want to stand by her? We'd be a family. Right?'

'Right. You said you'd come tomorrow?'

'As soon as I can get on that train. And Layla, we'll get through it together. It's all going to be alright.'

23

JONAN

THE HOUSE WASN'T WHAT HE'D EXPECTED. THE DETAILS described a character property, but Jonan had at least expected modern plumbing and electrics. With twilight falling outside, and the lights malfunctioning inside, it was impossible to get a good look at the place. The last three he'd seen hadn't been any good either. One had a weirdly intrusive landlord, another was covered in mould, and a rat ran across his foot when he was standing in the kitchen of the third. He had no idea how they were going to find anything liveable on their budget if Layla and Abi came back and they had to move out of Roland's house.

'What do you think?' The agent said with a fixed smile. 'Clearly it's a fixer upper, but it will be amazing when it's done.'

'Isn't it a rental?' Jonan frowned. 'I'm not looking to buy.'

'Oh, urm ...' The agent flicked through the paperwork. 'You're right. It's a rental.'

'And is the landlord planning to do any work before he lets it?'

The man swallowed. 'I believe not. But it is in a great location. Easy walking distance to both town and the station. You can't beat that.'

'Honestly, plumbing and electrics would beat that for me.'

'Get out!' A voice yelled from the street. Another voice rose in response. Jonan looked out the window. A couple were in each other's faces, yelling at the tops of their voices. The woman went into the adjacent house and slammed the door. The man stood in the front garden and kept yelling.

Jonan tried to imagine Beth here, but it wouldn't stick. He sighed. 'I'm sorry, this isn't for us. Do you have anything else worth looking at? Or is this the best you can do?'

'I'll call you when something new comes in,' the man said, but he was already scrolling on his phone and Jonan heard the dial tone going as he walked out the door.

Thank goodness Roland had offered him a room. He'd thought his life was coming together: Beth, the shop, all of it. Now he had no real home and Beth was miles away. Once upon a time everything had been clear. Now he had no idea what was going on.

There was banging and thumping from upstairs when Jonan got home. He took the stairs two at a time.

He knocked on Roland's door. 'Is everything alright?'

The door swung open and Roland stood there looking dishevelled.

'Come in.' He gestured for Jonan to sit on the end of the bed. 'Layla has invited me to visit. I'm going before she changes her mind. Do you want to come?'

Jonan grinned. 'Try and stop me! But shouldn't we do something about Amelia before we go? We left her in a fury.'

Roland smiled. 'Let's plant a new bombshell for her. She's

already tracking us on social media. Let's put out that advert for someone to work with Doriel and Mum on their tarot classes. Doriel's right. That will infuriate Amelia. She loves knowing her place in the Triad is still vacant.'

'I'm not convinced anyone else could work with Mum.'

'You don't actually need to hire anyone. Just put out an ad as bait, and wait to see what she does. Something will change. I'm sure of it.'

Jonan pulled his phone out of his pocket and opened an image creator app. A few clicks later, he sent a graphic to Roland.

Tarot and energy healing teacher needed, to join established team of two to facilitate workshops and healing groups. Contact Lunea for more information and to apply.

Roland grinned. 'She won't be able to resist that. And with us gone, she won't be able to get any information either. You know how vague Doriel and Mum are.'

'And she won't want to quiz them directly.'

Roland slammed the lid of his suitcase shut. 'Are you going to start packing, brother? I'm leaving first thing tomorrow whether you're ready or not.

'There's something I'd like to do in the morning first,' Jonan said. 'And I'd love to have your help.'

THE NEXT MORNING, THEY HAD TO RING THE BELL TO BE LET into the shop. The glass front was sparkling and the cabinets in the window displayed beautiful jewellery with eye-watering price tags.

'Aren't you from that crystal shop by the clocktower?' The woman said, as she led them to a desk.

'I am,' Jonan gave a tight smile. Was she one of Amelia's followers? 'Have you been into Lunea?'

'Oh yes, I'm a big fan. I've been to several of your workshops too. I'm looking forward to coming back.'

Jonan let out a sigh of relief. 'I'm glad you enjoyed your time in the shop. Would you mind not mentioning that I came in? I was hoping to keep my visit a secret for a little longer. I'm here to look at engagement rings.'

The woman beamed. 'Of course. Discretion is a huge part of my job. I promise not to spoil your proposal. What would you like? A diamond?'

'I'd prefer something colourful,' Jonan said. 'What do you have? A ruby? An emerald?'

The woman went to the other side of the shop. She unlocked a glass cabinet and took out a tray of rings, which she brought back to the desk. 'These are our emerald rings.'

Jonan leaned over the display. They were all beautiful, green stones surrounded by a ring of diamonds. 'What do you think, Roland?'

Roland trailed a finger over the gems. 'They're amazing, of course ... but I'm not sure they're Beth. Would you get a bigger stone if you didn't have the diamonds?'

Jonan raised an eyebrow at the woman.

'Well, I don't think we have ... Hang on.' She went into the back. They could see her talking to a man who was bent over a work bench.

'I'll just have a look around,' Roland got up as the woman came back out with a tray of gems.

'We could, of course, make something for you?'

She held out a tray filled with polished stones. 'They're

gorgeous,' Jonan said with a sigh. 'But I need a ring this morning.'

'What about this one,' Roland pointed into one of the displays.

The woman went behind the counter and pulled out a tray of rings. In the middle was a single ring with a deep blue teardrop.

'This is a sapphire in a white gold setting.' The woman took it out and handed it to Jonan.

A shiver ran down his spine. He took the ring and his skin tingled where the stone lay on his palm. He turned it around and looked at it from every angle. An image popped into his mind of a very similar ring on Beth's hand. A different Beth. A Beth from another lifetime, but his Beth all the same.

'It's perfect,' he said, his voice barely more than a whisper. 'Thank you, Roland.'

Roland's face lit up, his smile almost glowing. 'It gives me chills.'

The energy around Roland was clearer now, and Jonan's aura lifted in response. Amelia's influence was subsiding fast.

Jonan grinned, imagining the ring on Beth's hand. 'Me too. I'll take it now please.'

The woman talked as she buffed up the ring and put it in a deep blue velvet box. Jonan did his best to smile and nod in all the right places, but he wasn't listening. He was watching the image of the ring in his mind, Beth turning her hand this way and that, allowing the stone to sparkle in the light.

Once he'd paid and they'd gone back outside, Roland pulled Jonan into a rough hug. 'Well, brother, you're certainly showing Amelia where she stands now. You know she's going to hate this.'

Jonan shrugged as they started walking down the hill

towards the station. 'She will, but this isn't about her. It's about me, and Beth, and our destiny together. We've waited lifetimes for this, Roland. I won't allow Amelia to get in the way.'

'I'm right behind you.' Roland clapped his hand on Jonan's back. 'It's about time you got the girl. It gives me hope.'

24

BETH

BETH LAY IN BED, WIDE AWAKE, STARING AT THE CEILING. SHE'D been exhausted all week, but here she was at eight o'clock on a Saturday morning, her mind spinning.

She'd had a text from Jonan late last night saying he was arriving with Roland today. She'd known Layla was going to contact Roland, but she hadn't dared to hope things would move that quickly. The more she thought about seeing Jonan, the more she knew it was time to go home.

With a sigh, she got out of bed and pulled on a pair of leggings and a running top. She could at least work off some of this antsiness. The sun was bright and glittered on the glass-smooth ocean. Beth jogged along the clifftop, loving the birds eye view of boats and dog walkers on the promenade. Maybe they should move here. They could set up a second branch of Lunea. There was certainly the interest, and it would be amazing to live by the sea. After half an hour, she turned back and detoured via the bakery to pick up some cinnamon buns for breakfast.

She let herself into the flat, closing the door quietly on

the off-chance that Layla and Abi were still asleep, but she heard voices in the lounge.

'Is that you, Beth?'

Beth swung the door open. Layla was sitting on the sofa with a woman with long red hair. Abi sat in her lap, playing with strands of her hair and making little roaring noises.

The woman smiled and held out a hand. 'It's good to meet you, Beth. I'm Tabitha. Abi has told me a lot about you.'

'Tabitha is a friend of mine from home,' Layla said. 'I mean, from St Albans. She lives in Wildley Forest Village a couple of miles away.'

'It's lovely to meet you, Tabitha.' Beth smiled and put the bag of buns on the coffee table. 'I brought these for breakfast, but I didn't know we'd have company.'

'I've eaten,' Tabitha winked. 'But I reckon this little kitten would love one!'

'Meow,' Abi cooed.

Tabitha laughed, giving her a squeeze. 'Of course, cats don't eat cinnamon buns.'

'This one does.' Abi grabbed the biggest one from the bag and took a bite. 'This one loves all kinds of buns.'

Beth got plates from the kitchen and offered one to Tabitha.

'No, really, I've eaten. You have your cake. It looks like you've earned it.'

'And a coffee,' Layla said, pouring a cup from the pot on the side. 'You were up early for a Saturday!'

Beth grinned. 'I spoke to Jonan last night. You invited them to visit.'

Layla gave a shaky smile. 'They're coming this afternoon.'

Tabitha reached out and took her hand. 'This is good, no? Ten minutes ago you told me you wanted him to come.'

Layla nodded. 'But how can I face him after the way I left?'

'Don't worry about that.' Beth took a cinnamon bun from the bag, put it on her plate and cut it in half. 'Roland is used to what Amelia does to people. You couldn't have chosen someone who would understand more. He's trying to recover from her manipulation himself, and he was with her a long time so that runs deep. It will be okay. He's coming all this way to see you. That's how much he cares.'

Layla smiled, and it lit up her face. For a moment she looked like the woman Beth had first met. 'Maybe I'll dye my hair. See if the old me is still in there.'

'You definitely should.' Tabitha said, and then turned and did a double take. She was staring at the picture Beth had bought in Bournemouth. It was standing propped up near the window.

'Isn't it gorgeous?' Beth heard the excitement creep into her own voice. 'I bought it on a whim. I just couldn't leave it behind in the shop.'

'You should sign it, Tab.' Layla was beaming.

'Sign it?' Beth frowned. 'It's by Tara McLaughlin.'

Abi snuggled deeper into Tabitha's lap and growled.

Layla laughed. 'Beth, please meet Tara McLaughlin, known to her friends as Tabitha.'

Beth flushed, the heat beginning at her neckline and burning her face. She swallowed. 'Oh my God, what did I say? I can't even remember. I'm so embarrassed.'

Tabitha laughed. 'Please don't be. I'm flattered you love my painting. You should visit the gallery sometime, see some originals. Would you like me to sign your print?'

'Yes, please.' Beth lurched out of her chair, and then stopped herself and picked up the picture, reverently, from the table. She handed it to Tabitha who retrieved a fibre-tipped pen from her bag.

'Are you happy for me to take off the plastic covering? It would be worth framing it once I've signed it. You might want to sell it one day.'

'Yes, thank you. I'll put it somewhere safe. Hang on, does that mean you're ... that you're with ... Is he here?'

Tabitha rolled her eyes. 'I always wanted to be anonymous but being known as a rock star's girlfriend instead of an artist isn't what I had in mind. I'm afraid Dylan's on tour at the moment. Although I'm sure you'll meet him sometime soon. Layla tells us wonderful things about your shop. We'll pop by when he's back.'

'It would be lovely to see you there, and not just because of Dylan.' Beth grinned.

'Would you speak out against Amelia, Tab?' Layla leaned back in her chair and crossed her arms over her chest. 'At the moment she's got all the celebrity status on her side. You or Dylan would be wonderful advocates.'

'Climb down for a moment, kitten,' Tabitha said, pulling the cellophane off the picture. She signed the mount in purple ink, with an elaborate script and a flourish underneath. 'I'd be happy to, but I can't speak for Dylan. Still, I'm not sure you need me. You're doing a wonderful job and I think your authenticity and lack of celebrity are a big part of your charm. Playing her game would reduce you to her level. Here.' She handed Beth the picture.

'Now if you go broke from Amelia's trolling, at least you can sell that and eat for a while.' Layla winked.

Beth laughed. 'Thank you, Tabitha, for signing my picture, and for your support. It means a lot.'

Something brushed up against Beth's leg and she started,

turning around and frowning at the empty space behind her. 'I'm sure I felt ... but there's nothing there...'

'Don't worry about that,' Layla said, winking at Tabitha. 'We get that kind of thing here. I'm sure this flat is haunted.'

'Really?' Beth frowned. 'I usually notice that kind of thing.'

Abi giggled and climbed back into Tabitha's lap. Tabitha rolled her eyes at the girl. 'Behave,' she said, but pulled her closer.

A shiver shot down Beth's spine.

25

AMELIA

AMELIA WALKED ALONG THE MAIN STREET, DOING HER BEST TO look artfully casual. Laura walked ahead of her, and the Sheep was behind, as well as the six other hired security guards who paced at intervals all around her. She waved at a small girl who tugged at the sleeve of her mother's arm and pointed. The mother looked at her for a moment, and then ushered her daughter away. That wasn't what Amelia expected.

'Amelia!' a woman's voice floated through the air. She looked about twenty, and the look of adoration plastered across her face was decidedly false.

'Laura,' Amelia said through a fake grin, 'why have you set me up with paid admirers? I don't need them. The real ones are on their way.'

'But you didn't tell them you'd be here.' Laura chewed her lip. 'We can't have you seen out and about with no fuss.'

'Have faith,' Amelia's grin widened into something more real as three women dressed in black clustered around her, pushing copies of the Amelia's Haven notebooks into her hands for her to sign.

She chatted to them for a few minutes, and by the time they waved goodbye more people slipped forwards to fill their places. Buoyed up by the attention, she walked tall as she moved down the main street, waving, hugging people and posing for selfies. Her fans always alerted each other to her presence, and the crowd grew by the minute.

When she reached Lunea, she stood tall, her hands on her hips as she looked at the shop. She hoped they might come out to her, to speak in mutual territory, but Miranda simply looked up, met her gaze, and then looked back down at the book she was reading. Damn. That woman was impossible.

Amelia walked up to the door, but a huge man in a black suit stepped in front of her.

'You're not welcome. Take your preaching elsewhere.'

'Preaching?'

'You have been barred from this establishment.'

'I don't want to shop. I want to talk to Miranda,' she said, hating the desperation she could hear in her own voice. How did the woman make *her* feel small?

He looked at her through narrowed eyes. 'Disperse your followers and you can go in.'

'Are you serious?' She gestured to the buzzing crowd behind her. 'These are potential customers. Don't you think they might spend money in your shop?'

'That's the rule.'

Amelia sighed. Strike one to Miranda. She didn't know why it was important to speak to her right now, but this bloody security guard had made her even more determined. There was no way she was backing down now.

'My loves,' she said, turning to the crowd. 'Thank you for spending time with me today. But now I have business I must take care of alone. Please have a wonderful day and do come onto social media to tell me all about your fabulous experiences with Amelia's Haven.' There was silence for a moment, and then people started drifting off, beginning muttered conversations. Soon the pavement behind her was empty.

She spread her arms wide. 'Well?'

He stepped aside and opened the door.

Amelia pushed through. 'Miranda.' She plastered on her game face.

'What do you want, Amelia?' Miranda put her book down, leaned back on her chair and crossed her arms over her chest.

'I saw your advert for a third teacher for your classes. I wouldn't have thought you and Doriel would need anyone else.'

'We were always supposed to be a Triad, sister,' Doriel's voice came from the door at the bottom of the stairs.

Amelia swallowed. 'You look well.'

Doriel inclined her head. 'I've been through a lot, but I am recovering. I always do.'

'You've done well, sister,' Miranda said through gritted teeth, 'but what Amelia did when she kidnapped you matters. Don't let her off the hook.'

Amelia flushed. If anyone could make her feel like a naughty child, it was Miranda. 'I didn't do anything.'

'I saw you.' Miranda held her gaze. 'I was there at that abandoned barn. I saw you speeding in to retrieve Doriel and Bill when we came to rescue them. And I heard you yelling at your lackey for inadvertently letting us go. You can't fool me.'

'It doesn't sound as though she thinks we should be a Triad.' Amelia glared at Doriel.

'I don't.' Miranda stood up and walked over to Amelia. 'In fact, I don't think we need anyone else at all. But if Doriel wants a third, I will consider getting to know someone new, for her benefit. But you, Amelia, have done too much damage. I washed my hands of you a long time ago.'

'You're impossible,' Amelia said through gritted teeth. She clenched her fists, digging her fingernails into the palms of her hands as fury blazed through her, lifting her consciousness away from her body. In that place, watching her physical body try to find a fingerhold on self-control, she felt the fury and pain collide. These were the women she had built her life around, the sisters she had thought would always be by her side. She had assumed they would grow old together and, in that moment, she realised that was the biggest loss of all. It was greater than losing Jonan, who had never been hers to keep. It was greater than having to find a new life path and a new home. These women were everything.

'Want me to remove her?' the voice called her back and she landed in her body with a crash that winded her.

'Oh shush.' Doriel waved the security guard away. 'Can't you see she's hurting? If she threatens us you can do your thing. But I won't let you throw a broken woman out onto the street.'

The man flushed. 'But Ms McLaney, Mr McLaney said ...'

'Doriel is just as much your boss as Jonan.' Miranda's voice was sharp.

The man flushed an even deeper red, inclined his head and stepped back to the door.

Amelia swallowed and looked up at Miranda. 'Did you just stand up for me?'

'No,' she snapped. 'I won't see Doriel disrespected in her own shop.'

Amelia suppressed a smile. 'You won't get any argument from me. Talking about disrespect, what do you think of Robson Fall?'

Miranda narrowed her eyes. 'Why would you ask me a thing like that, as though I'm some kind of supportive friend?'

Amelia gave a harsh laugh. 'Don't worry, I would never mistake you for that. But whatever else I think of you, you are an Oracle, as is Doriel. I would appreciate your read on him. I suspect he might be trying to screw me over.'

'Oh, certainly,' Doriel said with a smile. 'He's been considering that for weeks. I think the delay is merely due to his indecision about the most profitable way of sealing the deal. He hasn't figured that out yet, but he will soon. Expect to be ditched in the most inconvenient moment possible.'

'Why would you tell her that?' Jonan's voice came from the doorway.

'Because she's my sister,' Doriel's voice cracked. 'Because whatever grudges you all hold, I want her back. I've always wanted her back and I've never pretended otherwise.' Doriel took Amelia's hands, and her skin was warm and soft. It brought a lump to Amelia's throat. 'I *do* want you back, sister. I always have and I always will.'

Amelia squeezed Doriel's hand.

'Good for you,' Miranda said, her voice dripping with sarcasm. 'But I am not as easily won over. What you did was wrong. It was wrong to sleep with your best friend's teenage son. It was wrong to go on television and lie about your conversations with Salu, pretending he was a dangerous predator. It was wrong to become that predator yourself, literally draining the souls you vowed to protect. And it was wrong to kidnap Doriel and Bill, to allow Bill to die on your watch, and to get your fingers into schools and whip up children and teachers so they turned on each other. Good for Layla, getting her child away from you. I would be doing the same if Jonan and Roland were young enough to do what I told them. The only way out now is to change your behaviour and start doing the right thing. Are you ready for that, Amelia?'

'You're so self-righteous.' Amelia tilted her head back so she could look down on Miranda. 'I'm not going to stick around while you paint me as a villain, as though you're some kind of saint. Doriel, we could do this without her. We wouldn't need a third member if it was the two of us. You know it. We were always the best of the three. Call me when your minder isn't glaring over your shoulder and we'll talk.'

'She's my sister too, Amelia. I won't choose between you. And she's right. For us to work, you have to commit to doing the right thing.'

'There's just no give, is there?'

'Not while you're terrorising people with fake threats.' Miranda shrugged. 'As soon as you are ready to let that go we can talk. Until then, you know where the door is.'

Amelia looked beseechingly at Doriel.

Doriel smiled at her, irritatingly serene. 'Tell the truth, Amelia. It's really not that hard.'

Amelia gritted her teeth, spun on her heel and walked out the door. She shoved it with more force than was necessary, waiting for the slam, but it closed with a soft click. She turned, but the man on the door was ignoring her.

That was maddening. She wasn't used to being ignored. None of her people had hung around for her so she strode down to the Inn, her anger growing with each step.

They had a nerve ordering her around, she raged, keeping her teeth locked firmly together so she couldn't speak her thoughts aloud. The morality act didn't cut it when she knew all their mistakes. They'd been arrogant. They always assumed they knew better than everyone else and tried to push their views on others. They were so convinced they were ushering in a golden age they refused to see that anything could go wrong. But she had seen it. Looked it in the eye and not backed down. They may not have liked what she became, but at least she acknowledged there was darkness in the world. People needed her. They needed Amelia's Haven. They needed something, someone to blame, and someone to look up to and follow. She gave them that.

She opened the door to the Inn and slammed it hard behind her. 'At least I can slam my own door,' she said to the room, enjoying the sound of her voice bouncing off the hard walls.

'Amelia?' Rose's voice came from the ballroom. 'Is everything okay?'

Amelia waited until Rose appeared in the doorway. 'Robson Fall is on the verge of ditching me. Miranda and Doriel are baiting me. Even Laura and Steve are starting to look at me as though I'm crazy. Things are going to shit and I have to turn them around.'

'Have you seen the media? Katherine Haversham has been talking about how awful she's felt since you went on the show. I think she's hitting back after my attempts to get you a slot. She's been speaking out against Robson Fall too. Are you sure this is the right time to put yourself out there with a big event?'

Amelia swallowed. 'Get me the footage. Let me see it. And yes, it's exactly the right time. I need to show my followers I am strong and unfazed. They need to know I'm still here for them.'

'But ...' Rose swallowed.

'But what, for God's sake?'

'Nothing.' Rose looked at the floor. 'I'll get on it now and get back to you as soon as I can.'

'I knew I could rely on you, darling. While everyone else questions me, you remain faithful. It is people like you I want to reward.'

Rose twisted her face into a pitiful approximation of a smile. 'Thank you, Amelia.'

26

AMELIA

AMELIA TOOK A DEEP BREATH AND THEN LET IT OUT SLOWLY. She was filled with fury, and she imagined it flowing through her like red-hot lava, before seeping out through the soles of her feet into the ground below her. She would not let them drag her down. She had walked away once before and managed perfectly well without them. As long as they were sitting in her head, soaking up her attention, they were in control. She would kick them out and spy on them in their own territory.

Imagining herself full of fiery light, she pictured Miranda in the shop behind the payment desk and reached her mind out to her.

She hit a brick wall and heard laughter in her mind. 'Bloody Miranda,' she muttered. She saw more of the lava seep into the ground.

This time she reached for Doriel, imagining her on one of the armchairs in the shop. Doriel looked up and smiled. *Welcome, Amelia, I hoped you would connect again. We belong together, you, Miranda and I.*

You can see me?

Of course. Did you think I wouldn't? I will always be an Oracle, whatever else I may become.

You look different. Amelia could hear the awe in her voice and felt a stab of irritation. She was here to spy, not shower Doriel with hero worship.

I am different. Everything that happens changes our energy. I went into a dark place after the kidnapping, but I am stronger. Are you stronger, Amelia? Can you pull the light from within yourself and shine it out to benefit the world?

I am very strong. My followers are good to me. They give me strength.

Yes, you pull it from them. You are draining them, sister. But you don't need their energy. You are strong all by yourself. Believe that.

I'm not. Amelia dug her nails into her palms in fury at the wobble in her voice. *That strength came from being part of the Triad and ended when I was cast out. I have to do things differently now.*

Your strength never came from the Triad. It was always your own.

Amelia shook her head. *You left me weak and defenceless. I'm strong now because I rebuilt in new ways and you hate that.*

Are those new ways working for you? Doriel tilted her head.

Stop it. You're trying to tie me in knots. I didn't come for this.

No, Doriel smiled. *You came to get into my head. But we've done that before and I've learned. I will never be less than before, Amelia. Only more. But you can be more too. You can be a part of this energy. Do you want that?*

Amelia breathed into the light that surrounded Doriel and her heart lifted. For once, the darkness dropped away, teasing her with a sense of hope she hadn't felt for a long time. She felt full of ... what was it?

Potential, Doriel whispered.

Amelia's eyes widened. *I can't go back, can I?*

Only forwards. The words drifted in the air around her. *But potential can be in your future as well as your past. You don't have to identify with The Fear.*

The Devil, Amelia whispered.

Is only your own fear. Only the fear that you inspire in others. I have moved through different cards more than once. Would you like to do the same?

It's too late. Amelia felt the light tug at her. She would only have to stop resisting and it would win. *But what if the light burns you?* The thought drifted through her mind. *It's too late. You've chosen your path. They don't want you really.*

'No!' she forced the words out through her voice box, heard the sound in the air around her even as it reverberated through her physical body. 'It's too late.'

It's never too late, sister. Doriel's words followed her as she retreated to her room at the Inn.

'You're wrong,' she said to the empty space, grief knifing through her. This was all that was real. The pain, the loss, the fear. They were all that she had. Anything else was false promise and she would never fall for that again.

Closing her eyes, she balled her hands into fists and screamed at the top of her voice, pushing her feet into the hard ground. She screamed the fear, screamed the anger, pouring it into the air around her. *Take it.* She sent out the thought to the monks. *Feed. Be strong.* She felt the pull of their energy and the swamping darkness. Pulling down a mental wall between herself and the energy she had exhaled, she stood up, kicked her shoes to the side and walked out of the room.

Rose must have left, because otherwise that almighty shriek would have summoned her in an instant. Instead, the Inn was cold and empty, filled only with Amelia's fear and the ghosts.

She padded down to the cellar, allowing the cold of the stone steps to seep into her skin through the soles of her feet. This building was drenched in history. The walls were steeped in pain and trauma, and she could access every bit of it. The chill laced over her skin as she went deeper into the cellar, and then pulled a blanket around her shoulders, hunching up on the chair in front of the computer screens. Reaching for the mouse, she clicked onto Lunea's webpage. There were the usual pictures of crystals and sparkly jewellery, but there was also a new events section. She clicked through. There they were. A picture of Doriel and Miranda, and an advert for divination classes.

> *Learn how to read tarot. In this class we will introduce you to the tarot archetypes and help you find your own way to read them, to aid self-development and decision-making. Allow the tarot to guide you to your best self.*

'Huh,' Amelia exhaled. 'As though they're being their best selves! If they were, I would still be with them and we'd be running those classes together.'

She shivered as an icy breeze drifted through the cellar. This old barn was far too big for one person. She was rattling around in it while those two were cosied up in their cute little Tudor cottage with Jonan. God, how she missed him. Beth had a lot to answer for. Before she'd come along, Amelia had still had a chance with Jonan, and she'd had Roland at her beck and call. Now she only had Rose, Laura and Steve. And she had to pay them for their loyalty. Beth had taken everything, and Doriel and Miranda were moving on without her.

She clicked in the address bar on the website, copied it, and then went onto her social media pages.

Avoid these classes run by Soul Snatchers. Let your friends know. They will be harvesting your energy and will keep that connection open forever.

She smirked. She did love her followers. Their gullibility was endless. She told them exactly what to look for, but they never spotted it when it came from her.

She watched as the shares exploded. Within moments, her post was everywhere. Doriel and Miranda were finished.

27

ROLAND

'ARE THEY COMING TO MEET US?' JONAN PEERED AROUND Bournemouth station.

Roland shook his head. 'I didn't want a public reunion. I'm far too nervous. I said we'd get a taxi.'

'Hey, Jonan!'

Jonan turned, and then frowned at Roland. 'Did you hear that? Do you see who it was?'

'There's a woman running towards you, waving. I don't recognise her though.'

'Jonan, could I get a selfie with you?' The woman was breathing heavily. She held up her phone and her hand shook slightly.

'A selfie? Why?'

'I'm a huge fan. Beth is incredible. She cleared me of Amelia's influence and a load of other stuff. I've never felt so good! I've been following you both online. I'm excited to meet you at last.'

Jonan raised one eyebrow, and then he smiled. 'Yes, of course.' He put an arm around her shoulders and she took a few photos. 'Please do tell your friends we'd be happy to help them in the same way, if they just contact the shop.'

'Can't Beth do it here?'

Jonan's smile was stilted this time. 'I'm hoping Beth will be heading home with me in the next couple of days. But we can do just as good a job from a distance, I promise.'

'That's a shame. But I suppose we can't keep her forever. Thank you for the picture. And have a lovely holiday!' She melted into the crowd.

'Beth wasn't lying when she said things were going well here.' Roland pulled his case towards the exit. 'I can't believe you have actual fans. Isn't that more Amelia's style?'

'You're not wrong.' Jonan hefted his rucksack onto his back. 'But we won't be anything like her.'

'If you are, I'll let you know.' Roland gave a tight smile and opened the door of the black cab at the front of the queue. He leaned in and gave the address. The driver nodded, and Roland climbed in, holding the door open for Jonan.

The drive would have been enjoyable if he hadn't been so nervous. The wide streets were lined with beautiful big houses and palm trees. The town gave way to a gorgeous cliff road with a view right out to sea sweeping down to the needles, huge standing stones in the ocean by the Isle of Wight. The sky was blue, and the sun shone bright on the sea, which was broken up by only a few small white waves.

'I can see why she came here,' Roland said, his voice small. 'How can I compete with this?'

'It's gorgeous, but a view is only ever pretty to look at. It doesn't make you happy. Only love can do that.'

Roland swallowed. 'I know you're right. I just hope it's enough.'

'You'll know soon,' Jonan said as the car pulled up on a street of houses.

'Thank you.' Roland's voice cracked as he handed a £20 note to the driver. 'Keep the change.'

They climbed out of the car and looked at the houses in front of them.

'I thought they lived in a flat.' Jonan peered up at the buildings, which glinted white in the bright sunlight.

'It's this one.' Roland walked up a narrow staircase to the side of one of the houses and rang the doorbell.

The door opened a crack and Abi peered through. 'Roland!' she screamed, flung the door open and threw her arms around his legs.

Roland laughed, untangled her arms, crouched down and wrapped them around his neck. 'It's good to see you too,' he said, smoothing down her long hair. 'Is your mummy here?'

'Will you take Jonan to Beth, sweetheart?' Layla's voice came from above. Roland stood up. Layla was smiling, her shoulder-length hair tucked behind her ears. She was wearing a bright pink dress and had dyed her hair to match. Her feet were bare. He swallowed.

'Come on, Jonan.' Abi grabbed his hand, and then turned and dragged him into the flat.

'You came.' Layla's voice was soft. She reached her hand towards him, and then dropped it before he could take it.

He smiled. 'I would travel through lifetimes for you, if you asked.'

Layla blushed and looked at her feet, before looking back up at him, her eyes damp. 'Have I pulled you away from your duty? I know that's important to you.'

'I don't know what my duty is anymore, apart from to

protect you and Abi from Amelia and, I hope, to make it safe for you to come home.'

She stood to the side of the hall and gestured him in. 'Maybe I am home?'

'Only you can decide that.'

She smiled and he was pretty sure he'd passed a test.

'Come on in,' Beth called as Roland came to the end of the hall. 'It's great to see you.' She pulled him into a tight hug, and then held him at arm's length. 'You look great. Can I get you a drink?' She walked over to the kitchen, pulled a beer from the inside of the fridge door and handed it to him. 'Have you met Tabitha?' She gestured behind him and he turned. A shiver ran down his spine when he saw the red-haired woman on the sofa. She was smiling, Abi hugged into her side. She looked benign and gentle, but there was something else to her. The tiger on the wall at home flashed through his mind and he stepped back.

'It's lovely to meet you.' Tabitha made to get up, but Abi snuggled in closer. Tabitha laughed and held her hand up to him instead. 'This one knows what she wants.'

He shook her hand. 'That's a good instinct to have, and not one all of us have mastered.'

'I've seen you on TV,' Tabitha inclined her head towards Jonan. 'You've had a rather chequered past.'

'Don't believe everything Amelia says.' Jonan rolled his eyes. 'I'm nowhere near as interesting as she makes out.'

Tabitha laughed. 'I know she's lying, but there's something fascinating about you in spite of that. I wish I could hang around to find out, but I promised to meet Dylan at the airport tonight.'

'Will you bring him to see us?' Abi put a thumb into her mouth. 'I like it when he sings to me.'

'You and everyone else!' Layla laughed.

'Ah, but Abi is more special than the others, aren't you, kitten.' Tabitha winked and pulled on her coat. She kissed Layla on the cheek and then waved to the others. I'll see you soon. Keep your spirits up. That woman's on a lucky streak, but it can't last forever. People will see through her in the end. And we will do what we can to help you.' She waved, and a few moments later the front door slammed behind her.

'I hope she's right,' Jonan said, pulling Beth close in to his side. 'I'm pretty sure we've all thought that in the past. I'm not sure what she could do to help though.'

Beth suppressed a smile. 'It's different here, further from Amelia. It makes you realise we only see part of the picture living in her shadow as we do. You'll see.'

'I think he already has,' Roland grinned. 'He was recognised at the station.'

'That keeps happening to me too.' Beth sat on the sofa in Tabitha's vacated space and put her arm around Abi. 'Layla, Jonan and I will spend some time with this one. Why don't you take Roland to the sea?'

'I don't need to be asked twice!' Layla grabbed her coat from the arm of the sofa. 'Come on, Roland. Let me take you to my favourite place.'

28

ROLAND

THE SUN WAS LOW IN THE SKY WHEN ROLAND AND LAYLA climbed out of the car and started walking across the windswept grassland on Hengistbury Head.

They walked side by side, wordless. The breeze was warm and the seagulls shrieking overhead filled the silence. They had crossed the wide flat grassy field and started up the hill into lush woodland by the time Layla cleared her throat. 'I shouldn't have spoken to you like that when Abi and I left.'

The tension in Roland's chest eased at her words. 'I know what Amelia's like. I know what she does to people.'

'Still, I wish I'd behaved differently. I've rewritten that scene in my head so many times since I saw you last.' She stopped by a pond to watch the dragonflies swooping over the water.

Roland leaned on a fence post. 'You did the right thing. I would have tried to persuade you to stay.'

'And now?'

'I would never ask you to bring Abi back. But that doesn't mean I don't dream about you doing just that.'

Layla smiled. 'I'm glad. I know you're as much Amelia's victim as anyone else, if not more. I want you in my life, but I don't know how to make that happen safely.' She gestured to the path and started walking up the hill again.

The air was buzzing with life. Roland thought he saw something move in the bushes off to the right, but when he looked properly, everything was still. 'Did you know I've moved into your house?'

She nodded. 'Have you done much to it?'

'I've painted a bedroom for Abi, just in case. I picked the big one at the back and put a tiger and a leopard on the wall.'

Layla stopped. She reached out, putting the flat of her hand on the trunk of the oak tree next to her. 'What made you choose a tiger and a leopard?'

'I don't know. It was a weird transcendental moment. The cats came to me. I couldn't not paint them. I'm not asking you to come back. Abi's safety is my top priority too. I just wanted you to know that she has her own space in my home, wherever you live.'

Layla started walking again, and then led him through the trees and out onto the beach. She sat on the sand, burying her hands in it, up to her wrists.

'Leopards and tigers are special to Abi. It's hard for me to explain why. You must be getting your gifts back if you painted those cats on her wall.'

'It's not just that,' he said with a sigh. 'I've been seeing and hearing you both in the house ever since I left. You're a part of the place.'

She shrugged. 'I'm sure that's just your memories.'

'Maybe, but, either way, I've felt you both with me every day. I've not been able to think about anything else. I need to help Beth and Jonan deal with Amelia. I have to put my mistakes right. But after that, maybe I could move out here? Would you wait for me?'

Layla pulled her hand out of the sand and linked her fingers through his. The sun was setting over the sea and the sky was painted a vivid red and gold. 'I've been waiting for you ever since I first saw you.'

Roland let out a long, slow exhale. Reaching up, he stroked a strand of hair away from her face and tucked it behind her ear. 'I would do anything for you, Layla.'

Her breath hitched as he leaned closer, and her fingers closed tighter around his. The wait lasted a lifetime and then their lips touched. Shivers laced over his skin. He reached up, threading his fingers through her hair and she pulled him closer.

'I can't,' she whispered a moment later.

He pulled back. Closing his eyes, he took a deep breath. 'No?'

'I mean, yes,' she said, a tear running down her cheek. 'I can't let you go.'

He lay down on the sand, his heart pounding as the adrenaline ebbed away. 'I thought you meant ...'

'I'm sorry,' she said, then let out a burst of laughter before falling silent. 'I want to hold you close forever, but I can't. I don't want you to go.'

'Then I won't,' he said, propping himself up on one elbow. 'I meant it when I said I'd do anything for you.'

'Anything?' She tilted her head, grinning at him. 'Anything at all?'

'Name it.' He sat up.

'Would you run into the ocean for me?'

'Is that all? I thought you were going to ask me to do something life altering.' Winking at her, he got up and ran into the waves. The water was icy and he gasped as it climbed his legs, but he didn't stop until he was waist deep. A wave caught him, lifting him from his feet and then depositing him back on the sandy seabed. 'Are you coming?' he called over the cries of the gulls, laughing as she jumped up, stripping off her cardigan and leaving it on the sand as she splashed into the sea.

'Oh God, it's freezing,' she yelled as she pushed through the waves. The sea was up to her chest and she shivered, but he reached out, pulling her close as he wrapped his arms around her. A seagull screeched and he looked up. A chill shot down his spine. His vision played through his memory: himself and Layla standing in the ocean, the seagull wheeling overhead. It was all coming to pass. He thought everything had gone wrong, that he was broken. But what if this was the way it was always supposed to happen?

Leaning down, he touched his lips to hers, feeling the cold and tasting salt as she pulled him closer, shivering in the icy water.

'You really will do anything for me, then?' she whispered.

'I'd do so much more than this. I'll make it safe for you to come back to St Albans, I'll sell up and move down here, or we can go somewhere completely new. Anything you want. My life has been blown apart. It's time for a new start and if you'll have me, I'll build that new start around you.'

She reached up and kissed him lightly on the lips. Then she turned and waded back out onto the sand. Picking up her cardigan, she wrapped it around her soaked shoulders.

Roland followed. 'I didn't think my fully clothed sea dive through properly,' he said with a grimace as a blast of cold air blew right through his soaked clothes. 'Let's get back and get warm.'

Layla led him through the woods. 'Your offer is amazing, but if it was safe, I would move back to St Albans in a heartbeat. I loved it there. Beth and Jonan are there, and Tabitha. That's where my people are.'

Roland threaded his fingers through hers. 'St Albans it is. Abi will have her bedroom. One way or another, we will make it happen.'

29

LAYLA

THE FIRE WAS CRACKLING IN THE GRATE. ABI WAS IN BED AND Layla was warm and dry, a soft blanket wrapped around her shoulders. Beth and Jonan had left shortly after she had arrived back with Roland, so they had the house to themselves.

Roland poured them each a glass of wine, handed one to Layla and then sat on the sofa next to her.

'Today is the best day I've had in a long time.' Layla threaded her fingers through his. 'Thank you for not giving up on me.'

He smiled. 'I wouldn't do that. Loyalty is kind of my thing.'

She tilted her head and looked at him, eyes narrowed. 'But I don't want your loyalty. We're not married. Abi isn't your child. You don't owe me anything right now. I'm only interested if you genuinely want to be here.'

He put his glass down and turned his body to face hers. Reaching out, he cupped her face with his hands. 'Can't you see I want to be here? Why would I be loyal if I didn't already love you?'

'You were loyal to Amelia.'

He sighed. 'I've learned from that. I thought I owed her because she took me in when I had nobody. And for a long time, I thought I loved her.'

Layla took his hands into her own and put them in her lap. 'You told me you had nothing right now. That you would rebuild around me. Isn't that what you did for her?'

He frowned and turned, his hands slipping from hers as he stared into the fire, cracking his knuckles, and watching the flames in silence.

She waited.

'I know this is different,' he said at last. 'But I'm not sure how to explain why. And I do see what you mean.'

'I don't want to be your next Amelia. I don't want you to build your life around me. I'd like you to take the time to figure out who you are when you don't have Amelia controlling you, and then we can meet in the middle. I think your gifts are starting to come back, but there's still so much more bubbling below the surface.'

'There is?' Roland looked at her, one eyebrow raised. 'What do you pick up?'

'That your talent lies in bringing harmony through love and loyalty. It's the opposite to what Amelia does. She refuels by sucking fear into herself from her surroundings. You put love and balance out. I think that's why Amelia wanted to control you.'

He swallowed. 'She didn't ever really love me, did she?'

Layla sighed. 'I can't possibly know. Maybe she did. Maybe she still does, in her own way. I've barely met her. You can get yourself back now, if you choose to, but you can't use me to fill the gap. I want the real you, not your perception of what I need.'

Roland took a deep breath and let out a long, slow exhale. 'That's very different.'

Layla smiled. 'I will wait for you.'

'You're not going to let me choose the easy route?'

'It wouldn't be easy in the long run. And I want this to work. You will sort things out with Amelia. You're the gamechanger. She will struggle now you're gone, because you brought the harmony and ease. Without you, she's just a needy, deranged woman trying to manipulate people.'

Roland chuckled. 'I can see it looks like that, but don't underestimate her. She had more than me up her sleeve, and she will have plans to blow everything we've thought of out the water.'

'Don't underestimate us either,' Layla squeezed his hand. 'She's not the only one who can work with energy. You have something special, Roland. Use it. Support Lunea. Go on record and tell everyone Amelia is not looking out for them. I know it's a tough thing to do when you've loved her, but she's hurting people. She hurt me, and Abi. She hurt Beth and Jonan, and she hurt you too. Don't dismiss that. Your support for Lunea could make all the difference. People have seen you with Amelia. They know you were hers. And they'll wonder why you walked away. You can also bring your grace and harmony to Lunea, and help the energy flow more easily. You can do that, Roland, if you choose.'

He swallowed. 'How do you know all of this?'

'Surely you don't think it's an accident that I ended up working at Lunea?'

'Are you in on this big destiny with Jonan and Beth?'

She smiled. 'I'm in on this big destiny with you and Abi.'

He stared at her. 'What makes you think I have any kind of destiny at all?'

'Where have you been, Roland McLaney? How can you have missed this?'

He sighed. 'I have missed an awful lot, lost in Amelia's fog. But do you really think I need to go public?'

She took his hand. 'I think it would help if you did. But obviously you've been through a lot and it may be too much for you.'

'No.' He took a deep breath and let out a slow exhale. 'We've all been through a lot. If we all back away, she will win.'

Layla's heart beat faster as he spoke, his fingers drawing circles on her palm. She couldn't believe that at one time she was going to let him walk away. Leaning forwards, she kissed him lightly, and then allowed him to pull her close, leaning into the reality of him in amongst the chaos. One day their moment would come. And she would be ready when it did.

30

JONAN

'Good call to leave Roland and Layla alone,' Jonan said as they went down the steps to the road. 'We definitely weren't welcome or needed.'

Beth slipped an arm around his waist and pulled him close, her shoulder fitting neatly under his arm. 'I wanted you to myself anyway. Let's go to the beach.'

'In the dark?' He breathed in the scent of her. God, he had missed her.

'Absolutely.' She grinned, her eyes glinting in the light from the streetlamp. 'You're not afraid of the dark, are you?'

He laughed as they crossed the road to the clifftop. 'Race you!'

'Hey!' she shouted as he ran towards the sea.

He veered off to the left, came to the fence at the edge of the clifftop and pulled up short. 'Damn. That must have been why she went to the right,' he thought. He chuckled, and followed the direction Beth had taken, finding the zigzag path down to the sea.

She was sitting on the sand waiting for him when he

reached the promenade. Her dark hair was whipping around her head, picked up by the wind. She looked wild and powerful. A shiver of anticipation shot down his spine.

He sat beside her, looping his arm around her waist. She leaned on his shoulder, her warmth seeping into him in the chill, night air. 'It's beautiful here,' he said, his voice quiet.

'I love it. I'm not surprised Layla bolted here when she had to run.'

He swallowed. 'Do you ever consider staying?'

Silence.

He could hear the blood pulsing through his brain as he waited. Was the lure of the sea too much?

'No, of course not,' she said at last. 'I mean, not unless you stayed with me. Anyway, we have things to do back home. Doriel, and the shop.'

He let out his breath in a rush.

'I mean, it's going to be a wrench to leave Layla and Abi,' she carried on, her voice just audible over the sound of the wind. 'And I loved meeting Tabitha, although she doesn't live here anyway.'

'Do you think Layla and Abi will ever come back?' he asked. She turned to look at him. Her eyebrows pulled into a frown. 'I have no idea. Layla would say no, unless something changed drastically with Amelia. But she's in love with Roland, so who knows. And I don't think Abi is as on board with this move as Layla likes to think. She was delighted to see Roland today.'

Jonan nodded. 'He's missed her too. Did you know he painted a giant tiger and leopard on the wall of one of the bedrooms in his house, and designated it a room for Abi?'

'A tiger? That's interesting. Tabitha is Tara McLaughlin, the artist who paints big cats. Abi's very close to her. She actually has an original painting. It must be worth a fortune.'

'Maybe don't tell Roland that.' Laughter bubbled up through Jonan's chest. 'It's an awful lot to live up to.'

They stared out to sea, watching the white of the surf crash against the dark sand. The tang of salt and the scents of seaweed and sand filled his nostrils, reminding him of holidays as a child, playing on the beach with Roland.

'We don't know whether Layla will come back, but what about you?' he said. 'Are you ready to come home?'

She put an arm around his waist and squeezed. 'I think I've done everything I can here.'

This was it. This was his moment. Adrenaline shot through him. If he went for it now, within minutes he could have everything he'd ever dreamed of. But what if she said no?'

'What is it?' She angled to face him. 'Something's wrong.'

'Nothing's wrong.' He gave a nervous smile. 'But I did want to ask you a question.'

She waited, her head tilted to one side.

He took her hand, running a finger around her left index finger, and then reached into his pocket and pulled out the box.

She gasped, covering her mouth with her hands. Her eyes were wide.

'Beth, I've missed you so much. I can't imagine life without you by my side. I have waited for you for lifetimes, and grieved you every time we were parted. If we choose it, this can be our chance. I choose it, Beth. Do you? Will you marry me?'

He opened the box.

A gull wheeled overhead, shrieking into the silence that

swallowed Jonan whole. Blood pounded through his head and his hands shook as he held the box open in front of her.

Beth let out a sob. 'Yes. Of course, yes. Yes a million times.' She threw her arms around him and pulled him towards her for a bruising kiss. When she drew back, her face was streaked with tears, but she was smiling broadly.

He grinned back as he took the sapphire ring out of the box. She held out her left hand, and he slid it onto her finger. It fitted perfectly.

'Can you even see it in this light?' he said with a strangled laugh. He dug in his pocket for his phone and then shone the torch at her hand.

'Oh my goodness, Jonan, it's beautiful.' She turned her hand and looked at the ring from all directions. 'It's giving me shivers. I think I've worn this ring before.'

'Not this one.' He shrugged. 'But one very similar, maybe. It reminded me of something too.'

'I love it.' She threw her arms around him. 'Thank you.'

'We're going to do this?' he said, his voice hoarse.

'We're going to do this,' she whispered back, squeezing his hand. 'But Amelia has no part in this. I don't want her to have any influence at all.'

Jonan kissed her, feeling her heartbeat and the warmth of her body through his clothes. 'It will never be about her. I promise you that.'

31

BETH

BETH TILTED HER HAND, ALLOWING THE SAPPHIRE TO SPARKLE IN the harsh train lights.

'It really suits you.' Roland smiled. 'I guess you will be my sister soon.'

'Are you okay with that?' Beth's heart pounded. She hadn't liked Roland when they'd first met, but he'd transformed since getting out from under Amelia's influence. She desperately wanted his approval.

'I'm delighted!' He beamed. 'And Mum will be too, even if she doesn't show it. Just remember she's not good at communicating with real live people. But she likes you. And she knows you're Jonan's destiny. You were the whole reason she fell out with Amelia.'

'She hadn't even met me then.'

'No, but we all knew you were coming.' Roland shrugged. 'Mum thought Amelia should have stayed out of Jonan's way. She was furious Amelia got involved where she wasn't destined to be. What if Jonan had committed to her and not felt able to walk away? If anyone has the ability to get into someone's head that much, it's Amelia.'

'It's nice to hear Mum had so little faith in me.' Jonan grimaced.

'I don't think any of us had faith in you at that moment.' Roland laughed. 'It's hard to overstate how big a mistake you had just made.'

Jonan rolled his eyes. 'One I will never live down.'

Roland shrugged. 'I wouldn't worry. You're not the only one to have made that mistake, after all. At least you realised you'd gone wrong quickly. It took me years.'

'You're free of her now,' Beth said, leaning back in her seat and rolling her shoulders. 'Layla and Abi will be back with us soon and then we'll all be together. I'm starting to think we might actually be able to stop her.'

'Did I tell you a journalist from the *Hertfordshire News* called me?' Roland raised one eyebrow.

Beth leaned forwards. 'What about?'

'They want me to do an exposé of Amelia, to let people know what it's really like being with her and why I left. I wasn't going to do it, but Layla thinks my voice matters. This could be the perfect way to be heard, since I have hardly any followers on social media.'

'Of course your voice matters.' Jonan frowned. 'But only do it if you want to. You've put Amelia first for too long. It's time to do what you think is right, not us or Layla.'

'Thank you.' Roland slumped back in his seat. 'I can't describe how much it means to hear you say that. But this is my battle. I may not have looked like a victim, but it's incredible to feel Amelia's influence wane. I won't let her do this to anyone else if I can stop it.'

'I think the interview is a great idea.' Beth smiled. 'Just

make sure you keep on track and don't say anything that could be taken out of context. Remember, you won't be asked for approval. They can publish what they want. Could I have the journalist's name? I'll do a bit of digging and see if I can find their angle on Amelia. Oh ... and have you actually looked at your social media recently? I think you'll find you have a lot of followers now.'

Roland tapped on his phone. 'Wow!' He slumped back in his chair. 'I haven't posted, or anything. Why would all those people follow me?'

'Because your voice matters.' Beth smiled.

Roland closed his eyes and took a few deep breaths. When he opened them again he looked calmer. He tapped on his phone and an email popped up on Beth's screen. It was from a journalist called Barbara Spencer. Beth recognised the name, but couldn't remember why.

'Thanks.' She smiled. 'Are you sure you're ready for us to move in with you, Roland?'

'Oh God, yes. I hate rattling around in that house by myself. You can stay as long as you like, although things may get crowded if Layla and Abi come back, which I really hope they will.'

Beth shrugged. 'I think they might. Layla is worried about Abi, but Amelia is the least of it right now. Abi believes she has the ability to manifest anything she focuses on, and I'm not sure she's wrong. She's terrified of manifesting bad things. I think she could really do with Doriel's support.'

Roland frowned. 'I didn't know that. We should talk to Doriel. Maybe she could give them some advice?'

'There's more going on than I've grasped,' Beth said, taking a bite of her sandwich. 'I don't think Layla has as tight a grip on Abi as she believes.'

'I'm sure they'll be fine.' Jonan took her hand in his. 'They're miles away from Amelia.'

'For now.' Beth looked out the window, watching the fields fly past with more than a little sadness. She'd loved her time in Bournemouth, and she really wasn't sure she was ready to head back into battle with Amelia.

32

AMELIA

AMELIA HAD BEEN TRACKING THE LUNEA WEBSITE ALL WEEKEND and getting angrier by the click.

Doriel and Miranda's first classes were fully booked. The advert for the extra teacher was still on the site, so she was pretty sure they hadn't hired anyone yet. But if the classes continued to be this popular, it would only be a matter of time before she was replaced.

'I don't know why you bother to keep track of them.' Rob waved his toast in the air and took a sip of coffee. 'They're small fry. You don't need to worry about them.'

'You don't understand,' Amelia said from between gritted teeth. 'They are capable of more than you will ever be.'

'Touchy today, aren't we.' He raised his eyebrows. 'I know they mean something to you, but your future lies with me. We should launch something together. Focus on the future not the past. We could run a conference, teach people how to keep themselves safe from Soul Snatchers, and run workshops on how to spot them. People will lap it up.' He got up, walked around the table and sat next to her. Putting his hand on her knee, he ran it slowly up her thigh. 'You and I will be spectacular.'

She slapped his hand away. 'Don't ever do that again.' She pushed her chair back. 'You may have stayed at the Inn last night, but you will never make it into my bedroom. You could be right about the conference though. We'll run something bigger and better than their puny workshops. We'll gain the upper hand on the airwaves and their support will collapse.'

'I knew you'd see things my way.' He smirked.

'Don't get ahead of yourself. You lifted that idea right out of my playbook and you know it.'

He rolled his eyes, stood up and pulled on his jacket. 'I'm going to leave you to cool off. You're very grumpy in the mornings. But think about my suggestion. We should get our people on it sooner rather than later.'

'Toddle off then,' Amelia muttered under her breath as he let the door swing shut behind him. 'Rose!'

The click of high heels was more sluggish than usual. When Rose finally poked her head around the door the fake smile plastered across her face did nothing to hide the dark circles under her eyes, or her pallid skin. 'Is everything okay?'

Amelia frowned. Should she be worried about Rose? No. The woman was an adult. She could look after herself. 'I want to run a conference.' She propped her feet on the chair next to her and crossed her arms over her chest. 'I'm going to teach everyone how to recognise a Soul Snatcher and how to protect against them. I will fill this place with Amelia's Haven supporters, have a global live feed, journalists and opinion-formers. I'll have merchandise and elite membership categories. Roland always said I needed to do more with the Haven. He was right. I will make him regret his excellent advice.'

Rose swallowed. 'When were you thinking of running the conference?'

'Next week. My followers adore me. They'll drop everything and run when I call. Getting numbers won't be a problem. And we'll make more of a splash if it's a surprise.'

Rose came into the room and sat down, leaning her forehead on her hand. 'Next week?' Her voice was strangled. 'You want me to put something big together in a week?'

'I have absolute faith in you, Rose.' Amelia tried to plaster an encouraging look on her face. 'I know you can do it. You are the safest pair of hands and I know you will help me shout loud about this.' She opened her computer and started firing off messages on social media. 'If we can make it really uncomfortable for Lunea to run classes, maybe they'll give up before they get properly started.'

Rose wiped her eye. 'I'll see what I can arrange.' Her voice cracked. Then she got up and left the room, leaning on the door frame for a moment before she went.

'What is wrong with her?' Amelia rolled her eyes. Everyone was becoming less dependable, and it was getting on her nerves.

'Roland,' she whispered the name as she typed it into a search engine. She clicked through to his social media pages, but in spite of his now huge follower count, he still hadn't posted anything since they split up. Damn. How was she supposed to stalk him if he never said anything?

She clicked on the news tab at the top of the search terms and adrenaline shot through her. There was an article by Barbara Spencer in the *Hertfordshire News* from that morning, but it had already been picked up across the national press websites and would undoubtedly be in their next print editions. She clicked on the link.

'I spent many years with Amelia. I loved her. But I have had to accept that she is consciously manipulating people. I believed her when she first told me about the Soul Snatchers. I believed she was trying to help people. But when we broke up I began to get some perspective. If you're in Amelia's Haven, have you ever actually wondered what would happen to you if you were declared infected? I can assure you there is no system to help you. And there is no way to substantiate whether anything untoward happened to you. It would be a witch hunt. Anyone could declare you infected, and you would have to defend yourself in a community that has no respect for reason, just complete adoration for the dictates of one unpredictable woman.'

Amelia put the heel of her hand into her forehead and pressed. Roland had always adored her. How could he betray her now? What would this do to her reputation? To her conference? Could she go ahead after this? *Yes*, a voice said in her mind. *Just shout louder*.

She let out a slow exhale. That was all she could do. She had invested too much time and effort to give up. If Roland was going to attack, she would make sure she destroyed his reputation before he did any damage.

33

ROLAND

'ROLAND.' BETH WALKED INTO THE DINING ROOM IN HER dressing gown, staring at her phone. 'I think you need to check your social media accounts. Amelia was on the rampage last night and she's aimed it all at you.'

'Of course she did. That was inevitable after the article. It'll blow over. I'd rather not engage.'

'That's very strong.' Beth grinned. 'But you might want to prepare for confrontation. I've never known her to stay behind the screen for long.'

Roland sighed. 'I've dealt with Amelia head-on many times. I'd rather not do it again, but I'm not going to avoid it either. She's expecting us to run scared. There's no way I'm giving her that.'

Beth slumped onto the sofa and frowned at her phone. 'Are you sure you don't want to see what she's saying?'

'I'm sure. I only started those accounts because Amelia wanted me to. They've never been mine. The fuss will go away as long as I don't feed the troll. I'll go into the shop with you. That way, she can find me without coming here. What time are you going in?'

'Eight. We need to do a stock check before the shop opens.'

'I'll come along later,' Roland said. 'I have some stuff to do first. Plus, if she was on a social media binge last night, she won't wake up until at least eleven.'

'Nice work if you can get it.' Beth yawned. 'I'd love to stay in bed until eleven. Have you seen Jonan, by the way?'

Roland pushed a note across the table to her.

'He's in the shop already?' She yawned again. 'He's keen.'

Roland's phone rang and he pushed himself to his feet, reaching across the breakfast bar to grab it from the worktop. 'Hello? She's what? Already? It's not even eight o'clock.' He sighed. 'Okay, I'm on my way. I'll see you in five.'

'What is it?'

'It turns out Amelia hasn't actually been to bed yet. She's turned up at Lunea looking for me, drunk and abusive.'

'Hang on.' Beth poured a cup of coffee from the filter pot. 'I'll throw some clothes on and come with you.'

'Take your time.' Roland tried for a reassuring smile. 'This is between Amelia and I. Drink your coffee. Get up slowly and give me a chance to deal with her. She will want an audience. I plan to deprive her of that.'

THE SUN WAS SHINING AND THE ROADS WERE EMPTY AS ROLAND walked to Lunea.

The door to the shop was locked, but he rapped on the wooden frame.

Jonan's face was grim when he opened the door. 'Good luck, brother. She's fuming.'

'What took you so long?' Amelia spat out the words, stalking over and squaring up to him.

'Is that the best you could come up with?' He raised one eyebrow, knowing it would infuriate her. 'I know you've been planning this moment. I was expecting something better.'

'You think you know everything. You think you need to punish me. But guess what, Roland, you left me, not the other way around. I'm the one who sobbed, alone, in the rain. I'm the one scrabbling around trying to fill your shoes at Amelia's Haven. Me.'

'Really? You mean Rose isn't taking up the slack?' Roland tried not to smile, but he couldn't help himself as her face darkened in fury.

'I wish I'd never got involved with you. I thought you were loyal. I never imagined you could hurt me so badly.'

'Leave him alone.' Miranda's voice came from the back of the shop. 'None of us are at your beck and call, Roland included. He tried to be there for you. It's not his fault you manipulated and used him while still holding a torch for his brother. Roland has a new life now. A life without you.'

'And what kind of life is that?' Amelia sidled up to him and slid her hand up his arm, her breath stinking of stale whiskey. 'Do you have a new lover?'

'If I did, that wouldn't be any business of yours.' Roland picked her hand off his arm and dropped it so it fell down by her side. 'What is it you want with me, Amelia?'

'You don't know?' Her voice was high-pitched. 'I've been posting on every social media channel all night.'

He shrugged. 'I joined social media for you. I don't look at it anymore.'

'But ...' she tailed off, turning to Miranda, who was

leaning against the payment desk, her arms crossed over her chest.

'What is it you want, Amelia?' Miranda raised one eyebrow. 'Do you want to rejoin the Triad? Because raging at us at eight in the morning after drinking all night isn't going to hit the spot.'

'Nor is it the right way to get me back.' Roland shoved his hands in his pockets. 'Go home and sleep it off. We can talk when you're sober.'

She reached for the lapels of his coat, and leaned against him, giving way to sobs. 'You're a traitor, Roland. You said you loved me, and then you abandoned me in the middle of the street. You left me alone in the rain with everyone watching.'

'That's the worst bit for you, isn't it: the idea of people watching. But do you know what? Nobody cared.' He unpicked her hands from his jacket and stepped back. 'I'm not coming back. You need to move on. I have. You know who hasn't? Doriel. She would take you back in an instant if you got your act together. Stop the booze. Stop the fearmongering and manipulation. Rediscover the woman you were born to be. The door isn't closed here, Amelia. You can come back. You can have what you always wanted. You just need to stop hurting people.'

She hiccupped and slumped into one of the armchairs. Her eyelids fluttered, and then she lurched upright. She paled, clasped her arm around her stomach and began to heave. Jonan grabbed her arm, but she shook her head and crouched low on the floor, holding the chair with one hand and clamping the other over her mouth.

'No,' she rasped. 'I'm okay. Leave me be.' A single tear ran down one cheek. 'Roland,' she said, her voice choked. 'I miss you. I need you to come back. It's been long enough. You've made your point.'

He got down on his knees so he could meet her gaze, and took one of her hands in his. 'Amelia, I know you're lonely. I know you're having a rough time. But I'm not making a point. This is forever. I have moved on and you need to do the same.'

She pushed him away and lurched to her feet. 'You're a traitor. A bastard and a traitor. I will make sure no woman ever wants anything to do with you again.' She held his gaze as he stood up, and then gaped. 'Oh my God. There really is someone else, isn't there? That's why you don't care what I say. You have your new woman in the bag already.'

Roland said nothing.

'You are a sleaze and a two-timing bastard,' she yelled. 'I hate you, Roland McLaney, and I hate you too, Jonan. You have ruined my life.'

They said nothing. Roland, Miranda and Jonan just watched her, arms crossed over their chests in identical poses.

'Aghhhh,' she yelled, picking up a crystal ball and swinging it up above her head.

Doriel ducked out from the stairwell and lifted it out of her hands before she could throw it. 'Don't do that, darling. I know you're angry with them, but please, don't damage my shop. You'll be here with me one day, I hope. We'll be running this place together as we were always supposed to.'

Amelia looked at Doriel. She swallowed. 'You see that?'

'I want that.'

Amelia held her gaze for an impossibly long moment, and then shook her head. 'I'm not well.'

'Of course not.' Miranda walked over, placing herself

between Amelia and Doriel. 'You're wasted. Go home. Sober up and think about what you've said and done here. We all mean what we say, Amelia, including Doriel. Think about what that could mean for you. Think about what you will give up if you let this opportunity pass.'

'You've always pushed me away. You thought you were better than me even before I hooked up with Jonan.'

'And I was right.'

'Miranda, stop embarrassing yourself.' Doriel's voice was sharp and Roland tried not to laugh. He didn't quite manage, and a small snort escaped him.

Amelia caught his eye, and for a moment it felt like he'd gone back in time. The world shrank down to just the two of them and that connection.

He shook his head. 'Don't. Do. That.'

Amelia took a step towards him, but he lurched back.

'It always used to be like that, Roland, it could be again. We don't have to be on opposing sides.'

'The only way we are going to be on the same side is if you shut down Amelia's Haven and take up Doriel's offer.'

'But ... I can't give everything up.'

Roland shrugged. 'That's your choice. Nobody is pushing you out. You are leaving yourself out in the cold.'

'There's nothing cold about where I am.' She stood tall, trying to appear steady, even as she swayed and grabbed a shelf of crystals.

Doriel leaned forward and anchored the stack as it swayed under Amelia's weight.

'I am going back to my glorious and luxurious mansion. I shall leave you to squash into your tiny flat upstairs and work all day in this shop while I get paid for existing. I'm not the one who made the wrong choices: you are.' She wove her way towards the door, her nose in the air. She reached for the door handle and missed, but then fumbled and grabbed it, slamming it open so hard the glass shook. She tripped over the step but managed to stay upright as she disappeared down the road towards the Inn.

34

LAYLA

A SCREAM PROPELLED LAYLA OUT OF BED AND TO HER FEET. She bent over, leaning her hands on her thighs and pulling in air, trying to control the nausea that swept up from her stomach.

Another scream.

'Abi!' Layla ran.

The little girl was sitting bolt upright in bed, tears streaming down her face.

'What happened, pumpkin?' Layla slumped on the side of the bed and gathered Abi into her arms.

'I had a bad dream, Mummy. It was about Roland. We have to go to him.'

Layla sighed. 'It was just a dream, sweetie. Roland is fine. He's a grown-up and he's good at looking after himself. Plus, it's 3 a.m. He will be tucked up in bed, asleep. He's not in danger at all. I promise.'

'Not right now. Soon.' Abi choked out the words as she collapsed into sobs. 'We have to go. We're in the wrong place.'

'Abi, honey.' Layla put her hands on the little girl's upper arms and held her gaze. 'Everything will feel a lot more normal in the morning.'

'No.' Abi's voice was quiet, but surprisingly firm. 'We have to go to Roland. He's not safe.'

'Sweetie ...'

'Promise me, Mummy.'

'I promise we will talk about this in the morning, and you can tell me whether you're still concerned.'

Abi frowned at her, and then nodded as she lay back down. 'Will you get in with me?'

Layla climbed in next to her. She had barely closed her eyes when sleep took her.

'Get up, Mummy. We have to go.'

Layla's head was pounding and her throat was dry. 'What time is it?'

'Five o'clock. Time to leave.'

'Five in the morning?' Layla yawned. 'Go back to sleep.'

'We have to find Roland.'

Layla groaned as she sat up. 'Pumpkin, we are not going to find Roland. He's perfectly safe and he has Beth, Jonan, Doriel and Miranda looking out for him. I won't take you anywhere near Amelia.'

'I'll be okay. Let's go now.'

Layla groaned again. 'Talk to me later.'

'Mummy, will they let me go on a train on my own? I have pocket money saved.'

Layla blinked. 'On your own? What do you mean?'

'You don't want to go, but I have to see Roland.'

'Are you telling me you'll go without me if I say no?'

Abi nodded, but her eyes were wide and innocent. There

was no trace of defiance. Layla shook her head and swung her legs off the bed. 'Let me get a coffee and wake up, and then we'll talk about it.'

'Okay but be quick. The train leaves soon.'

Layla sighed. This was clearly going to be a long day.

35

BETH

BETH HAD BEEN ON HER FEET ALL DAY, FIELDING ENQUIRIES, booking sessions and clearing people of Amelia's energy. People were travelling a surprisingly long way for treatments, and she was staggered by the faith they had in her.

Roland gazed around the packed shop. 'This is amazing.' He kissed Beth on the cheek. 'Business is clearly booming despite Amelia's attempts to clip your wings.'

'The word has spread from Bournemouth. I couldn't get anyone interested a few weeks ago. Now look!'

'Amelia won't like that.' Roland chuckled. 'And if she causes a scene now, she'll confirm everything I said in that interview.'

'Will this even be on her radar?' Beth frowned as she rearranged a display of tarot decks that had been knocked over. 'We haven't said anything publicly.'

Roland raised one eyebrow. 'Amelia draws energy from every person she's tied up in her knots. If you disentangle them, she becomes weaker. Plus, she's on your website several times a day, searching for information about each and every one of you. Of us. She knows.'

'And isn't that a comforting thought.' Jonan came over and pulled Roland into a quick hug. 'It's good to see you.'

Roland grinned. 'I reckon there'll be a show at some point. I have to keep popping in or I'll miss it.'

'Did someone mention a show?' The voice was familiar. Beth spun around. She gaped, and then stepped back, clapping her hands over her mouth.

Dylan McKenzie was standing right there, in her shop, Tabitha at his side. He was wearing a baseball cap and sunglasses, trying to blend in. But the quirk of his smile was unmistakable, as was the tiger tattooed on his bicep.

Tabitha rolled her eyes. 'Don't freak them out. Not everyone is used to having the voice from their playlist pop up behind them.'

'I ... um ...' Beth tailed off. 'Is it really you?'

Dylan laughed. 'Layla said you'd had some bad luck and suggested we pop in to support you. I think Tabitha wants to do some shopping as well. This is her kind of joint.'

'It certainly is.' Tabitha grinned. 'Let me introduce you all properly. Dylan, this is Beth, Roland and Jonan. Beth and Jonan are the ones Layla has told us so much about. And Roland is, well, you know ...'

'I do know.' Dylan smiled.

'And I'm Doriel.' They all turned at the voice from the bottom of the stairs.

A mental image of Doriel after the abduction flashed into Beth's mind: cowed, washed out and dressed entirely in black. Now she was like a kingfisher in a gorgeous turquoise jumpsuit, her bright red hair full of tiny gems.

'So this is the wonderful Tabitha. Your reputation precedes you.' Doriel pulled Tabitha into a hug.

The younger woman froze for a moment, and then relaxed into the contact and sighed. 'I do a lot to escape my reputation, although Dylan likes to blow my cover with his rock star routine.'

'Rock star routine?' Dylan raised his eyebrows. 'I came incognito.'

Doriel laughed. 'Sorry, I wasn't clear. I didn't mean your artistic reputation, although that does certainly precede you. I've heard all about you from Abi and I trust her instincts one hundred percent.'

Tabitha grinned. 'Abi told me I'd like you too. We may have been set up.'

'Undoubtedly.' Doriel laughed, and the sound was like bells. 'Did Abi tell you she thought we should create a tarot deck together?'

'The plan involved a lot of cats as I remember,' Tabitha said. 'Tarot isn't my usual fare, but I am certainly intrigued by the idea.'

'It's Dylan McKenzie!' A voice rang across the shop. The customer was staring wide-eyed at him. 'Dylan McKenzie is in here right now!'

Within moments, Dylan was surrounded by fans.

'You go upstairs with Doriel,' Beth said to Tabitha, trying not to laugh. 'You can watch the end of the workshop she's running with Miranda, and then chat about tarot cards. I'll look after Dylan and bring him up when he's finished with his fans.'

Doriel linked her arm through Tabitha's. 'I know it's a little on the nose, but I do believe you are our Strength card.'

Tabitha gave a short burst of laughter. 'Are you sure that's not Abi?'

Doriel ushered her up the stairs and closed the door behind them.

36

BETH

DYLAN HAD ABANDONED HIS HAT AND SUNGLASSES, AND WAS chatting openly to the fans, signing autographs and posing for selfies.

'Here, Beth.' He gestured her over. 'Your expertise is needed.' He backed away as she started explaining the services on offer.

'Does he come in here often?' one woman asked.

Beth smiled. 'Today is the first time. You lucked out. How did you hear about us?'

'You treated my friend in Bournemouth. I've travelled a long way to visit. Is there any chance you could fit me in?'

'Of course!' Beth looked in the book, but all the slots were full. 'We've booked up fast. But you've come a long way. I'll figure something out. Roland? Could you manage the shop while I see this lady?'

'Roland, do this. Roland do that.' A voice came from the door and a chill shot down Beth's spine.

Amelia looked dishevelled and pale with dark circles

under her eyes. 'I see you've slotted straight in here, Roland. Not as loyal as your reputation suggests.'

'Back so soon, Amelia?' Jonan put his hands on his hips. 'I thought you'd sleep for a lot longer after your drunk early-morning visit. But since you're here, let me get you a strong coffee and we can chat in private.'

'So you can shut me up?'

'So we can talk things through. I'm tired of arguing. Let's figure out a way to move on.'

'You think you can stop me causing a scene that easily?'

'Not a chance.' Jonan chuckled. 'I know you love nothing better than making a scene. But from memory, you also love coffee.'

Amelia hesitated. But then she shook her head, rolled her shoulders and straightened her back. 'Come with me, people,' she called out to the room. 'Jonan and Beth are trying to get into your heads, to force you into the hands of the Soul Snatchers. They will destroy your peace of mind and eat into your thoughts.'

Roland shoved his hands into his pockets. 'Amelia, these people are here because you have already destroyed their peace of mind and eaten into their thoughts. You're preaching to the wrong audience.'

'How dare you?' She stepped closer, tilting her chin up and holding his gaze. 'You abandoned me. Now you do everything you can to discredit me in public. That interview hurt me, Roland.'

Beth heard a faint growl and turned to look, but there was nothing out of the ordinary. She tuned into her psychic sight and looked at Amelia. There were grey cords coming from her hands, snaking their way towards Roland. She sent a blast of light at them, and they shrivelled back.

'Stop it!' Amelia glared at Beth.

'Nobody did anything.' Roland rolled his eyes. 'You're imagining problems now.'

'It was her.' She pointed at Beth.

Beth shrugged. 'We've been here before. I'm not getting into another one of these showdowns and our customers aren't interested in your wind-ups. What do you want, Amelia? This is a shop. Are you going to buy something?'

'I want to stop them.'

Beth frowned. 'Stop who?'

'Doriel and Miranda. They're trying to replace me. Someone just messaged to say a red-haired woman went upstairs with Doriel. Is she the one? Have I been wiped out that easily?'

'Leave Tabitha out of this.' Dylan walked towards them, his smile gone, hands clenched into fists at his side.

Amelia gaped. She stepped back. 'Dylan McKenzie? What are you doing here?'

'Shopping,' he held up a crystal and a packet of sage. 'Why else would I be here?'

'You did this to spite me,' Amelia hissed at Jonan. 'Dylan McKenzie may be a superstar, but his fans only listen to his music. I have a truly devoted following. They have changed their lives for me, and I am an ever-present fixture in their homes and their minds.'

As she spoke, the grey cords snaked out again. Beth blasted them with light, but this time they shivered and then continued. The room was silent. Everyone had turned to watch Amelia. Dylan had his arms folded across his chest and was looking at her, but his gaze continually flitted to the door at the bottom of the stairs.

Amelia turned.

'No!' He lurched forwards.

Amelia darted across, putting herself between Dylan and the door.

'The woman with the red hair. Doriel and Miranda. They're all upstairs, aren't they? Replacing me.' Her voice was low, hypnotic. Dylan blinked, and then shook his head and drew himself up taller. Roland stepped over and stood next to Dylan. 'We're not going to let you up there, Amelia.' Jonan stepped to Dylan's other side.

'Look at you all clubbing together like good little boys.' In a slow, exaggerated movement, Amelia reached down and grasped the handle.

Dylan darted towards her, but he hit an invisible wall and ricocheted back. He doubled over, leaning his hands on his thighs as he tried to catch his breath.

'So loyal.' Amelia ran a hand across Dylan's shoulder.

He shuddered and jerked away. 'Don't touch me.'

'Why? Would your redhead not like it?'

A growl rumbled through the air. Beth spun around, but there was nothing there. Roland and Jonan were looking around the shop too, but Dylan was more steadfast than before.

The door slammed open, sending Amelia tumbling into the room. She tripped on her high heels and fell into a stack of crystals. There was a crack as they tumbled to the floor. One landed on her toe and she screamed. Grabbing her foot, she rocked backwards and forwards in pain, her eyes tightly shut.

Doriel stood at the bottom of the stairs, her eyes a deep purple, ears sharpened into points.

'Abi?' Her voice cracked. 'What are you doing here?'

Beth turned to the door. Abi stalked forwards, her face

dark with thunder as she stared Amelia down. She seemed so much bigger and older than her age, and an aura of danger fizzed around her. Another growl shivered through the air.

Amelia paled. She stood up slowly, unsteady on her feet.

'I thought you had left,' she said through gritted teeth.

'I bet you wish I had stayed away.' Abi's laugh sent a shiver down Beth's spine. 'I bet you wish you had asked what I was before you bullied me. Now it's too late. I know all about you, but you know nothing about me.'

Dylan, Jonan and Roland stood frozen, staring at Abi and Amelia locked in standoff. Then as one, they lurched forwards.

Amelia darted to one side and they all ran at her. But she ducked past them and up the stairs faster than Beth could have believed possible.

37

BETH

'No!' Dylan bolted after her, Roland close on his heels.

'Roland!' Abi screamed, and followed. Beth tried to grab her, but the girl dodged easily and disappeared, slamming the door shut behind her.

The bells on the door to the shop tinkled and Beth turned. Layla stood there looking hot and flustered, her face bare of make-up, her Doc Martens back in place. She almost looked like her old self.

'Upstairs,' Beth yelled at her, and then started sprinting up the steps. 'Abi. Amelia.' She shifted to the side just in time to let Layla bolt past her, and then followed, closing the distance to the second floor, dimly remembering that she was leaving the shop completely unattended.

'Abi!' Layla yelled as she almost fell into the event room. Beth stumbled through behind her.

Abi stood in front of them, her arms stretched wide, her face steely with determination. A roar cut the air and Beth caught flashes of a huge shadow-like cat stalking Amelia, its gold spotted fur coming in and out of focus.

Roland staggered towards Abi, his face pale. Beth could see the grey cords binding him to Amelia, coiling around him and reaching out to everyone else in the room.

Then Abi raised her arms higher and roared as the room filled with blinding light.

'Abi!' Layla screamed.

Beth fell back against the wall as the energy that wasn't hers lifted away. She had been stripped bare. In that light she was just Beth, Betalia from the throne room. The woman who walked with Jonan to incarnate. The light being who promised to help people.

This is it, she heard Lunea's voice ripple through the light. Everything changes now. You can do this, if you really try.

A soft growl reverberated around the room.

Beth blinked, trying to clear her vision of the coloured spots that followed the over-bright light. Everyone looked stunned. Most of the workshop guests were sitting on the floor. One or two had their hands over their eyes. Another was sobbing.

'Abi,' Layla gasped, crawling towards the girl and pulling her into her arms. But Abi was glowing. And she was staring at Amelia. 'Leave Roland alone,' she said, her voice high-pitched.

Amelia squeezed her grip on Roland's arm tighter and her knuckles turned white. 'Why? What will you do if I don't, little girl?' She grinned, her face pale, dark circles shadowing her eyes. She stepped closer, but her body sagged, weakened.

Abi grinned. The growl that shivered through the room was louder this time. 'I make things happen. I make things real. Who knows what I might do?'

Amelia blanched, her gaze darting around the room. 'What was that? It sounded like a lion or something!'

Abi grinned wider.

Tabitha walked over to Abi, bent down and whispered in her ear. Abi wrinkled her nose and shook her head sharply.

Tabitha looked her in the eye and raised her eyebrows.

Abi rolled her eyes and relaxed her posture. Layla slumped too, all the fight going out of her. She covered her face with her hands and her shoulders shook, but she didn't make a sound.

There was a murmuring around the room.

Roland walked over to Abi and took both of her hands in his. 'Thank you. I don't know what you did but thank you. I haven't felt this good in years.'

'She was tying you up.' Abi glared at Amelia. 'I didn't like it. I untied you. And you too,' she said, gesturing around the room.

Beth swallowed. Abi was right. Amelia's grey cords were gone. The room shone with a new iridescence. Amelia looked furious, but also exhausted as she leaned against the wall, hunched, her hands shaking.

Roland put a hand on Amelia's arm. 'I suggest you sit down. You only have your own energy to draw on now.'

'Screw you, Roland.' Amelia sneered. 'You think you know everything? You think you've weakened me with your little kitten, but I assure you it's not that easy. I am strong. I will always be strong. And people will always love me.'

His smile was bland.

'You.' Amelia gestured around the room at Roland, Doriel and Miranda, and then at Jonan, Beth, Abi and Layla. 'You are ruining everything.' She swung the door open and slammed it behind her. Everyone in the room let out a collective sigh of relief.

Beth took a deep breath, and then made towards the door.

'No.' Miranda's voice was firm.

'I have to.' Beth swung the door open. 'There's nobody to stop her destroying the shop.'

'I will go.' Miranda walked past her. 'I'll close the shop while I'm down there.'

Beth stepped back.

'Right.' Doriel clapped her hands. 'That's it for the day. You've all had some pretty amazing energy work, courtesy of Abi, and we don't want to overdo it. Go home, chill out, drink lots of water. Take care of yourselves. Enjoy it!' She ushered the guests out with a touch on the shoulder here, a hug or a word in the ear there. Within a few minutes they had all left.

38

LAYLA

Upstairs, Layla pulled Abi into a big hug.

'You're squeezing me, Mummy. I can't breathe.'

Layla forced herself to relax her arms and moved backwards. 'I was scared. Please don't ever do that again.'

'Roland needed me.' Abi stuck her lip out.

Layla looked up at Roland.

'She's not wrong. Although I have no idea how she did that, or where the growl came from. Amelia was right. It did sound like a lion.'

Abi giggled. 'A leopard,' she said, and giggled again.

'Can you tell us what happened, Abi?' Doriel asked, handing her a glass of juice.

Abi gulped it down and then shrugged. 'Amelia was tying people up with her grey ropes. Especially Roland. I stopped her.'

'How?' Doriel sat on the sofa and patted the seat next to her. 'How did you stop her, sweetie?'

'I burned her webs away.'

'How did you learn to do that?'

Abi tilted her head to one side and frowned at Doriel. 'Salu showed me, of course.'

'Salu?' Layla's voice was hoarse. 'Beth, isn't that ...?'

Beth nodded. 'My brother.'

'He loves me too.' Abi grinned, pleased with herself.

'Did Salu tell you to do it, pumpkin?' Layla said, blinking back tears. 'Does he tell you what to do?'

'Never.' Abi shook her head, her face earnest. 'They can't do that. They can only help if you ask them to.'

'That sounds like Salu,' Beth said with a nervous laugh.

'Roland needed help. I asked Salu what I could do and he told me how. I had to help Roland. That's why we came back.'

Roland sat on the sofa on the other side of Abi. 'Sweetheart, I really appreciate what you did, but it's not your job to look after me. I'm a grown-up.'

'I told her that,' Layla said, her voice soft. 'But she was ready to get the train up here on her own if I didn't bring her.'

Abi shrugged. 'I won't let anyone hurt my people like those kids hurt me, Mummy. I know how to make it stop now.'

Doriel pulled Abi into a hug. 'You must be exhausted, sweetie. Why don't you go into my room. There's a TV in there. You could watch some cartoons?'

'Can I lie on your bed?' Abi crossed her fingers.

Doriel laughed. 'Of course. I'll bring you some more juice in a few minutes. You settle in.'

Abi ran into Doriel's bedroom, slamming the door behind her.

Doriel leaned back on the sofa. 'I think Abi did need to come back to help Roland. We all have our parts to play, and hers is manifestation. She is the Magician card and has everything she needs to bring things into the real world.'

Tabitha snorted.

Doriel raised her eyebrows.

'Sorry. It's nothing.' Tabitha said, suppressing a smile. 'I'm just remembering some of Abi's manifestations. They were pretty spectacular.'

'She's just a child.' Layla's voice was rough. 'She isn't responsible for anyone's wellbeing, and I won't let you put that on her. If she wants to opt in to this big destiny when she's an adult, that's fine. But for now, you leave her out of it.'

'We did leave her out of it.' Doriel held Layla's gaze. 'But she chose this. You said that yourself.'

'I won't let you use her.'

'We wouldn't dream of using her. But I won't turn her away either.' Doriel's voice was gentle. 'She has some interesting abilities and a very strong connection with you.' She inclined her head towards Tabitha.

Tabitha smiled but said nothing.

Miranda came back in and sat on the sofa, her back ramrod straight. 'She's gone. She won't be back any time soon and the shop is shut. How is Abi?'

'As bright as anything.' Doriel reached out and took Layla's hand. 'But Layla is worried.'

Miranda nodded. 'Amelia is unstable and Abi just challenged her. Maybe it would be safest to take her away again?'

'I'd love to,' Layla said, her chest tightening. 'But she says this is her home and she needs to be near Tabitha and Doriel.'

'I will help protect her.' Tabitha held Layla's gaze. 'You know I can.'

'Yes, you can.' A smile played around Miranda's lips. 'I'd love to talk to you about that talent of yours, and your connection to Abi.'

'Listen.' Beth leaned forwards. 'I'm sure you're really fierce, Tabitha, but taking on Amelia is something different. If all of us combined were unable to protect Abi, I don't see how you'll manage by yourself.'

Tabitha nodded. 'I get it. It's hard to understand. And you should increase security at the shop in case Amelia sends her thugs again. But if Amelia goes for Abi, I've got it. You can trust me.'

'I trust her, Beth,' Layla said with a growing certainty. 'I know what Tab can do, and I would trust her with Abi's life.'

A growl shivered through the air.

39

ROLAND

ROLAND COULDN'T BELIEVE THE HOUSE HAD BEEN EMPTY A couple of weeks ago. Now it was full to bursting with Layla and Abi back to stay, and Jonan and Beth in the spare room.

When he'd brought Abi up to her bedroom she had stared at the mural, wide-eyed. 'It's me,' she whispered. 'Me and Tabitha.'

'There are no people on there,' he said, 'just a tiger and a leopard.'

'Yes.' She walked up to the painting and laid her hands on the leopard. 'This is me.' Then she ran a single finger over the face of the white tiger. 'And this is Tabitha.'

Roland shook his head. He had no idea what game she was playing, but he might as well play along. 'What about me? Am I there?'

She looked at him as though he was crazy. 'You said, remember? There are no people there.'

'So only you and Tabitha get to be cats?'

'Are you a cat?' she said, something lighting up in her eyes. 'I would love more cat friends.'

'I could be,' he said, and got down onto all fours, meowing and rubbing his head against the side of the sofa.

She watched him, eyebrows raised, lips pursed. She said nothing, but a shiver ran down his spine as a growl reverberated through the room. Her eyes shone with a fire he hadn't seen before. He got up awkwardly and cleared his throat. 'Er, Abi, what was that?'

'What was what?' she tilted her head. 'I didn't see anything.' Then she skipped over to the door. 'Thank you for my amazing room, Roland. I love the painting. I'm going to bring my things up now.'

He leaned against the wall as her footsteps faded. What just happened? Painting this room had been a strange and transcendental experience. But that growl? It gave him chills in an entirely new way.

Layla poked her head around the door. 'Are you okay in there? Abi sent me up to look at the picture. She said you'd had a funny turn.'

Roland swallowed. 'What skills does Abi have? If I'm going to help protect her, I need to know what I'm dealing with.'

Layla sighed as she came in and shut the door behind her. She sat on the bed and fiddled with a loose thread on her trousers. 'Nothing is developed. It's all hard to understand at the moment.'

'Still, I'd like to know.'

The door slammed open and Abi came in with armfuls of stuffed toys. 'Mummy, this is my room. Go somewhere else.' She dumped the teddies on the bed.

Relief flickered across Layla's face as she all but leapt from the bed, out the door and down the stairs. She fiddled nervously with her hair as she perched on the edge of the sofa in the lounge.

He wondered what she had to tell him that an extra moment made so much difference. 'What's going on, Layla?'

'You know Doriel has pegged Abi as the Magician? The card relating to manifestation?'

Roland nodded.

'That does fit. Things happen when she's around. And as she's been focusing on that, she's started having strange experiences. She's been talking to Tabitha about it, and ...'

'I was wondering how Tabitha fitted into it all.'

'She's ... kind of ... training Abi. She's helping her understand how to manage her gift safely.'

'Safely?' Roland frowned. 'What kind of experiences is Abi having?'

Layla took a deep breath and let it out slowly. 'Well ... when she chooses to, she can astral project. She leaves her body and can travel anywhere she likes.'

'That's great!' Relief swept through Roland. 'I always wished I could do that. Perhaps she could teach me.'

'That's not all.' Layla grimaced. 'When she travels, she looks like a ... a leopard.'

Roland gaped. 'A leopard?' A shiver shot down his spine. 'Like the leopard I painted? When I created that there was a presence with me. Was that Abi?'

Layla swallowed. She shook her head. 'That was Tabitha.'

'Tabitha? How can she teach Abi to be a leopard?'

'She has the same gift. She astral projects as a white tiger.'

Roland closed his eyes, seeing the picture on Abi's wall clearly on the backs of his lids. He opened them again and held Layla's gaze.

She cleared her throat. 'Tabitha is her private name. When she works, she's known as Tara McLaughlin.'

Adrenaline shot through Roland. He took a deep breath and released it slowly. 'The artist?'

She nodded. 'The artist who paints tigers.'

'I heard the growl in the room above the shop. I wasn't sure what to make of it, but now it makes sense. Is she safe? How wild is she when she turns?'

'Abi, or Tabitha?' Layla smiled.

He shrugged. 'Both, I guess.'

'They don't turn, as such. Their human bodies are still here and the same, but they travel outside of them. Abi's spirit looks like a leopard, and Tabitha's looks like a tiger. At the moment Abi is invisible to most people, and she can't make herself solid. Tabitha thinks it won't be long before she masters that though.'

'I'm guessing Tabitha has that nailed?'

Layla nodded. 'She even interacted with the real tigers at the zoo before they went to the sanctuary in India.'

Roland stood up and started pacing. 'So, I channelled a world-famous artist, who's still alive, to paint that bedroom mural? Why would she bother?'

Layla grinned. 'Abi means a lot to Tabitha. They are connected by their gifts. There's power in that mural. You and Tabitha combined your energies to give that to Abi. That's incredibly special.'

'Do you think her abilities have anything to do with what we're doing here?'

Layla shrugged. 'I don't think they can. It's too new. And she's really young. I just need to protect her from Amelia. That's my job.'

'You know Doriel thinks your card is the Star?'

'She told me that, but I don't really know what it means.'

'It's a card of healing and balance. I think it means you bring true, deep and soothing healing to people.'

'That's lovely, but I don't see how I do that.'

'You're healing me.' Roland's voice cracked. 'You and Abi both. Coming into my life, helping me wash away Amelia's interference. I didn't even know who I was anymore. I can't say I've figured it out yet, but I'm starting to see myself more clearly outside of Amelia's shadow.'

Layla swallowed. 'I'm healing, you're loyalty and Abi is manifestation. That's quite a combination. Surely our journey can't be all about Amelia?'

'I know it's not,' Roland whispered as he moved closer and put his lips gently to hers. He kissed her, leaning into the rightness of it, into her warmth and the prickle of her nearness over his skin. This was where he was supposed to be. His time with Amelia seemed insipid compared to the feelings that flowed through him now, waking every cell in his body.

When they drew back, he held her gaze and swallowed. 'You can stay here for as long as you like. Stay forever if you're not going back to Bournemouth.'

'I wanted to go back. I wanted to get Abi as far away from Amelia as possible. But she doesn't want that for herself. Tabitha thinks Abi is strong enough now, and she promises to help protect her. I think if anyone can stand up to Amelia, Tabitha can.'

'I'm sure you're right. I've never seen anyone take her on successfully, apart from Beth. But a tiger? That's something new. Have you seen Tabitha?'

Layla's face lit up. 'Her coat is so thick. It's thrilling to be near her. But even as you run your fingers through her fur, feel the warmth of her body, her wildness is everywhere. I never know whether I am truly safe in her company, but I love it all the same. I know I should be dreading Abi manifesting fully. Keeping a young child from wreaking havoc with that kind of strength is a huge responsibility. But I can't wait, and I don't know why.'

'Because you will be with her more fully.' Roland squeezed her hand. 'And however wild she may be, Abi is the kindest, gentlest child. You can trust her.'

'I thought you would walk away when you knew.'

Roland tilted his head. 'You really thought I was capable of leaving you and Abi?'

'Who wouldn't? It's an impossible situation.'

'It's an exciting situation.' He smiled. 'I'm used to different. And I trust you and Abi. Whatever happens with Amelia, I know there is something special waiting for Abi down the line. I can't wait to see where this life takes her. Whatever happens, I am here for you both.'

40

BETH

BETH LOCKED UP, LEANING ON THE DOOR FOR A MOMENT, trying to ground into the solidity of the wooden frame, the cold metal of the key and the glinting pavement. She was still buzzing from the after-effects of the bright light, but it hadn't integrated yet. She felt as though she were floating somewhere above her own head.

'Are you in a rush to get back?' Jonan raised one eyebrow.

'Why? Do you have plans?'

He smiled. 'I have something I'd like to show you.' He crooked his arm and she threaded her own through it, leaning into the warmth of his body as they walked. The streetlights glinted on the slick pavement, creating an otherworldly glow. The occasional person walked past, eyes cast down at phones, or staring blankly ahead. A man sat in the doorway of one of the shops, huddled in a sleeping bag. Jonan threw a coin into the cup in front of him and the man raised a hand in thanks.

'This way.' He tugged her down a side street.

'Where are we going?'

Jonan chuckled. 'Patience.'

They came around the corner and he stopped in front of a small stone cottage set back from the road, a garden full of brambles flanking a narrow path up to a deep blue front door. There was a sign declaring it 'To Let' stuck in the flowerbed on the right.

'Is this what I think it is?' Beth whispered.

Jonan beamed, his eyes glinting in the orange streetlight. 'Do you love it?'

'From here I do, but can we go inside?'

'You certainly can,' a voice said from behind her. She turned to see a suited man with slicked-back hair. He walked past them, up the path, unlocked the door and held it open.

The hall was narrow and led straight to a farmhouse kitchen at the back of the cottage. It had been newly renovated and the appliances all looked unused. The window at the back looked out over a ramshackle garden with roses crowding in at the edges of the glass. Beth put her hand flat on the stone worktop. She could ground in here.

'Look at this,' Jonan called from another room.

Going back down the hall, she turned right into a cute little lounge with a thick carpet, a wood-burning stove and deep, squishy sofas. The ceiling was an inch higher than Jonan's head.

'What do you think?' He spread his arms wide, his face beaming.

'It's gorgeous. But can we afford it?'

'It's on at a low price,' the agent said, 'but you'll have to pass an interview if you want it. The owner is less interested in money than in having people in here who will care for and treasure the house.'

'And it hasn't gone yet?' Beth asked, unable to stop the excitement bubbling up inside her.

'They have interviewed a fair few people.' The man frowned. 'But they haven't been happy with anybody. You seem to love the place though. I'm sure you'll be the ones.'

Beth raised her eyebrows. 'I bet you say that to all the tenants.'

The man smirked. 'Would you like to see upstairs?'

They followed him back out into the hall and up a narrow staircase. Beth peered into a gorgeous modern bathroom with black, marble-effect walls and a cute corner bath, but the man led them straight into the main bedroom.

It was a modest room, painted in a soft off-white with just a double bed against one wall and a fitted wardrobe. But even in the dark, Beth could see that the view would be spectacular. The cathedral was lit up, surrounded by trees and the cityscape. Beth sighed. 'I could get used to this.'

Jonan slid his arm around her waist. 'Shall we? Shall we see if they'll give us a chance to get used to it?'

She spun around, looking up into his eyes, which were a deep purple. She wondered whether the estate agent could see the points on his ears, or whether that was reserved only for her. 'Definitely,' she whispered. 'I have a good feeling about this place.'

The agent's phone rang. He looked at the screen. 'Excuse me,' he said, leaving them alone.

'I can't pick up any traces of Amelia here.' Beth sat on the bed, her gaze drawn once again to the view.

'It's been empty for a while.' Jonan sat next to her. 'The last tenants left a few months ago and the house has been refurbished since then. It would be great to get our own place now Layla and Abi are back. I promised we'd give them space when that happened.'

'And it would give us space too.' Beth leaned towards him, kissing him lightly on the lips. She glanced towards the door but it was shut, so she leaned in, kissing him more firmly.

'Oh, I'm sorry,' the agent spluttered.

They sprang apart. 'Sorry. Didn't hear the door open,' Jonan said. 'We'd like to request an interview, if possible?'

'Bizarrely, that was the owner on the phone. She's on her way now if you're up for meeting her straight away?'

'Now? That's amazing!' Beth stood up. 'What will she ask us, do you know?'

The agent led the way downstairs. 'It's not a test, as such, she just wants to get a feel for who you are, and how much you love the place. She's looking for someone who will treat it as their own and nurture it. Those are her words. If she thinks that's you, you can move in as soon as the paperwork is complete.'

As they walked into the living room, Beth did a double take. A woman was standing in the doorway to the hall, leaning on the doorframe. Her smile widened as Jonan walked into the room. 'I thought it was you,' she said, crossing the room and wrapping him into a hug.

'Celia?' He pulled back and looked at her, one eyebrow raised. 'Is this your house?'

'It is.' She sat on one of the sofas and indicated for the rest of them to sit down. 'I bought this place when Doriel moved here so I could spend lots of time with her. But when David, my husband, started working in London more often, we bought a bigger house and moved here permanently. Didn't Doriel tell you?'

Jonan shook his head. 'She hasn't mentioned you in years. I had no idea you were still in touch.'

Beth coughed, and then raised her eyebrows at Jonan.

'Sorry, Celia, this is Beth.'

'I know who she is.' The woman tilted her head and held Beth's gaze. 'The similarity is remarkable. I still remember that dream as clear as day, and here you are right in front of me. Potential.'

'I'm sorry, have we met?' Beth frowned. She didn't recognise her at all.

'Beth,' Jonan took her hand. 'Celia is the artist who illustrated *The Starfolk Tarot*.'

Beth gaped. She looked from the woman to Jonan, and then back again. Finally, she took a deep breath and leaned back on the sofa. 'I always wondered how I came to be in that deck. Jonan explained that you knew his family, but *we've* never met. It sounds like you saw me in a dream?'

'You and others. Many others. That deck was a manifestation of years of dreams. But you were particularly vivid. I'm pleased to see you found each other at last. And now here you are, in my house. I have to say, I was starting to lose hope that you would come. I was getting well and truly sick of doing these silly interviews.'

Jonan raised one eyebrow. 'Another dream?'

'And spot on it was, as ever.' She grinned. 'I'm not even going to pretend that I'm not smug right now. Anyway, I assume Rob here has given you all the proper information, the rent and terms? The place is yours if you want it, of course.'

'Really?' Beth clapped her hands together. 'We can have it? I never dared hope we could live somewhere like this.'

'Yes, well. I'd rather have kindred spirits in here. I don't want any of that Amelia stuff seeded in my house. I trust you will keep the energy clear?'

'Of course.' Jonan cast a glance at Rob, who was frowning now, and looking backwards and forwards between them. 'You can trust us to look after the place as though it were our own. Shall we do it, Beth?'

'Where do we sign?' She looked at Rob, who was now fumbling around in his satchel.

'I have the paperwork here if you'd like to fill it in. You can move in a week's time.'

'That would be perfect.' Jonan squeezed Beth's hand. 'We're staying at my brother's house, and we need to get out of his hair.'

'Your brother? Is Roland here too?' Celia clapped her hands together. 'I saw his interview. I'm delighted he got away from Amelia. I liked her all those years ago, but I can't believe all the rubbish she's spouting now. I must pop over to her place sometime. I can't help thinking the woman needs a good talking to. Surely we could make her drop all this nonsense. No?'

'Be our guest,' Jonan said with a chuckle. 'Maybe you will be the answer to more of our problems.'

'Ha, I doubt it. She never forgave me for casting her as the Devil in my tarot deck and drawing your Beth here as Potential. She ranted at me for a good hour about that one. But what do you think of my strange decision now, eh?'

'Ahem,' Rob said, standing up. 'I'm sorry to break up the reunion, but I do need to get to my next appointment.'

'Ah, never mind, poppet. Jonan and Beth here were about to take me to see some old friends, weren't you darlings.'

'Of course.' Jonan stood up and held his hand out. 'We'll wait to hear from you, Rob.'

He let them out and they waved as he locked the door and dashed out to his car.

'Now, take me to see that brother of yours. I believe he might be living with the Star and the Magician, and I'm dying to see them!'

'I think it's Abi's bedtime,' Beth put a hand on Jonan's arm.

Celia beamed. 'Don't worry about that. I'll only be a moment, and then I'll head over to see Doriel and Miranda. How exciting! The gang is finally gathering together.'

41

ROLAND

THE FIRE WAS BLAZING, AND THE TABLE WAS LAID WITH takeaway for two and deep goblet wine glasses. Roland sighed. He'd been so lonely here, but now he had everything he wanted. More in fact. It was going to get crowded here fast. But for now, Layla was putting Abi to bed and then they would have the house to themselves. He poured the wine.

The key turned in the lock. He had thought Jonan and Beth would be gone for hours after visiting that gorgeous cottage. He'd assumed they'd go out for a romantic meal, not come straight home to interrupt his plans.

He padded through to the hall in his socks, only to be met by a small woman with faded blond hair streaked with grey, and a smile that set off a million memories. 'Celia?'

'That's right, my beautiful boy. It's wonderful to see you.'

Jonan and Beth followed her in and shut the door softly.

He gaped. 'What are you doing here? I haven't seen you in years!'

'I've come to see that pink-haired lass of yours. Is she here? And the little girl? I saw her on the news after that awful attack. I knew she'd come through. She's strong, that one. Amelia will have her work cut out if she doesn't smooth things over with the girl before she's fully grown.'

Roland frowned. 'What do you know?'

'Me?' She wandered through to the dining room. 'I'm just an artist. I don't know anything.'

'Your random musings turned out pretty on point last time.'

She looked at the laid table and then turned, taking both of his hands in her own. 'I see you have plans and I'm interrupting. But could I meet your girls before I go? I'd love to know whether or not I did them justice.'

'Layla is just putting Abi to bed, but ...'

There was a thumping sound and Abi flew into the room dressed in pyjamas, her long hair braided into two plaits. 'I knew it was you.' She threw her arms around the woman's waist.

'Abi!' Layla ran after her and pulled up abruptly in front of Celia. 'I'm sorry. Abi, please let our visitor go.'

'Ah, please don't.' Celia smiled and hugged Abi back. 'I've been waiting a long time to meet your kitten. And you for that matter. You're quite a shining star, my dear.'

Layla frowned and looked at Roland. Then she stepped forward and untangled Abi's arms from Celia, stepping her firmly backwards. 'Do I know you?'

'Not yet, but you will.'

Roland slid his hand into hers. 'Celia is an old family friend. She illustrated *The Starfolk Tarot*, the deck Doriel told you about.'

'Where I'm the Star, you're the Lovers and Abi is the Magician? I get it. But please don't be so familiar with my daughter. We don't know you, for all that you may have dreamed us up once upon a time. And we don't have a good history with Roland's family friends.'

'Of course, of course. You have no reason to trust strangers with your daughter's welfare. And I can see I've come at a bad time. I'll leave you lovely people alone. It was wonderful to meet you, and I hope to see you all again soon. I have been speaking to Doriel and Miranda about running workshops with them, so you may see me more than any of us expected!' She waved and then disappeared out into the hall. 'Oh no,' she said as Jonan made to follow her. 'You go back in. Rob will be in contact about the house. I do hope you are happy there.'

There was silence as the front door slammed.

'What the hell was that?' Layla crossed her arms over her chest. 'Abi, go upstairs to bed, darling. I'll be up in a minute.'

'Like I said, she's the tarot illustrator …' Roland tailed off at the look on Layla's face.

'That's not what I meant. Why was she here? What is her agenda? If you know her from that far back, she could easily be one of Amelia's cronies.'

'She's not.' Beth reached out and touched Layla's arm. 'She's our new landlady. We've found somewhere to live.'

'You're moving out?' Layla looked stricken.

'You don't want us here really.' Beth pulled her friend into a hug. 'I know we've got used to each other recently, but we'll only be around the corner. You need your space. So do we.'

'Did anyone else think it sounded like Doriel and Mum had actually replaced Amelia with Celia?' Jonan sat down on one of the kitchen chairs. 'I thought that was a ruse to wind Amelia up. I didn't think they'd actually do it.'

'If they're going to replace her, Celia is the perfect choice.' Roland leaned against the wall. 'Amelia will be enraged.'

'But do we really want to enrage Amelia that much?' Jonan frowned. 'I thought this whole thing was about creating a situation we could calm down. I think we might be losing control of this narrative.'

'I'm going to get Abi to bed,' Layla disappeared up the stairs.

'Jonan,' Beth put her hands on his shoulders and nudged him to stand up. 'Celia was right about one thing. Roland and Layla have plans.'

'Oh ... yes. Sorry.' Jonan lurched up. 'Let's talk tomorrow.'

'Honestly, you don't have to rush off that fast,' Roland followed them into the hall. 'I appreciate your tact, but Layla's still putting Abi to bed.'

'You enjoy your evening, brother.' Jonan pulled him into a tight hug. 'You deserve it. We're going to celebrate our big news. I'll tell you all about the house tomorrow.'

They were gone so fast, Roland was left standing in the hall staring at the closed door. They were really leaving. He, Layla and Abi would have this place all to themselves. Could he be about to get the life he'd always dreamed of?

42

AMELIA

'THESE ARE A GIFT FROM ME, AS A THANK YOU FOR YOUR loyalty.' Amelia handed Laura and the Sheep identical jackets. They were branded with Amelia's Haven across the back and had gold emblems on the front. 'They will identify you as being on my team. I would really appreciate if you wore them all the time, particularly when you're doing any work for me.'

'Of course, Amelia.' Laura gave a strained smile.

The Sheep nodded. He put on the coat, but said nothing.

'These are valuable and I will be selling them to my followers. You are deeply fortunate to be getting them for free. If anyone asks, please do tell them they are available for sale on my website.'

'Of course.' Laura nodded again, but her gaze kept twitching to the door.

Amelia frowned. What was with the woman? 'I would like you to go to Lunea. Break in. Damage the shop. You know the drill.'

The Sheep sighed. 'They'll know it's us. It's always us.'

'They have security cameras now,' Laura said, her impatience obvious. 'I've seen them.'

'Then do something about them. Just sort it.' Amelia waved her hand dismissively. 'Go. Do my work and be proud to be part of Amelia's Haven.'

They trudged out the door and let it slam behind them.

Amelia gave them a moment, and then ran to the basement stairs.

Rose was sitting in front of the monitors, eating a packet of crisps. 'Did they have any idea there was something dodgy about those jackets?'

'Not even a flicker. They're getting more cynical, but hopefully they figured it was all about the marketing. Are the cameras working?'

Rose nodded. 'Although having them embedded into the jackets makes for odd and bumpy viewing. I'm not sure how long I'll be able to watch this without getting sick.'

'You'll be fine.' Amelia took a huge crisp from Rose's packet.

The grainy pictures jerked on the screen, rocking as Laura and the Sheep walked. When they got to Lunea, the Sheep rattled the door. An alarm pierced the night. Amelia lurched back and covered her ears. The images on the screens started jumping violently.

'Stop,' a voice shouted. The images kept lurching. 'Stop or I will release my dog.' The images stilled, and a thick-set man with a dark blue uniform and a huge German Shepard appeared. 'The shop is closed.'

'Oh, sorry, I didn't realise ... We wanted to buy some sage,' Laura said, her voice high-pitched.

Amelia snorted.

'At this time of night?' The man glared at them. 'What kind of idiot do you think I am?'

Amelia snorted again.

The dog snarled, its lips peeled back from sharp teeth.

'Leave now.' The man's voice was menacing. 'My dog might not wait for the police.'

'Yes, of course.' The Sheep's voice was shaking. 'We didn't mean any harm. We're going.'

'I thought you might.' The guard smirked and gave his dog a little more slack on the lead. It lurched forwards.

The world spun again as Laura and the Sheep ran.

'Damn.' Amelia slapped her palm on the desk. 'Someone defanged my Brute. I need a new plan. How are we going to get in?'

Rose pushed her chair back. 'We've targeted the shop so many times. It's not surprising they've increased their security. Could we get them where they're not expecting it?'

Amelia narrowed her eyes. Rose's aura was pulsing a muddy red colour. Her skin was pale and her hands gripped the arms of her chair. Good. She was terrified and that was exactly how Amelia liked her. Still, it wouldn't hurt to give the kicked puppy a stroke. 'That's not a bad idea. Brainstorm and come back with a suggested plan of action.'

'Yes, Amelia.' Rose turned back to the screen, her shaking hands clasped in her lap.

Amelia stood up to go, but the screens stopped lurching and she found herself looking into the Sheep's face. On another screen, Laura was gazing up. 'What are they doing?'

'Why don't we sit down,' Laura's voice was soft over the noise of the wind in the microphone, but it was still clear.

The Sheep bent down and touched the grass. He took off his jacket and laid it down for Laura to sit on.

'No! My camera is getting wet! Damn his chivalry.' Amelia took another of Rose's crisps and leaned forward to see more. They only had one screen now. Laura was facing out over the hill by the abbey, looking towards the lake. The nearby trees moved in the wind, lit by the lights on the cathedral behind them. Further away, the world fell into blackness.

'What will Amelia say when she realises we've failed?' Laura's voice was quiet.

'She'll say you're useless,' Amelia muttered, taking the entire packet of crisps from Rose and starting to munch her way through them.

'She won't be pleased, but don't worry. I'll take the brunt of it. I'm used to her. And she's not big enough to hurt me seriously.'

'Not big enough to hurt you physically,' Laura said, turning to face the Sheep. 'She has hurt you seriously many times.'

The Sheep shrugged, but just stared into the darkness. 'I must have done something pretty bad to have ended up with her. But now she has so much on me. I'll never get away.'

'Am I imagining it, or is she getting increasingly unpredictable?'

The Sheep looked straight into the camera now. 'It's been getting worse for a while. She hates not getting her own way. She's lost Jonan, the two women, and now Roland. She's furious that Doriel and Miranda are working without her. We can't fix that. We have to stay out of her way as much as possible.'

Laura sighed. 'That's easier said than done.'

'Don't worry.' The Sheep reached towards Laura. 'I will protect you.'

'But what if it's you I'm worried about?'

The Sheep stared at Laura, his eyes wide, lips parted. 'Er ... I don't know what to—'

A dog barked and they jumped, the camera lurching one more time. Then Laura began to laugh. She doubled over, leaning one hand on the Sheep's thigh. His big hand covered it, as he started shaking with laughter too.

When Laura looked back up at him, still at last, his face was more open than Amelia had ever seen it.

'I didn't know he could look like that,' she said, her voice barely more than a whisper. Laura's hand rose, and then disappeared off the top of the screen. He leaned down and then the view disappeared and all they could see was his coat.

'Turn it off.' Amelia shoved her chair back, relishing the screech it made on the stone floor. 'I don't want to listen to their squelchy kissing noises.'

Rose shut her laptop and the screens went black.

'I don't like the way they're talking about me. What does she see in him? He's revolting.'

'Er,' Rose pushed her chair back.

Amelia was pacing now. 'He's disgusting.'

Rose swallowed. She stood up and went over to the door.

Amelia raised her eyebrows but said nothing.

'Steve has been very loyal to you.' Rose gripped the edge of the door so hard her knuckles went white. 'I'm pleased he's finding happiness with Laura. Goodness knows he hasn't had much.' She edged backwards until she was at the bottom of the stairs, the door ready to swing between her and Amelia if necessary.

Amelia narrowed her eyes. She had planned to keep Rose on edge, but maybe she'd gone a bit far. She didn't want the woman to leave her with no backup.

She rearranged her face into something she hoped was friendlier. 'Of course he does. Both ... Steve and Laura have been unfailingly loyal and they will be rewarded. As will you.'

Rose's shoulders slumped. 'I'm going to ...'

'Yes, of course,' Amelia cut her off, not wanting to hear whatever made-up excuse the woman was preparing. 'I'm clocking off for the night anyway. You do the same. We'll figure things out tomorrow.'

Rose vanished up the stairs without a word, the sound of her heels fading surprisingly fast.

Amelia sighed. Rose was right about one thing. She needed a new plan. Her support system was disintegrating faster than a sandcastle in the tide.

43

BETH

'ARE WE REALLY GOING TO DO THIS?' A THRILL OF EXCITEMENT shot through Beth.

'If you mean the house, then I hope so! Are you getting cold feet?'

'No, I just can't believe we get to live in a place like that. Life is changing so fast. And on that note, I really don't think we should go home tonight. Roland and Layla need their space.'

'Agreed. I'm sure they'll put up with us for another week, but we could stay there tonight?' He nodded towards a big hotel at the top of the high street. 'We wouldn't have too far to roll to work tomorrow morning.'

'Shall we go to dinner first?'

They booked a double room and then went into a bar a couple of doors down.

They were shown to a table right in the middle of the restaurant. Beth looked around, but nobody was watching them. Could they have found the one place not riddled with Amelia's followers?

The waitress handed them menus. 'Can I get you a drink?'

'Gin and tonic, please.' Beth smiled.

'And a beer.' Jonan put a hand over Beth's as the waitress walked away. 'Nobody has recognised us.'

'At last.' She put the menu down. 'Every time I think I've got her out of my head, I realise another way she's wormed her way in.'

Jonan smiled. 'One day she will be out of our hair, and we will look back at this time and think how crazy it was, but how it brought us together at last.'

'Yeah, yeah, I know. Character-building and all that. But let's not spend tonight talking about Amelia. This house is a new start. I'm sure of it.'

'A new start for us, and for Roland and Layla. I hope they go the distance.'

Beth frowned. 'There's something Layla's not telling me. I have no idea what it is, but I'm pretty sure Tabitha's in on the joke. Abi too.'

'I know what you mean.' Jonan smiled. 'But they'll tell us if we need to know.'

'Maybe.' Beth narrowed her eyes. 'But do you have any idea what Abi did when she ran into that room and blasted Amelia's cords away?'

Jonan shook his head. 'I've never seen anything like it. It was incredibly powerful. I do know Doriel's been talking about her gifts, and she's convinced Abi is the Magician from the tarot deck, but she's being typically cryptic.'

'Has Roland said anything?'

Jonan shook his head. 'He wouldn't. He's far too loyal to betray a confidence. He did have a transcendental experience when he painted that mural, though. Have you seen it? It's incredible. Roland has always had a talent for art, but he's never been that good.'

Beth laughed. 'I saw the mural. It reminds me of Tabitha's paintings.'

Jonan narrowed his eyes. 'Does Tabitha fit into our story? Didn't Doriel say something about her being the Strength card?'

'She said that was on the nose. Any idea why?'

'The strength card usually has a woman and a lion, or some kind of big cat. Doesn't Tabitha paint tigers?'

'That's probably it. I'm not sure how all of this ties together, though, or what it says about Abi, apart from that she's attached to Tabitha.'

Jonan shrugged. 'If we need to know, someone will tell us. I'm glad Abi has Tabitha in her corner. I can't put my finger on why, but she seems ... powerful.'

Beth laughed. 'Maybe it's spending all that time with predators. It must rub off on her.'

As the food arrived, Beth spotted movement out of the corner of her eye. Turning, she saw Laura, her face bright red, the Brute following behind her. They wore matching Amelia's Haven jackets. The Brute froze as Beth caught his eye, looked around, and then hurried past their table to sit with Laura, his back to Beth. Laura looked at Beth for a moment and held her gaze. Last time Beth had seen her, she had been furious. Now there was a quiet desperation in her eyes that Beth couldn't explain. She frowned at her old friend, but Laura just shook her head, and then turned back to the Brute.

Beth leaned closer to Jonan. 'Did you see that?'

He nodded. 'Something is shifting. Amelia will be furious!'

Beth didn't even try to suppress her smirk.

Jonan reached over and took her hand. 'Things will change. Amelia is losing her hold on people and we have a new home waiting for us. We just have to try and navigate this time without any more disasters.'

Beth smiled. 'Here's to that.'

44

JONAN

JONAN TOOK IN A DEEP BREATH WHEN HE STEPPED OUT OF THE hotel the next morning, taking in the unexpected sunshine, the birds singing in the trees that lined the road, and the man who whistled as he set up his market stall.

'What a beautiful day,' Beth said as she followed him out. 'Maybe this bodes well for our new start.'

'Wouldn't that be nice!' Jonan slipped his hand into hers as they walked down the street towards the shop. 'Maybe Amelia will have found someone else to bother overnight and we'll be left in blissful peace.'

Beth laughed and the sound was freer than he'd heard it in weeks. 'Maybe she'll have decided to give up Amelia's Haven and rejoin the Triad.'

'That's how life was always supposed to look,' Jonan said, as sadness seeped through his muscles and settled bone deep. 'The three of them working together, talking, laughing, moving life forwards for themselves and others.'

'It will be that way again.' Beth squeezed his hand. 'We will make it so, one way or another.'

'I so wish that were possible.' Jonan stopped.

The bins outside the shop were lying on their side. He walked up to the front door and tried the handle, but the door was locked as he'd expected.

'Wait here.' He unlocked the door, went inside and checked every inch of the shop. Nothing was out of place. It was exactly as he'd left it at closing time the day before.

He nodded to Beth and then called up the stairs. 'Doriel? Mum? Are you okay?'

'We're meditating.' Miranda's voice was sharp even from two floors up.

'We're fine, love,' Doriel called. 'Why would you ask?'

Beth pushed the door open, setting off the bells.

'Doriel, focus.'

Jonan couldn't help smiling at his Mum's irritation. Years in seclusion had done nothing for her patience levels.

He heard footsteps on the stairs, and then the door swung open. Doriel stepped into the room, wrapping a long cardigan more tightly around her middle. 'Is something wrong?' She squinted into the bright light that streamed through the window.

'Someone's been messing with the bins. I thought we'd been broken into, but there's no sign of trouble in here.'

'I didn't hear anything.' Doriel frowned.

There was a knock at the door and Jonan turned to see the security guard he'd hired, his huge dog on a short lead. He opened the door. 'Come in.'

The man stepped inside, his dog at his heel.

'There were two people trying to get into the shop last night.'

'Can you describe them?' Beth asked.

'There was a man. Big. Dark hair, pale skin. And a

woman. Small. Petite. Brown hair. They were both wearing Amelia's Haven branded jackets.'

'Smooth.' Jonan rolled his eyes. 'She sends her saboteurs to do over the shop, and writes her name all over their clothes!'

'It sounds like Laura and Steve.' Beth sat down on one of the chairs. 'I wonder whether that was before or after we saw them in the restaurant.'

'Anything else?' the man asked.

'No, I think we know what we're dealing with. Thank you for your work. Will we see you tonight?' Jonan held out his hand and the man shook it.

'It will be my colleague tonight. He will look after you well.'

'You hired good people.' Doriel padded over to the door in her bare feet.

'Doriel.' Jonan's voice came out over-loud in the quiet room.

'We're fine, Jonan, stop fussing.' Doriel's smile was kind, but there was no give in her expression.

'You didn't hear anything?'

'I was probably fast asleep. Or maybe I was listening to music. You should be pleased I'm not hyper-alert anymore. You've hired excellent security and they're doing an amazing job. I'm putting my trust in them and getting on with my life. And don't forget, Miranda and I aren't helpless.'

Jonan raised one eyebrow.

'Don't look at me like that. I know I turned out to be pretty helpless last time. But there's been a lot of water under the bridge since then. And Miranda has got into their heads before.'

'Are you coming, Doriel?' The voice floated through the stairwell.

Doriel rolled her eyes. 'Who would mess with that?'

Jonan could hear her laughter all the way up the stairs.

Beth hooked her arm through his and pulled him close. 'She's right. We should be pleased she's learned to relax again. That's no easy task once Amelia has been in your head.'

'I'm worried she's not being careful enough.'

'I know.' Beth pulled him into a hug, leaning her cheek against his chest. 'But you're being careful for her. You have great security. They stopped Laura and Steve getting in, and they helped you identify them. You didn't have that last time.'

'I won't let her keep infiltrating my home.'

'It's not your home anymore, though, is it.' Her voice was quiet, but it landed deep. This place had been home for so long and although he'd left, he hadn't let go. But this was Doriel and Miranda's space now and he couldn't tell them how to live in it.

'Come on.' Beth pulled him back to the present. 'It's time to open the shop.'

45

ROLAND

ROLAND COULDN'T SEE A REASON FOR THE EDGY ATMOSPHERE at Lunea. His high from a night spent with Layla was dissipating fast and that wasn't in his game plan for the day.

Beth gave him a tight hug. 'Someone tried to break in last night.'

'They tried?' He raised one eyebrow. 'Do we have any idea who the someone was?'

The bell on the door rang and Layla came in with Abi.

'Where's Doriel?' The little girl jiggled on the spot.

'Upstairs.' Jonan held the door open and Abi bounded up, slamming the door shut behind her.

'Abi!' Layla called, but there was no reply. 'I'd better go after her.'

Jonan grinned widely and let out a long breath. 'Abi certainly knows how to bring a breath of fresh air to this place. I'm not sure whether Mum will agree though. She's already annoyed I interrupted their meditation to ask about intruders. And yes, we know exactly who it was.' Jonan picked up a pair of scissors and stabbed it into the tape at the top of a bulging cardboard box. 'Who is it every single time?'

'Did they say why they were here?'

'I assume for obvious reasons. Amelia is getting less subtle by the minute. She used to be the master of the unexpected. Now she's just using the same tired play over and over.'

Roland sighed. 'Her support system is dropping away and she's getting desperate. We should be pleased she's becoming predictable. At least that limits the damage.'

'Or she's lulling us into a false sense of security.' Beth shrugged. 'I just don't believe this falling apart narrative, and I think we'd be naive to put too much store by it.'

The door at the bottom of the stairs opened and Layla came through. 'Abi and Doriel are playing cards. Miranda wasn't impressed, but Doriel told her to see to her own soul and leave her alone.'

Jonan laughed. 'That sounds like Doriel. They are spending so much time closeted away. I know they have these workshops to plan but, honestly, they know that stuff inside out. I can't understand what they're getting up to.'

'We'll never know.' Roland shrugged. 'You know what Mum's like.'

'What's your plan now, Layla?' Beth handed Layla a mug of tea.

'Abi is determined not to go back to Southbourne. She wants to stay near Doriel and Roland. I've tried to talk her out of it. We've told her Roland will come with us, but this is where she wants to be. She told me she would leave by herself if I took her back, so it's safer to stick together. That does increase the pressure to deal with Amelia, but I feel better knowing Tabitha and Dylan have Abi's back.'

'We all have Abi's back.' Jonan put a hand on Layla's arm. 'Any one of us would put ourselves between Abi and Amelia without a thought.'

'Thank you. That means a lot.' Layla gave a tentative smile. 'And does the job offer still stand? I know it won't be a designer's salary, but I was getting by on my wage from the bookshop in Southbourne.'

'We'd love to have you.' Jonan pulled her into a hug. 'I could do with more help. Doriel is too distracted to be much use, and it's a long time since Mum's been on this planet. Beth and I are doing everything at the moment, but we're moving house in a week so we'll need to take time off. You can start straight away if you like.'

Layla frowned. 'I hope you're not moving out because of me? Abi isn't disruptive, I promise.'

Beth put her arm around Layla. 'I've stayed with you. I know that better than anyone. But you and Roland need your space. And so do we. We have a wedding to plan and a new life to build. And the cottage is gorgeous. Wait until you see it. Life is about to take a turn for the better. I just know it.'

46

BETH

BETH LOCKED THE DOOR AND TURNED THE SIGN TO CLOSED.

Jonan stretched. 'Is it that time already?'

'Not only is it that time, you're needed upstairs in the flat.' Layla grinned.

'Did something happen?' Beth frowned. 'Did someone call us?'

'Nope.' Layla's smile widened. 'I was asked to send you up at closing time. That's now.'

Abi poked her head around the door and giggled. 'Are you coming?'

Beth let out a long breath. This was no emergency. 'I am.' She walked over to the bottom of the stairs and held a hand out to Abi. 'What are you plotting?'

Abi ignored her hand and giggled, darting back up the stairs.

Jonan reached out and took it instead. 'Shall we go and see?'

Beth opened the door at the top of the stairs and gasped. The lights were off and the room was full of candles and fairy lights. It was pure magic. 'What is this?' She stepped into the room and spun around, absorbing the beauty of it.

'It's your engagement party!' Abi giggled, and threw her arms around Beth's middle. Look, everyone's here.'

As Beth's eyes adjusted to the dark, she looked around. Doriel and Miranda were there, but so were Tabitha, Dylan and Celia. Jonan, Roland and Layla had all followed her up. Abi was right. They really were all there. Together.

'You did this for us?' Jonan's voice was rough.

'Did you really think we wouldn't?' Doriel pulled him into her arms. 'You deserve all the happy memories, love. You have been the light of my life and I'm so glad you finally found Beth. You deserve it all.'

'You do.' Miranda's voice was soft. I'll never say it as well as Doriel, but she's absolutely right as usual.'

Doriel let go of Jonan and pulled Beth into her arms. 'Love, you are everything. You have brought joy and magic into our lives in the most challenging of circumstances. I know you will look after my boy. That you will take him forwards when I cannot. That together you will become all you have the potential for.'

'Is this congratulations, or goodbye?' Beth said as Doriel held her tight.

'Oh, you.' Doriel let her go, stepped back, and wiped her eyes. 'I'm just emotional about Jonan's dream coming true after lifetimes of grief.'

'This seems like a good moment to open the champagne!' Layla popped the cork off a bottle. Roland was ready with the glasses, and everyone let out a cheer as she poured two and he passed them to Beth and Jonan.

'To the bride and groom.' Roland held his own glass high

as he nodded at his brother. 'Welcome to the family, Beth. I will be proud to call you sister.'

'You'll be my Aunty Beth now,' Abi said, jumping up and down.

'No, pumpkin, she'd only be your aunty if I had a brother, and she was marrying him.'

'Or if you married Roland.' Abi ducked out of reach as Layla flushed bright red.

Doriel laughed loudly. 'You need to get used to this if you're going surround yourself with psychics, Layla.'

Roland smiled without a hint of embarrassment, but said nothing.

Beth tapped on her phone and Dylan's voice blared out of the speakers making them all jump.

Doriel shrieked with laughter, and Layla followed suit, doubling over in hysterics. Jonan grabbed Beth's hand and pulled her to him, swaying with the music.

'I'm glad you're home. I can't wait to marry you.'

'Beth McLaney,' Beth said and he squeezed her tighter. 'That works.'

'I think we can do better than that,' Dylan said as the song came to an end. He turned the stereo off and settled onto the sofa with his guitar. 'This is my new song. I'd love to hear what you think.'

Beth held her breath as he started to sing, his gaze firmly fixed on Tabitha, who smiled as she swayed with the music. It was haunting, sweet and raw at once. A growl shivered through the air and Beth swallowed, feeling herself expand into the energy, soaring on the depth of feeling. One hand was clasped in Jonan's palm, and she felt Layla reach for the other. She could feel Salu and Lunea, feel the past, present and future intertwined. There were traces of sadness and hope, but standing there, next to Jonan, there was an overwhelming sense of joy.

As the final chord rang out, they stood in silence, hands linked together, drinking in the symmetry of it. In that moment they were all together in harmony. In that moment, everything was perfect.

47

JONAN

THE SHOP HAD BEEN BUSY ALL DAY, AND THE MOMENT OF CALM was like a reward. Doriel and Miranda had made a rare appearance and were sitting with Roland in the squishy shop armchairs, drinking tea. Beth was leaning against the edge of a bookshelf, telling them all about Celia and the cottage, and Doriel was exclaiming with delight, waving her hands around. Jonan took some deep breaths and closed his eyes as a glorious beam of sunshine warmed his face. These moments were priceless.

The crash jerked him out of trance and set his heart racing as he threw himself out of the chair. Amelia stood in the doorway breathing heavily. Her face was flushed with fury, eyes blazing.

She advanced on him, her voice low. 'The ad is gone. Who did you replace me with?'

Jonan sighed, trying to slow his heart rate back to normal. 'None of your business. You weren't interested.'

She stood shaking.

Roland stood up and shoved his hands in his pockets, but

he didn't step closer. 'You didn't think they'd do it, did you? You thought they'd stay as predictable as you. Your standards have slipped since I left.'

'So have yours,' she said from between gritted teeth. 'I can't believe you're slumming it with that pink-haired woman after being with me. Do you have no self-respect?'

Roland shrugged. 'You were never going to like seeing me with someone else. Just be thankful you've never actually loved me. You'll be over this before you know it.'

'Of course I loved you. I'm not the monster you make me out to be.' Amelia's voice cracked and a tear slid down her cheek. She swallowed. 'I loved you too,' she said, turning to Doriel and Miranda, her voice quiet now. 'And I can't believe you're moving on without me.'

'So come back.' Doriel reached out to take her hands. 'I've asked you enough times. Take your place beside us in the Triad. It doesn't have to be over. Leave Amelia's Haven behind and let your followers heal. We've always needed you, Amelia.'

Miranda snorted.

Amelia's nostrils flared and her face reddened. 'Don't worry, Miranda, we all know you don't need anyone.'

'You're wrong.' Miranda faced her, straight-backed, chin raised. 'I needed you.' She paused for a moment, closing her eyes, but when she opened them, they were steely. 'That's why I was so devastated when you betrayed me. Letting you go was one of the hardest things I've ever done. It has left scars that will never heal. Why should I trust you again?'

Amelia's breath was ragged. She held Miranda's gaze, mirroring her stance. 'You shouldn't.' Her voice was little more than a whisper.

Doriel reached for Amelia's hand and then Miranda's.

She clutched them both to her chest. 'Please, Amelia. Please come back. Roland and Jonan have their own paths, but the three of us are supposed to stand side by side. Sisters. We've missed you so much. Please?'

Amelia clutched Doriel's hand so tightly her knuckles went white, but Doriel didn't flinch. She held the other woman's gaze with a pleading intensity that made Jonan's heart race. He had always known his aunt grieved the Triad, and the sister she had lost, but until that moment he hadn't truly realised how much he had taken away from her.

When Amelia let her breath out, the whole room breathed again. Her posture relaxed and she smiled. 'I'll come back, but I'm not giving up Amelia's Haven.'

Miranda raised one eyebrow. 'I told you, Doriel. She will never agree. Amelia just wants to integrate Lunea into her Haven. The rhetoric won't change. She'll still pedal fear and use Salu for her own ridiculous purposes. As of this moment the Triad is finished.'

Amelia tugged her hand from Doriel's and stepped back, her eyes blazing. 'Why should I give it up? You left my life in ruins and I've worked harder than you will ever know to rebuild. What I have now, a following, a platform, people who adore and trust me, that is everything. Those people are all I have, and you want me to give everything up to teach tarot? What kind of idiot do you think I am?'

Doriel swallowed. 'I think you're someone who's chosen the wrong path and wants to put things right.' Her voice was melodic and soothing, but Amelia shook her head.

'You always were over-optimistic.'

Miranda laughed, a belly laugh that made Jonan gape. He'd never heard that sound come out of his mother's mouth before.

'There we are agreed, sister.'

Doriel slumped. 'I'm sad you feel like that, Amelia. I've always hoped there was a way back for us.'

Miranda sat back down, picked up her phone and started scrolling. 'In another life, maybe.'

Amelia closed her eyes. 'This is why I left. She's impossible. She's not willing to connect on any level.'

'The words pot and kettle spring to mind,' Roland muttered under his breath.

Jonan would have laughed if he hadn't seen the look on Amelia's face.

Grabbing a huge crystal ball from the shelf next to her, Amelia held it up over her head.

'And what are you going to do with that?' Roland raised one eyebrow. 'Throw it at me? Knock me over like a bowling pin? You know, your followers are surprisingly attached to me. You may lose support if you're not careful.'

Amelia lowered the sphere, flushing red. 'This is pointless. There is no place for me here. You want an Amelia you can change and mould, but she doesn't exist.' She lurched towards the door, but Jonan zipped past her and held it open, not budging when she tried to pull it out of his hands to slam it.

'You are insufferable!' she yelled, before walking out into a barrage of camera flashes.

'Thank you, there's nothing to see here.' Jonan closed the door behind her and locked it. He turned the sign to closed and walked back over to the others. 'Pleased with yourself?' He looked at Miranda and raised one eyebrow.

She shrugged. 'That woman broke us, and she hasn't done anything to redeem herself. My door is open if she chooses to change. Until then, I'm not interested.'

48

BETH

'It's beautiful. I love it.' Layla put an arm around Beth's shoulders as she admired the front garden, which was bathed in morning sunlight.

Beth grinned and pulled Layla into a hug. 'Thank you. As soon as we're settled, you, Roland and Abi should come to dinner. I can't wait to get inside. I wonder how long Jonan will be with the keys.'

Beth walked up the path and put her hand on the rough wood of the door. Having her own home had been an impossible dream, but this cottage was everything she'd ever wanted.

A car door slammed and she turned.

'I've got them!' Jonan bounded down the path to slide the key into the lock. He paused for a moment, holding Beth's gaze.

'Enough of the suspense,' Layla shouted.

Beth snorted. She reached out, turned the handle and pushed the door open. The house felt new, empty, as though its history had been erased. Beth ran a hand over the wall, loving the solidity of it, and sending her own energy into the fabric of the building. They would fill this house with love and hope. It would be their new beginning.

'Ooh,' Layla said as she walked through the hall into the cosy living room, running her fingertips along the walls. 'This is beautiful. I hope you're going to let me help you decorate it.'

Jonan laughed. 'I don't think we can afford you.'

'Don't be silly.' She waved a hand. 'You're my family. There's obviously no charge. It's so cosy, but with some throws, a rug and the right pictures it could be even better.'

'Just wait until you see the bedroom.' Beth led her upstairs and grinned as she cooed over the low beams and the incredible view. She poked into every corner of the house and had so many plans Beth was quite overwhelmed by the time they got back downstairs.

Roland put a box in the middle of the living room floor and dusted his hands off on his jeans. 'We've only got a few more to bring in before we head back for the next lot. Where do you want me to put this?'

Beth looked inside. 'You can leave it here. Layla and I will start unpacking while you get the rest.'

'I haven't seen any of this before.' Layla rooted around in a box, and then pulled out a lamp with a base in the shape of a hare.

Beth took out a few books. 'That was from the flat I shared with Laura.'

'The one who tried to rob the shop the other night?'

Beth put down the books and leaned back on the radiator. 'Yet another of Amelia's victims.'

'I don't know.' Layla tilted her head to one side. 'Things are changing for her. I don't know why.'

'I hope you're right. We had an odd friendship, but I hate to see her manipulated.' Beth stood up and picked up one of the bigger boxes. I'm going to take this upstairs.'

'Go for it. I'm going to see what I can do with these soft furnishings. I'll try to surprise you. Don't come down until I call you.'

An hour later, Beth picked up the empty box and surveyed her work. The room was still a long way from homey, but it was starting to feel a little more lived in.

'Wow!' She heard Jonan's voice from downstairs.

'Can I come and see?' she called to Layla.

'Wait ... yes now!'

Beth could hear the smile in Layla's voice as she hurried down the stairs. When she rounded the corner into the living room, she gaped. Layla had filled the room with twinkly fairy lights. She had put throws over the aging sofas and plumped them up with colourful cushions as well as rolling out a thick rug. 'This is incredible,' Beth said, running her hand along the soft throw over the back of the sofa. 'I'd forgotten I had some of this stuff.'

Layla grinned. 'You see, it didn't cost a penny.'

'Is it too early to celebrate?' Jonan pulled out a bottle of Prosecco and held it up. 'I'm not sure where the glasses are, but if we all hunt, I'm sure we'll find them soon enough.'

'Now there's an incentive to get unpacked.' Beth laughed. 'We'll be settled in no time.'

49

BETH

A BIRD WAS SINGING. BETH OPENED HER EYES AND SQUINTED into the light that flooded the bedroom through and around the thin curtains. A breeze wafted over her from the open window. She sighed and stretched. She could get used to waking up like this.

Jonan mumbled something in his sleep and turned over. The alarm went off and he groaned. 'What time is it?'

'Time to get up.' She swung her legs out of bed and threw open the curtains. Leaning on the windowsill, she took a deep breath of fresh air. 'I can't believe this is real.'

'You'd better get used to it.' Jonan yawned and hauled himself up. He stretched, walked around the bed and slid his arms around her waist. 'Life is about to get a lot better, Miss Meyer.'

When they arrived at Lunea, Doriel was already downstairs, thumbing through the display of tarot cards.

'You're not usually about this early.' Jonan raised one eyebrow.

She grinned. 'Beth, it's time we talked tarot. Is now good?'

'I have to get the shop ready ...'

'I can do that. You go ahead.' Jonan nodded towards the stairs.

Doriel's room smelled of jasmine, and Beth let out a sigh as she sank into the comfortable chair. The memory of that first reading was so vivid. She ran her finger over the amethyst cathedral, drawing in a long breath and closing her eyes as she let it out.

'You always did like that one, didn't you.'

When Beth opened her eyes, Doriel was sitting opposite her, shuffling *The Starfolk Tarot*. She smiled and laid down a card. Justice. She paused for a moment, her fingers hovering over the card, and then dealt two more: Intention and Judgement.

Beth leaned forwards, resting her elbows on her thighs. 'What do they mean?'

'Why don't you tell me?' Doriel looked up at her. A smile played across her lips and her eyes sparkled.

Beth frowned. 'Justice keeps coming up.'

Doriel's smile widened. 'And?'

'Salu said I'm changing from Potential to Justice.'

Doriel was full-on grinning now. She leaned back in her chair and crossed her legs. 'How does that make you feel?'

'A little bemused. I'm not sure I like the suggestion that I have to bring Amelia to justice, but I guess I knew that already.'

'Amelia's world is all about shadows.' Doriel leaned forwards. 'What's real is irrelevant to her. It's not about effort, balance, or what's right. It's not about any of the things the Justice card represents. You came from the same place, you and Amelia. You both started out as Potential, but she went to a place of murk and fears to become the Devil card. You are coming out into the light of Justice. There's nowhere to hide here. You're shining a spotlight into Amelia's gloom. She doesn't like that. You bring balance where she tries to knock people out of alignment. And you stand up for truth where she tries to obscure reason. You started at the same point and became polar opposites.'

Beth stared at Doriel. Her mouth was dry and a shiver ran down her spine. 'The other cards? Intention?'

'You know that's Jonan.'

Beth nodded. 'And ... Judgement?'

Doriel smiled again, but this time her eyes looked sad. 'You're not the only one to have changed card.'

Beth swallowed. 'You?'

Doriel nodded. 'But we're not here to talk about me.'

'No,' Beth said, her heart hammering in her chest. 'We're here to talk about tarot. And I'd like to hear your take on Judgement. I've read about that card so many times, but I still don't really get it.'

Doriel sighed. 'Judgement is about ascending to the next level. It means I'm moving onto the next stage of my journey.'

'And what's that?' Beth frowned.

'Never mind me.' Doriel looked down at the cards, avoiding Beth's gaze.

'Is it to do with the concept of Judgement Day?'

'The cards are based on those traditional ideas, but what they can mean to us has evolved. Judgement is a card of Ascension, of rising above that which has been holding you back. It's about achieving goals and taking a higher focal point. I am at peace with my change, Beth, what about you?'

Beth sighed and leaned back in the chair. 'I don't feel any different. I understand that potential, or the Fool, is a card of beginnings, and I am no longer a beginner in this process. I have a history with all of you now, Amelia included. So change is inevitable. But Justice? For all my talk about balance and holding Amelia to account, it's still pretty elusive.'

Doriel shrugged. 'And it will be until it's completed. The key is working out what it means to you right now, and how you can use it to move forward. What do you need from Justice today?'

'Is any of this ever about what I need?' Beth's voice came out strangled and she cleared her throat.

'Yes. Even if you don't understand how or why. It's what you chose before you came here.'

'That's not really me though, is it.' Beth stood up and started pacing the tiny room. 'This story about the elusive Betalia who incarnated with this big destiny, what does that mean to me? What can it mean? It's a fairy story; something you tell children to help them understand the world. But it's no help at all when you're standing opposite Amelia and her thug, trying to figure out how to protect the people you love. Because she wants to hurt them, Doriel. She wants to hurt you all.'

'And you want to hold her to account, to do what's right?'

'Yes.'

Doriel folded her arms over her chest. 'And you say you don't understand what Justice means to you?'

'Stop it.' Beth rubbed the back of her neck. 'You're so smug.'

'So Jonan tells me.' Doriel leaned back. 'But I'm not worried about how you see me. My interest is how you see yourself and your path. I won't always be here to help you understand. But right now, I'm focused entirely on you. I'm here to help you, Beth. What do you need from me?'

'I need you to make up with Amelia. I need you to deactivate the storm you set off when the three of you smashed the Triad in a tantrum about the behaviour of a teenage boy. I need you to mend what you broke, so we can focus on what is ours. We are trying to solve your problems, yours and Miranda's. And you both act as though it's all on us.'

'That's not true.' For the first time, Doriel looked defeated. 'I have been reaching out to Amelia continually. I feel a deep sense of responsibility for what happened, and I want my sister back. If it were only about me, I would have fixed it by now. But as much as you'd like to put this onto us, when Jonan got involved with Amelia, he brought all of you into the mix. This is as much his to solve as it is ours. And, no, Miranda is not helping. But if Amelia showed one speck of remorse for what she's been doing to people, Miranda would welcome her back. She's a lot more forgiving than she appears, but Amelia isn't ready for forgiveness. She wants us to get in line behind her and support Amelia's Haven. Is that really what you want us to do?'

Beth swallowed and sat down. 'Of course not. I'm just angry and feeling hopeless.'

Doriel put a hand on her knee. 'It's all part of the process, love. It's your key to understanding what this means to you, and how you are best placed to deal with it. You are involved because you are uniquely able to impact this awful situation. You just need to figure out what type of magic you hold. That is where the tarot comes in. It can help you access the understanding you need, and give you an overview of which options might be most aligned for you.'

She stood up and walked over to the bookshelf behind her. Running a finger along the spines, she pulled one out, walked back and handed it to Beth before sitting back down.

'Read this. It might help.' Picking up the deck again, she dealt three more cards: Judgement, The Tower and Death. She paled and closed her eyes for a moment, but when she opened them, they were bright. 'We've already talked about Judgement. What do you know about the Tower?'

Beth frowned. 'It's pretty disastrous, isn't it?'

Doriel ran a finger over the card. 'It doesn't have to be. It can mean that your obstacles drop away suddenly. It can be a card of freedom, of release from blockages. But it can also bring sudden and disorientating lessons.'

'Death doesn't sound good.'

'Death is an ending, and a final one. But some endings are helpful, and most deaths aren't physical. Most of the time, it's the end of a situation or life stage.'

'And in this case?'

'In this case ...' Doriel paused. 'Something is coming, something unpredictable, transformational and unexpected. We may not like it, but whatever it is, we would do well to be ready.'

'Did you ...' Beth narrowed her eyes to watch Doriel's energy. 'Did you know those cards would come up?'

'Did I know?' Doriel's laugh was edgy. 'You saw me shuffle. I had no way of knowing which cards I would deal.'

'But you've seen these cards before. Recently. I could see it in your eyes.'

Doriel sighed and her shoulders sagged. 'It doesn't matter what I've seen. This reading was for you. The cards will have different meanings for each of us. I can give you guidance, but this deck is for you to form a relationship with. It's part of your blood and heritage, just as it is mine. You will find your own resonance with these cards, and that won't be the same as mine.'

'You read for people all the time.' Beth tried to keep the irritation out of her voice. 'Surely that's always the case, but they're not all going to go off and learn to read tarot.'

Doriel shrugged. 'You're different. You're deeply embedded in this narrative. And I won't always be here to read for you. You need to start finding your own way through the maze.'

'You talk as though you're dying. Are you ill?'

'No!' Doriel laughed, but the sparkle didn't reach her eyes. 'I'm as fit as a fiddle.'

Beth couldn't see anything in Doriel's energy to suggest she was lying, but something was off.

'You're reading too much into this.' Doriel slumped in her chair. 'Don't let scare stories distract you. It's what Amelia wants.'

That much, at least, was true. But Beth couldn't help thinking there was more to Doriel's words than she had understood.

Doriel stood up. 'Stay in here. Play with the cards. Meditate with the crystals. Find your own sense of things. Treat this room as your own at any time. I'm going to leave you to it.'

'But ...' Beth reached for Doriel's hand, but the woman slipped out the door and was gone.

'I'm fine.' She called as the door closed behind her. 'I promise you that.'

50

AMELIA

The doorbell rang.

Amelia clutched her pounding head and waited to hear Rose's footsteps and whiney voice.

Nothing.

She gulped down a bottle of water, wanting it to be a miracle hangover cure, but the cold water turned her stomach.

The bell rang again.

Still nothing.

'Do I have to do everything around here?' she yelled into the emptiness, kicking a wine bottle into the corner of the room.

Sliding her feet into the flip-flops by the door, she went into the reception area. Bile rose in her throat, and she gripped the desk to steady herself as the room span. Not far to the door, she whispered as she walked carefully, trying not to jar her head or nauseous stomach any more than necessary.

She tugged at the handle. The ancient wood stuck, and

then creaked open.

Laura stepped back, grimacing as she met Amelia's gaze. The Sheep was watching Laura with an irritatingly gooey expression, but when he saw Amelia, his gaze hardened and his eyes went blank. Interesting.

'Come in,' she croaked. She cleared her throat. 'I need to sit down.'

They stared at her, frozen, and then the Sheep stepped in, staying as far from Amelia as possible. Laura followed.

Amelia slumped into the single armchair by the cold, empty fireplace. Laura shifted from one foot to the other and then back again. The Sheep stood behind Laura like a guard dog, his gaze darting around the room on constant alert.

'Steve?' Amelia kept her voice soft and sweet. 'Steve, look at me.'

He coughed and looked out the window at the front of the hotel.

'Steve.' Her voice was firmer now.

'You can talk to me,' Laura snapped.

Amelia turned to Laura, narrowing her eyes. 'I know what happened at Lunea. I know you achieved nothing. I need you to cause havoc. That's what I pay you for.'

Laura straightened, pushing her shoulders back. 'I'm sorry you were unhappy. They have increased their security, and honestly, I don't think I can continue to collect my pay cheque from you in good faith. We can't do what you want. We are stepping back to allow you to hire someone with more specialised skills.'

'Stepping back?' Amelia could hear how shrill her voice sounded, but she didn't care. Fury thrummed through her as she lurched from her chair. 'You're stepping back? What exactly do you think gives you the right to walk away from something you've committed to?' She advanced on Laura, her hands clenched at her sides.

The Sheep cleared his throat. She looked up, sending him a glare that would have terrified him once upon a time. Instead, he stepped towards her, his face dark with fury. 'If you touch Laura, I will not be responsible for my actions. I will not let you hurt her anymore.'

Amelia stared, and then she slapped him hard across the face. He didn't flinch. She slapped him again and again. His eyes watered, but he didn't move.

'Amelia, stop!' Laura tugged her backwards. 'Get control of yourself.'

Amelia took a deep breath. They were staring at her, fear etched across their features, but their posture was strong. They held hands, united, their feet planted firmly.

Amelia forced her voice back under control. 'Steve has been working for me for a long time. His skills are highly specialised. That kind of history is irreplaceable. I will not accept his resignation. Do you want to leave alone, Laura? I would not stand for any employee fraternising with someone who had deserted the fold. If you go, it's you against the might of Amelia's Haven.'

Come. Amelia sent out a mental call to the monks and felt the whisp of cold as they began to drift towards her.

Laura flinched. Her jaw hardened and she glared at Amelia. The moment stretched out. Steve shuffled from one foot to the other. A crow cawed from outside.

Laura was pale now and sweat began to gleam on her forehead and upper lip. She reached back and grasped Steve's hand so hard he winced. 'That ... erm ... that wasn't what I meant. I didn't want to take your money if I couldn't provide value. If you value what I *can* do, of course I will stay.'

Amelia's smile was languid. 'Good,' she tipped her head back. 'It's time to raise your game. Arrange protests. Push my followers to troll Lunea online. Do everything you can to put Beth and Jonan down and keep people away from Lunea. We've caused them so much disruption, they must be near their limit.'

'I'm not sure about that.' Laura's voice was small. 'I went in disguise and discovered their appointments are fully booked for the next few weeks. Their courses are full too. The queues for the shop are huge every day. Business is booming.'

Amelia gritted her teeth. 'Make it stop. Find their weaknesses and cut off their strengths. I have more profile than them, and a lot more money. This should not be difficult.'

'Yes, Amelia.' Laura looked at her feet.

'Where are your branded coats? I want you to wear them at all times so people know you are affiliated with me.'

'Sometimes it works better to go undercover.' Laura didn't meet Amelia's gaze.

'You are my representative and should be proud of that. Shout it out loud. You are either all in, or all out. Which will it be?' Amelia called the monks in closer, drawing them around Laura and tightening their hold as her face turned ashen.

'All in.' Laura's voice was no more than a whisper and a tear ran down her cheek.

Amelia looked up at the Sheep. 'You used to frighten them. What happened?'

He shrugged. 'They got used to me. Hired their own muscle. Anyway, they weren't scared of me really. Maybe the red-haired one.'

'Doriel? Don't be ridiculous. That wasn't real. She doesn't

frighten easily. Get your jackets and get to it straight away.' She stood up.

'Get to what?' Laura wrung her hands.

'Cause mayhem and damage. Do I really have to spoon-feed you? I thought you were a self-starter. That's why I put you together, so you could lead ... Steve.'

'I don't need to be led.' Steve's voice was level. There was a steel in his eyes she had never seen before.

She raised her eyebrows. 'In that case, show me this new mettle. I would be delighted to see what you are made of.'

He nodded and then turned and walked back to the front door. He held it open for Laura. When she went through, he glared at Amelia but said nothing.

'Wear your jackets,' she called just before the door slammed.

'That did not go how I expected,' she muttered to herself. She wrapped her arms around her middle. 'I thought I had them figured out, but I really don't know what they'll do next. Will they even get the jackets so I can watch them?' She shivered as she went down the stone staircase to the basement. This place was horrible and damp. Something needed to be done if she was going to keep spending time down here. These old buildings were a curse.

She flipped the switches on the screens and watched as the cameras came to life. One set of cameras was obscured, but the other pointed at a wardrobe that had been left flung open. Colourful clothes were lined up neatly on the rail, but to the right was a whole section of black, and these were falling out of the wardrobe and flung across the bit of the bed she could see. That must be Laura's room.

Amelia heard the creak of a door, and then a blurred arm reached in front of the camera and the room started to spin.

She looked away from the camera, and when she turned back, the room was the right way up and the banister was flying by to the left. Laura thrust the second jacket at the Sheep. 'Are you going to put it on?'

The Sheep sighed. 'If I must.'

Amelia ground her teeth. If even the Sheep was losing interest, what hope did she have with the rest of them?

51

AMELIA

Amelia pulled a blanket round her shoulders and pulled her legs up, resting her feet on the chair in front of her and hugging her knees. The image on the screen in front of her was bouncing around and was in serious danger of making her sick, but there was no way she was walking away.

'Amelia has lost her calm, and you're getting irritated with her? My world is turning upside down.' Laura gave a nervous laugh.

Amelia ground her teeth. She had thought Laura idolised her.

The Sheep sighed. 'Amelia has never been calm. She's always been unpredictable, fickle and abusive, interspersed with charm and generosity. She keeps people by her side with a mix of promises and threats. You've been lucky so far, but the tide was always going to turn. I've had enough. I'm leaving and I'm hoping you'll come with me.'

'You've become very verbal all of a sudden.' Amelia grimaced at the computer screen. 'How the worms are turning.'

'But you heard her.' Laura's voice was small.

'We need to get away. Maybe leave the country. I don't know how far her power reaches.' The Sheep's camera burst into life and the screen was a jumbled mix of movement until it settled. Amelia could see Laura now, pale, chewing her lip.

'Leave the country?'

'I think it would be safest.'

She nodded but didn't look at him. 'Can you give me a bit of time to think about it?'

He shrugged. 'I'm not leaving without you.'

Laura's shoulders relaxed and colour returned to her cheeks. 'Thank you.' She turned to look at him.

'Urgh, talk about puppy-dog eyes. Those two make me sick.' Amelia made retching sounds and then burst out laughing. 'He's punching way above his weight with that one. I wonder what it would take to make her leave him?'

Lunea came into view and Amelia leaned forwards. They walked up to the door, but a security guard stepped in front of them.

'I'm going to have to ask you to leave.' The man stared forwards, his face blank.

'It's okay. We just want to do some shopping, and I'd like to see my friend Beth. She works here.' Laura's voice sounded false. Would the guard notice?

'I have orders not to let either of you in. Ever. Please move on.'

The Brute's camera zoomed in on the guard. He must have stepped closer. 'My girlfriend wants to shop. You will let her in.'

'Good Sheep.' Amelia grinned. 'Maybe he's getting his mojo back.'

The guard spoke into a microphone on his lapel and

another man came round the corner with a large dog on a short lead. 'Do we have a problem?'

Laura looked from one man to the other, and then at the Sheep.

He glared at the guards, and then stepped back. 'Let's go over the road to eat. You can look through the window and see what you would have spent your money on if this place didn't discriminate.'

The tension was palpable, but the man didn't take the bait. Steve slumped and then led the way to the restaurant over the road.

'Damn.' Amelia slammed her hand on the desk. 'I do not pay you to give up so easily!' she yelled at the computer screen. Picking up her phone, she dialled Rose's number. It went to voicemail. She hung up and called again. Voicemail. 'Damn you, Rose,' she yelled. The final time she gave in and left a message. 'Rose? Where are you? You were supposed to be at work today and I need you. Things are going all kinds of wrong. Laura and the Sheep have been denied access to Lunea so they're eating instead of stirring the pot. How are you getting on with my conference? It's in two days. Please arrange for a team of cleaners and decorators to come. I will work on the content. You need to fill the venue and sort food and ambiance. Get the invite list from the Amelia's Haven database. Every member should be invited. Everyone who comes will receive a welcome gift of an embossed notebook and pen. I will do signings. Sort it. Let me know when it's done.'

She hung up.

Rose would get back to her any minute. The conference would be a huge success and would put Jonan on the back foot. Doriel and Miranda too. And Beth? Beth, she would obliterate.

52

BETH

Beth tried to read the look Laura was throwing her. Was it desperation? A plea for help? Or something different? Steve was stony-faced, staring down at the cinnamon swirl he was picking to bits on his plate.

Beth took a deep breath and let it out slowly. Then she walked over to their table, a fake smile fixed on her face. 'Laura.'

Laura cleared her throat and then started fiddling with her lapel. 'Why did you follow us?'

'The security guard said you wanted to speak to me. Is something wrong?'

'Ha!' Laura's laugh was high-pitched.

Beth stepped back.

'Why would you think there was anything wrong?' Laura's voice cracked. She reached into her pocket, pulled out a piece of paper and dropped it on the floor.

Beth frowned. 'Is this yours?' She bent down and picked up the paper.

'It's nothing to do with me.' Laura held her gaze, her eyes beseeching.

'My mistake.' Beth slipped the piece of paper into her pocket.

She walked over to the counter, and ordered a coffee before pulling the paper from her pocket. *We've been bugged somehow. Amelia has turned on us and is watching our every move. Don't take anything I say seriously. I will contact you when I've figured out how she's stalking us.*

Beth pulled a pen from her pocket and scribbled on the back of the note. *Find me when you're ready.*

Steve was still staring at his cinnamon roll when Beth returned to their table, coffee in hand. She dropped the piece of paper on the floor by Laura's feet.

'I know you tried to break into the shop again.' Beth put both hands flat on the table and leaned towards them.

Steve glared at her.

'Leave us alone. You won't be allowed in the shop, and you will not be able to interfere with it at night either. Your time here is done.'

'Oh, get over yourself.' Laura picked at the skin around her nails. 'We're just not that into you, Beth.'

Beth stared at them, and they both glared back, expressionless. 'Bye then.' She turned and walked out the door.

'What's wrong?' Jonan frowned as she walked back into Lunea, resisting the urge to slam the glass door behind her.

'There's something weird going on with Laura and Steve. Laura passed me a note saying Amelia had bugged them. She said they'd come and speak to us when they'd figured out how to evade the surveillance, but I'm not sure whether to believe them.' She got out her phone.

'What are you going to do?' Jonan sliced open a box and started unpacking tarot decks.

Beth put the phone on the counter and clicked speaker.

'*Deep and Dark*,' A voice said on the other end of the phone.

'It's Beth Meyer. I noticed Katherine Haversham hasn't seemed right since Amelia inducted her into the Haven. I have helped many of Amelia's victims get rid of her influence and would be happy to do that for Katherine, for free, if you would consider covering it on the show? I'd be happy to offer you an exclusive if you'd like to talk about my feud with Amelia.'

'Thank you, we'll get back to you if we need you.'

'Could I speak to Katherine?' Beth said before the woman could hang up.

'She doesn't deal with scheduling or answer the phones. As I said, we'll get back to you if we need you.'

'Will you tell her I offered?'

The woman sighed. 'If we told Katherine about every freebie she was offered, we'd never get the show recorded. If we need you, we will contact you. Goodbye.'

The phone went dead.

Beth stared at it. 'Damn. If I could have helped Katherine, I might have been able to help Laura at the same time. I was sure that was where this was all going to end. I have to get to her somehow.'

53

BETH

Abi ran into the shop and threw her arms around Beth's middle. 'I did it! I had my first day at school.' She jumped up and down on the spot. 'I even made a friend.'

Beth swung her up into a hug. 'That's great news, pumpkin. I'm so pleased you've found a good place. I can't wait to hear all about it.'

Roland, Layla and Tabitha followed her in, smiling when they saw her in Beth's arms. 'You have a break.' Roland smiled at Beth. 'Let Abi tell you and Doriel all her news. I'll stay here and watch the shop.'

'Thank you.' Beth put Abi down. 'I'll race you to the top!'

Abi shrieked, ran to the bottom of the stairs and bounded up faster than Beth could have imagined. She disappeared into the lounge before Beth had even started and the door in front of her banged as a faint growl echoed down the stairs. Beth shivered.

Layla and Tabitha followed Beth upstairs, where they found Abi prancing around the living room, telling Doriel and Miranda all about her day. Doriel was grinning. Miranda looked bored.

'Come on in, Layla, Tabitha, grab a seat.' Doriel stood in one fluid motion and ushered them all into chairs by the fire. 'What can I get you?'

'Ooh.' Abi clapped her hands. 'It's my tiger. Look!'

Beth turned to where Abi was pointing and froze.

A huge white tiger was walking towards her. Beth's scream froze in her throat. She forced her feet backwards, pushing inch by inch, trying to loop around towards the door. There was a small growl behind the tiger, and it turned just as a leopard cub flickered into sight. Beth let out her breath in a rush, and then made a leap for the door. She could hear Jonan yelling, and Layla talking in soothing tones. Why weren't any of them following her out of the room?

Tabitha's voice cut through, firm and commanding. 'Abi. Stop it.'

'Why?' Abi's voice was petulant. Why didn't she sound more panicked?

'It's not fair to scare people.' Tabitha's voice was almost a growl.

Abi sighed. 'Okay.'

Beth peered around the door. The tiger was fading right in front of her eyes. She could see through it and the leopard cub was already gone. She stepped back into the room, keeping her hand on the doorknob. 'I don't understand. Am I the only one who saw that?' She looked from one to the other of them. Jonan was pale, his hand shaking where he gripped the table. Doriel was still sitting on the sofa, her expression weirdly benign. Miranda was leaning forwards, her face animated. But Layla looked embarrassed.

Jonan shook his head and cleared his throat. 'I don't understand either.'

'Sit down, everyone,' Layla said. 'We have something to tell you.'

Beth scanned the room as she walked over to the sofa and sat close to Jonan, taking comfort from the warmth of his leg next to hers.

Layla perched on the arm of the sofa. 'I'm not sure where to start.'

'I'll do it.' Tabitha smiled. 'It's my story to tell, at least some of it. When I paint, I astral project, and my energy appears in the form of a white tiger. Most of the time I'm invisible, but occasionally I choose to make myself solid. Recently, Abi's manifestation abilities have increased to the point that she can make me visible without my permission.'

'That was you?' Jonan's voice cracked.

Tabitha nodded.

'And me too!' Abi jumped up and down, beaming. 'I was the leopard.' She gave a little growl.

It was so human and unthreatening that Beth couldn't help laughing. 'That was you, Abi? I'm not sure what to make of all this.'

'I'm good at man-i-fest-ing.' Abi sounded the word out slowly. 'Doriel told me so.'

Doriel sighed. 'That's true, sweetie, but I also told you to be careful with it.'

Layla sucked in her breath.

'I know your concerns Layla, but that wasn't what I meant. Abi needs to learn how to control her projection so people can't see her leopard. And she mustn't manifest hidden aspects of other people. That isn't fair on anyone.'

Layla sighed. 'Agreed. But she's so powerful and so young.

I know she's trying to control it, but it's a lot for her to handle right now. And I have no idea how to help her.'

'I do.' Tabitha took Layla's hand in her own. 'And I love her as a niece. Do you trust me, Layla?'

'You know I do.' Layla gave a shaky smile. 'I trust you and Roland completely.'

Doriel frowned but said nothing.

'It's fun being a leopard.' Abi's voice was small. 'Do I really have to stop, Mummy?'

'You don't need to stop.' Layla pulled the little girl into her lap and wrapped her arms around her. 'But you do need to save it for when we're at home, or somewhere else safe and private. When you're bigger, you'll be able to make sure nobody can see you, and then you'll have more freedom.'

'I want to run with the tigers like Tabitha.'

'You're not a tiger, sweetie.' Tabitha's voice was firm. 'You need to find yourself a leopard.'

'Humph.' Abi pouted.

Beth tried not to laugh.

'Abi,' she said, sitting forwards and reaching her hands towards the fire. 'We all know now, and this is a safe place. I would love to see your leopard properly. Would you show me? I was so shocked before I didn't get to enjoy it.'

'Yes!' Abi jumped off Layla's lap and scrunched up her face.

'Wait!' Tabitha's voice resonated through the room, but a small leopard was already running circles around the furniture.

'For goodness' sake.' Tabitha slumped onto the sofa, staring vacantly into the fire. A moment later, the white tiger shivered into existence and growled at the leopard, which pulled up short, tilted its head and looked at the larger cat.

The cub pounced, landing on the tiger's front paws before jumping away and pouncing again. The tiger licked the cub's head, but remained on the ground, watching her play, taking in every movement.

'How do you do it, Tabitha?' Beth asked, but the woman ignored her, not moving a muscle.

'She can't hear you.' Layla's voice was hypnotic. 'Tabitha is completely focused on Abi right now. We have no idea when Abi will learn to make herself solid, so Tabitha is making sure she doesn't hurt anyone unintentionally.'

The white tiger lay on the rug in front of the fire right by their feet, and the cub played around her, pouncing, rubbing her head on the tiger's flank and finally collapsing between her paws. The tiger licked her fur and then laid her huge head down by the cub and closed her eyes.

Beth let out a long, slow breath as the cats faded into nothing. 'That was incredible. I can't believe I just saw that!'

Tabitha and Abi were curled up on the sofa together now. Abi was fast asleep in Tabitha's arms and the woman was clearly trying hard to keep her eyes open. Tabitha smiled as her eyes flickered. 'I will help you with Amelia in any way I can. And I will keep Abi safe. Please don't worry.' Her eyes flickered one last time and she fell asleep.

54

JONAN

'Doriel wasn't wrong when she flagged Abi as the Magician.' Jonan chuckled. 'That's manifestation like I've never seen it before. And Tabitha as Strength! There's nearly always some kind of big cat on that card.'

'Tabitha is the strongest person I know.' Layla's voice was thick with emotion. 'She has faced so much, and she doesn't let anything stand in her way. She knows her limits and, rightly, believes in herself. I'm so grateful she's there for Abi. I would be lost in this strange shadow world without her.'

'Where did she come from, Layla?' Jonan started restocking the bookshelf, hoping Layla might speak more easily if she wasn't being watched. For a rare moment, the shop was empty, so he wanted to get as much information as he could before someone came in. 'I've obviously heard of Tara McLaughlin, but people with psychic talents tend to be drawn to this shop like a moth to a flame. I'm surprised I haven't met her before.'

'She hasn't been here long.' Layla shrugged. 'But we go

way back. I trust her completely if that's what you're worried about?'

Jonan swallowed. 'I worry about you. You're family.'

Layla's eyes shone. 'Thank you. That means a lot.'

The door banged open. Roland strode in and dumped a load of sandwich bags on the reception desk. 'Amelia's lot are out today. It looked like they were heading here.'

'Great.' Jonan rolled his eyes. 'That's just what we need.' The bell on the door rang again as a woman walked in. She smiled at them and then wandered over to a display of crystals. She had crystal chip bracelets on one wrist and several pendants hanging at intervals over her jumper. Surely she wasn't one of Amelia's? Jonan let his breath out, but the smile froze on his lips as a different crowd piled in.

A short man with dark hair gave a hoarse laugh as he fell down the step and his friends jeered as they shoved him in further.

'Careful please.' Jonan steadied a display of crystals as the men lumbered past and started poking at a shelf of tarot cards. The man laughed again and then wandered over to the reception desk. He coughed. 'I have an appointment. You're going to clear Amelia out of my system.' He laughed again.

'Want to stop dreaming about her, do you?' his friend yelled, and they all guffawed.

'Name please?' Jonan asked, gritting his teeth. He wanted to throw them out, but if the man genuinely had an appointment, he would have to honour it.

'Saul Snatcha,' he said, doubling up with laughter.

Jonan sighed. How had they missed that when they booked the appointment? 'Do you want this appointment? That slot has been saved for you. You have to pay for it.'

One of the men in the group got out a phone, tapped on

it, and then pointed it at Jonan. Jonan looked from him to the man with the appointment. Whatever was about to happen, it was all going to be filmed and uploaded to the internet before Jonan had time to process it.

'I'm not giving you a penny,' the man leered, leaning closer to Jonan and blasting him with garlicy beer breath. 'You're a Soul Snatcher, you are. You deserve to lose everything. You're all Soul Snatchers!' he yelled at the top of his voice as Beth stepped into the room. 'We're going to take you down.'

Jonan stepped towards Beth, but she seemed to grow in height as she moved closer to the man, eyes flashing. 'You think you're so terrifying?' she said, her voice whisper quiet. 'You think we'll be scared by a few macho words?'

'I've got more than words for you.' The man cackled.

'Now,' a voice yelled from the growing group of men at the back. 'Go.'

They lurched towards the door, laughing, and destabilising a huge crystal on a stand. Jonan lunged and just caught it before it hit the ground. He took in a deep breath, and his airways filled with the thick, cloying stench of rotten egg. The few genuine customers were now rushing for the door.

Holding his breath while he did a quick mental inventory of the room, Jonan followed Beth and Layla out the door into the fresh air.

'Stink bombs?' Layla's voice was high-pitched when she'd finished coughing. 'I can't believe she's transitioned from actual threat to ridiculous playground tactics.'

'I'm not sure they are ridiculous.' Dread settled in Jonan's stomach as Amelia's energy prodded at his shields. 'I think she's trying to distract us and wear us down for something bigger.'

'Layla is right though.' Beth shrugged her shoulders. 'This we can deal with. We just need to make sure she doesn't have the opportunity to go back to anything dangerous.' Beth's phone beeped. She pulled it out and frowned at the device.

'What is it? Have they posted the video already?' Anxiety bubbled up through Jonan's legs from the soles of his feet.

'No. It's worse. She's running a big conference at the Inn. St Albans is going to be flooded with her supporters. She's promising lessons, lectures, free gifts, one-on-one time. This will radicalise people even more.'

'When is it?' Jonan peered over her shoulder. 'This weekend? She must have been organising it on the quiet for ages. It's unlike her to keep something like that on the down-low.'

'Or she's trying to throw it together at the last minute?'

Jonan sighed. 'That would be more in character.'

'Look.' Beth held up the news clip on her phone. 'She's got Robson Fall involved, so they're still working together. I guess that gives her access to his huge audience, and they'll be primed for her kind of stories.'

Amelia and Robson Fall were being interviewed now. Amelia was ranting about Lunea. Jonan rolled his eyes. 'Do you think people really believe this claptrap?'

Beth shrugged. 'I think those men did.'

'Or they just wanted to cause trouble. She could have paid them to do that.'

Beth nodded. 'I think a lot of people won't believe her, but I suspect enough will. I hate that.'

Robson Fall was talking now and, as he spoke, he put one hand on Amelia's thigh. She batted his hand away and moved her leg to the other side of the chair, but he leaned forward and planted his palm firmly on her leg.

Jonan wondered if the rest of the world could see how furious she was, or if it was only obvious to him.

When Robson Fall moved his hand a little higher, Amelia stood up, and he lurched back.

Jonan didn't miss the smirk she sent his way before she stretched her arms out wide. 'Lunea is trying to undermine the help and protection I am offering, because they are in league with the Soul Snatchers. Do not believe what they tell you. Do not believe what they say about me. You know who I am. I have lived in the public eye for years. I am yours. Who are they? What were they doing before they started attacking me publicly? You know the truth deep in your hearts. I know you do. I know you will rise above the negativity. Stay in the light and support me.'

'Erm, yes ... well,' the interviewer spluttered. 'Clearly this is Amelia's opinion and not endorsed by this channel. Now to sport.'

Jonan burst out laughing. 'She certainly got their number.'

'I'm not so sure.' Beth frowned. 'That woman just humiliated Amelia at one of her most powerful moments, and in front of Robson Fall. That's going to smart. She will be furious. We need to watch our backs.'

Jonan let out a sigh. 'As always. It doesn't take much to infuriate her, and she normally decides everything is our fault. I don't really see any difference. At least we know what happened this time.'

'Her hold is slipping.' Beth put the phone down on the desk. 'She's lost people she relied on, and her supporters are deserting her. I think she's becoming desperate. With so little to lose, she might be more dangerous than she has ever been before.'

55

BETH

When they opened the next morning, the smell was almost gone. Since Beth's visit to Bournemouth, interest in Lunea had blossomed. Their healing sessions and readings were booked weeks in advance, stock was being sold before it hit the shelves and they were building a solid core of loyal customers and collectors who regularly came in for coffee and a mooch around the crystals and decks.

Jonan was deep in conversation with a customer and Beth had a long queue of people to serve at the till when Amelia was stopped at the door by the security guard, flanked by Laura and Steve in their matching Amelia's Haven jackets.

The people in the queue turned to watch. One woman smirked, another put her headphones on with exaggerated care, a third turned her back on Amelia and scrolled on her phone.

'The original Soul Snatchers are here, in this shop, targeting people under false pretences and offering fake treatments. Instead of helping you, they're getting into your head and manipulating you,' Amelia yelled from outside.

'Why do you think they won't let me in? They don't want me to protect you from their manipulations.' The customers responded by increasing their own volume until she could barely be heard. There was a shifting and a sniggering, a gradual turning until not a single person in the shop was facing Amelia. As one, they blocked her out without a word.

Beth carried on serving customers, trying not to laugh. The last time Amelia had tried something like this, Beth's life had been put at risk and the shop was destroyed. This time, Amelia's undoing was subtle and silent, but brutal for a woman who breathed attention and publicity.

There was a commotion at the entrance, and Beth looked up to see a TV camera pointing at the door.

Amelia stopped mid-sentence, coughed, and then pulled herself up to her full height, tilting her chin up.

'Excuse me.' A woman from the queue pushed through to the reception desk. 'Can I leave these here?' She held up an armful of sage, tarot cards and crystals. 'I want to talk to that reporter.'

'Of course.' Beth forced her face into a polite smile, hoping the woman couldn't see her trepidation. 'Take your time.'

Beth strained to hear the TV interview while she carried on serving customers, and as she listened, her shoulders relaxed. People really were seeing through Amelia now, and to hear one of her own customers speak out filled Beth with hope.

'Amelia is throwing her weight around, trying to manipulate and intimidate people.' The woman's voice was rising in pitch. 'She thinks we owe her something, even though she's done nothing but push people around and peddle dangerously divisive lies. I wouldn't go anywhere near her, except that I really want the gorgeous things stocked by this shop, and she's standing right by the door.'

Amelia was frozen, her face blanched, teeth gritted. Her fists were clenched so tight her knuckles were almost blue.

The interviewer laughed and nodded as the camera man lowered his kit. He said something to the woman, but Beth couldn't hear the words.

The woman came back in, picked up her purchases and headed for the back of the queue.

'No,' the woman at the front called. 'Come in front of me. We all owe you for that.'

'I can't push in front of everyone but thank you.' The woman blushed, clutching her purchases more tightly.

Everyone nudged her to the front, muttering thanks.

Beth packed up her things and handed them to her, waving her card away. 'This is on the house. Thank you for your support.' She grinned at the woman's obvious delight and then met Amelia's gaze. It was steely, furious and undoubtedly dangerous. Beth rang a bell on the counter and then carried on serving.

A few minutes later, Doriel poked her head around the door. 'Is everything okay?'

Beth nodded at Amelia and then leaned towards Doriel to whisper in her ear. 'She's just taken a major hit and it was very public. I don't think it will end well if I interfere. Would you mind?'

Doriel's face lit up. 'I'd be delighted. Amelia, love.' She walked out the door with her arms held wide. 'Come here. It's so good to see you. Let's go for coffee. I'd love to chat.'

Amelia froze. She looked around, took in Laura and Steve watching her, and swallowed. 'I could do with a coffee.'

'Fabulous. Beth, would you look after Amelia's friends?'

Doriel raised one eyebrow. 'I would like to have her all to myself for a while. It's been far too long.'

The woman who had given the interview stared at Doriel, her mouth slack with astonishment. Doriel didn't care. Beth smiled. These women never failed to surprise, her or anyone else.

As Doriel and Amelia disappeared down the street and Beth finished serving the last person in the queue, Laura cleared her throat from the doorway. 'May I come in?' she asked, shoving her jacket at Steve who was standing outside the shop. 'It's been so long.'

Beth nodded. 'I think you wanted it that way.'

Laura took in a deep breath, held it for a moment, and then shook her head as she released it and walked towards Beth. 'I don't know what to say. Amelia is my boss.'

'I understand,' Beth shrugged her shoulders. You have conflicted loyalties. But I hope you don't think I'm a Soul Snatcher anymore?'

Laura swallowed. 'I don't know what I think anymore. I'm so confused. But I do miss you. Is that enough?'

'I think we should go.' Steve poked his head around the door. 'I don't want to be seen in here without Amelia. It could play out badly later.'

'I'll see you another time, Beth.' Laura held her gaze as Steve led her out the door.

Beth let out a breath, her eyes misting over. Laura may not have been warm, but that was closer to an apology than she had expected. Maybe the tides really were turning.

56

AMELIA

Amelia followed Doriel up the stairs, gripping the banister tightly. This place smelled like home. The moment she stepped into the stairwell she paused, closed her eyes and breathed it all in. The memories came back in such vivid detail that she had to blink back tears. She had lost so much, and it had been right here all along.

'Come on up,' Doriel called down the stairs.

Amelia realised she had frozen halfway. 'Coming.' She wiped a stray tear from her cheek. What was wrong with her? This was not the moment to lose her edge.

Miranda was sitting bolt upright on a squashy armchair when she stepped into the room at the top. Amelia had never been in here before, but if she could have designed Doriel as a room, this would have been it.

'Amelia.' Miranda held her gaze. 'Doriel, what is she doing here?'

'Miranda.' Amelia wanted to snort, to burst out laughing, anything to break the tension, but Miranda's gaze held her locked. 'Stop it,' she said at last. 'I was invited.'

Miranda sighed and the pressure released.

'We went out for coffee and got on so well I brought her home.' Doriel handed Amelia a steaming cup of tea.

She took a sip and closed her eyes. She hadn't drunk tea in years. The taste immersed her in memory: drinking tea late into the night with Doriel and Miranda, chatting, meditating and practising tarot. 'Thank you.' She sat on the sofa, wishing she felt relaxed enough to pull her legs up onto the seat as Doriel was doing.

Doriel took a sip of her own drink. 'Amelia, can we end this now? We want you back. You know that, right? We belong together. I miss you so much. We're the Triad. We're supposed to work and live together. I hate being at odds like this. I know you and Miranda fell out, but that's in the past. Surely we can move on?'

Amelia swallowed. 'I would love to make up. You know I would. But we'd all have to want it. Look at Miranda. She can't even look at me without accusation.'

Miranda held her gaze for an uncomfortably long time. 'You know how I feel, Amelia. Jonan was young and vulnerable when you took advantage of him. Then when he left, you moved onto Roland, who was even younger and even more vulnerable.'

'I took care of Roland when you didn't,' Amelia said through gritted teeth. 'We didn't become romantically involved until he was an adult. If you were so concerned, you could have stayed in his life and been the mother he so badly needed.'

'I messed up.' Miranda tilted her chin in the air, glaring at Amelia. 'I let Roland down. I will always regret that. What will you regret, Amelia?'

'You always have to set traps, don't you, sister.' Amelia rolled her eyes.

Miranda raised one eyebrow.

'Come on now, we're supposed to be making up.' Doriel leaned forwards, looking from one to the other. 'We have spent years going over our hurts. It's time to move on and find peace. Miranda, your time in seclusion is over whether you like it or not. You are needed here in the outside world.

'Amelia, you are needed too. *We* need you. Please, stop hurting people and come back. Together we could do so much good. I want you at my side, sister. And I know you miss us too.'

'I lost a part of myself when we were severed.' Amelia's voice cracked. 'And I don't want you to replace me with some stranger.' She paused and frowned. 'Wait. Stop hurting people? What do you mean by that? Are you suggesting I'm the only one here who has ever hurt anyone?'

'I'm suggesting that with Amelia's Haven you are spreading toxic lies that are hurting a lot of people.' Doriel's voice was firm.

'You want me to give up Amelia's Haven? To walk away from everything I've worked for? To abandon those who follow me and to whom I have promised protection?'

'Love, you're not protecting them. You're putting them in harm's way and that's not fair. It's not what they came to you for.'

Amelia slammed her hand down on the table. 'Enough!' Her voice ricocheted around the small room. 'Either you want the real me, or you don't want me at all. You don't get to mould me anymore.' She stretched her arms out wide. 'This is who I am now. Do you love me this way?'

Doriel stood up and walked over to Amelia. She pulled Amelia up and clutched her hands to her own heart. 'Darling, I will always love and adore you just as you are, but I don't love what you are doing. You are hurting people and I cannot support that. You will always be my dear friend and sister, but if you want to work with me, you must close Amelia's Haven.'

'I can't.' Amelia's voice was strangled. She coughed. 'I can't turn around now.'

'This is what you were born for, sweetheart.' Doriel pulled her into a tight hug and held her as she sobbed. 'I'm simply urging you to come back and live your destiny. You can bring your followers with you, but not under the banner of Amelia's Haven. Rebrand. Isn't that one of your talents?'

Amelia clung to Doriel for a moment, and then pushed her away, wiping the tears from her eyes. 'I might be able to do that. I need to think about it. This is huge.'

'Of course.' Doriel stepped back. Her eyes glinted with moisture. 'Take all the time you need but, please remember, if you don't agree to work with us soon, we will offer the partnership to someone else.'

Amelia nodded. Her eyes were heavy, and a headache was starting to throb in the middle of her forehead. 'It was lovely to see you both,' she said, her voice catching in her throat. Forcing herself to turn, she walked over to the door, stepped down onto the stairs and shut the door behind her. Leaning back on the solid wood, she allowed herself to release the tears that had been building since she walked into that living room. The Amelia she had been longed to come home, but she had been through so much and the woman she was now couldn't let go of everything she had worked for.

At the bottom of the stairs, she pushed the door open a crack and put her ear up to the gap.

'She's actually up there with Doriel and Mum?' Jonan's voice was incredulous.

Amelia squeezed the banister with an iron grip that hurt the skin on her palm.

'I'd love to be a fly on the wall for that conversation. They must be the two least flexible women in existence. I know Doriel is good, but surely even she can't make those two bend that far?'

'And can they really work together after everything Amelia's done?' Beth's voice was sharp. 'She almost killed Doriel. And Bill is gone because of her. Can Doriel really forget? I don't think I can in spite of everything Salu told me. We may have made agreements before we incarnated, but the Amelia on earth right now is toxic.'

Amelia took a deep breath and released it slowly. She straightened her hair, lengthened her spine, and then strode out, pausing for a moment by the payment desk. Jonan and Beth stared at her, horror etched into every line of their faces. She spun around and strode out of the shop, walking a little down the path to lean on the wall where they couldn't see her. She doubled over, heaving breath into her lungs, gasping for control, and fighting back tears.

'Amelia?'

Dread settled in her stomach. She didn't want Laura to see her like this. But it was done now, and the woman had strength she could use. She clung to the sound of her voice, allowing herself to draw from the other woman. Energy flowed into her as the colour drained from Laura's face.

Amelia straightened.

'Are you okay?' Laura's voice was small. 'Do you need help?'

'I'm fine, thank you.' Amelia's voice was steady and her

breathing slowed to normal. 'The energy in that shop is not beneficial, but I have recovered myself. What's going on out here?'

For the first time she took in the scene around her. Robson Fall stood a few feet away, deep in conversation with a journalist while a camera filmed. People wearing Amelia's Haven merchandise milled around, some watching Rob, some staring at her. Others peered in through the window of Lunea.

A woman with a clipboard walked over. 'Ms Faustus, would you mind answering some questions?'

Amelia swallowed. Doriel stood just outside the doorway to Lunea now, her arm looped through Miranda's. Doriel held her gaze, eyes pleading. Amelia took a deep breath. Doriel was the one she wanted. She couldn't let Beth and Jonan get in her way anymore. She needed to be reunited with the sisters she had grieved for so many years. She drew in breath to speak, but Beth and Jonan walked out of the shop. Beth put her arm around Doriel and then looked directly at Amelia, holding her gaze without flinching. A red-haired woman walked up with Layla and the little girl. They stood, arms linked, and one by one they looked at Amelia. Fury shot through her. She was not supposed to be on the outside. One mistake and she had spent a lifetime being judged and excluded.

'Amelia?' the woman with the clipboard said with a cough.

'Yes. Of course,' she barked at the woman, who stepped back and then scribbled on her clipboard, backing away and then turning to walk over to the camera.

Laura frowned. 'Is everything okay?'

Amelia nodded, trying to control the anger that seared

her brain. 'What has Rob been saying? Has he set traps for me?'

Laura looked over at Robson Fall. 'I don't think so, but I didn't know you were expecting him to. I assumed he was on message.'

'He'd better be.' Amelia painted a smile on her face that she hoped would be convincing. 'Why would he betray me, after all? Why would anyone betray me?'

Laura's throat worked and she stepped back. 'I'm just going to ... erm ...'

'Of course. Off you go.' Amelia waved her away and turned to the interviewer. She would find her revenge in the way she understood best. The media. She would take Lunea down.

She walked towards the interviewer, but a peal of laughter pulled her up short. With a sinking dread she turned. They were all laughing. Doriel was doubled up now, and when she stood up, slowly, her sparkling eyes met Amelia's. They were laughing at her. They were always laughing at her. Beth squeezed Doriel's shoulders and then looked at Amelia, her eyes bright as she laughed uncontrollably. Even the kid with her big, haunted eyes laughed at Amelia. On the other side of the women, Jonan and Roland stood together. They were talking seriously, but then Roland let out a bark of laughter. She was a joke. She always had been a joke and she always would be.

Amelia yelled in fury, forcing the noise out through her teeth as she ran at the group, arms wide. She pulled every scrap of energy she could muster and hurled her grey cords at them. She would ensnare them so tightly they would never get free.

Miranda held her gaze and the energy hit a brick wall.

The cords rebounded, swamping Amelia with her own fury. She dropped to her knees, gasping for breath. Her mind fogged with red-hot anger and she gritted her teeth, squeezing her hand as tight as she could around a brick that lay on the ground. She imagined it crumbling from the strength of her grip, but no. It held annoyingly firm. She picked it up, turning it over and focusing all her rage on it. She would not look at them. She would not face their laughter.

'Amelia?' Doriel's voice pierced the fog.

'Don't.' Amelia forced out the word, her jaw clenched tight.

'Amelia, we didn't mean …'

'I said don't!' Amelia screamed. She kicked off her shoes and ran, flailing her arms. Forcing fury into every strike. She would not let them make her a victim.

Hands grasped her wrists, but she wrenched them away, waving the brick around her, creating a barrier.

'Amelia' Jonan's voice was panicked. Amelia hit out harder, putting years of fury into the swipe.

There was a sickening crunch.

Amelia froze. Lightheaded. The brick felt suddenly hard and cold in her hand. No, not just cold. Slippery. Why was it slippery? Why was she still holding it?

Doriel staggered and then dropped to the ground, her head covered in blood.

The world lurched. Amelia tried to grab on to something, to find her balance, but there was nothing to hold her upright. She fell. The impact screamed through her bones. Every stone in the tarmac dug into the sensitive skin of her knees and palms. Someone was yelling. Was it her? Doriel? How badly had she hurt Doriel? She wanted to find out, but the world was spinning and she was about to be sick. She dry-retched, pulling herself onto all fours. Where was that TV camera? Was it trained on her? Could she stop it? She tried to stand but collapsed and retched again.

A strong pair of hands caught her under her armpits and picked her up, putting her back onto her feet and holding her upright. 'You'll get trampled if you stay down there.' The Sheep was frowning at her. 'You need to get out of here before the police arrive.'

'The police? What happened? Is Doriel okay?'

The Sheep looked surprised. 'I can't be sure, but she looks like a goner to me. There's a lot of blood and she hasn't regained consciousness. You did the job properly this time. If you don't want to be done for murder, put your escape plan into action. You do have a plan?'

She stared. 'Escape plan? Murder? Don't be ridiculous.'

He frowned and bent at the knee so he was on her level. 'You will be arrested. You hit Doriel over the head in front of a load of witnesses and TV cameras. There was a brick in your hand covered in blood. I think she's dead.'

Amelia looked around her, trying to make sense of the chaos. She remembered the brick and how it felt to dig her fingers into its pitted sides. She remembered a thud. But that must have been someone else. She would never have done anything bad to Doriel. This was a joke.

But Jonan didn't find it funny. He was crouched over Doriel's blood-stained body, yelling and pleading by turns. Miranda stood behind him, eyes closed. Beth stood, her hands resting on Jonan's shoulders, not caring that tears streamed down her face. The Sheep was still looking at her. What did he expect? She would never hurt Doriel. Everyone knew that. The world loved her. She was the media's darling and she had the police in her pocket. All she had to do was provide a scapegoat.

'You hurt Doriel,' she said, her voice cracking.

The Sheep frowned. 'What?'

'You heard me.' She lurched to her right to grab hold of a lamp post and held on tight. 'You hurt Doriel,' she said, louder now. 'YOU HURT DORIEL!' She wasn't in control. She didn't care. The Sheep had to pay. He was built to take whatever she threw at him. She pummelled him with years of fury and every ounce of the confusion that pounded through her veins. 'I can't believe you would be so brutal. She might be dead because of you. How could you? You'll be arrested.'

The Sheep didn't even try to stop her. He ducked his head out the way and accepted the blows she rained down on his chest, staring at her, face pale and pasty, mouth gaping.

'Don't be ridiculous, Amelia,' Laura's voice said from behind her. 'Everyone saw what happened. It was caught on camera. There's no way out. Steve was on the other side of the street.'

'Everyone will believe me,' she hissed from between gritted teeth. 'You plotted with him. You hurt Doriel and tried to frame me, even though I have cared for you.' Amelia sobbed, grief blooming from her chest. Her mind narrowed until all she could sense was the pain. 'Get off me!' she screamed, as a hand touched her arm. She was vaguely aware of Laura and the Sheep retreating but didn't care anymore. She could feel Miranda looming over her. Could feel the emptiness in Doriel's body. She slumped onto the ground, hugging her knees to her chest, and allowed the grief to take her.

57

BETH

BETH WOULD NEVER UNSEE THAT MOMENT.

Amelia rushing towards them, flailing her arms around and lashing out with the brick. Doriel crouching, her arms wrapped over her head, while Jonan and Roland did their best to hold Amelia off, gripping one arm each. Beth had no idea how Amelia had accessed so much strength, or why she thought she needed it. She would also never understand why Doriel took her arms down and reached out to Amelia.

The blank look in Amelia's eyes as she brought the brick down on Doriel's head, and the crunch it made, would haunt Beth for the rest of her life.

As would Jonan's scream as Doriel sank to the ground.

Beth allowed tears to engulf her as the images played on a loop in her mind. Crouching down she pushed her palms into the smooth, warm bricks, bringing herself back to the moment. Jonan was bent over Doriel, doing compressions and yelling.

'Excuse me, sir.' A man put a hand on Jonan's back, and then took off his coat. 'I'm a doctor. Can I take over please?'

Jonan crumpled backwards and the man slid seamlessly into place.

Jonan bent double, clutching at his middle as his body wracked with sobs. Beth wrapped her arms around him. Pulling him close, she leaned into his back and they rocked together. Alone in the chaos.

Beth was dimly aware of Miranda standing beside them. Impassive. Blank.

The world around them was a blur. The doctor kept on with compressions and mouth to mouth, intermittently speaking to someone on the phone, reeling off staccato updates and instructions. Tabitha stood on a concrete flowerpot issuing orders to the crowd, who watched her, stunned and silent. None of it seemed real.

Amelia's voice cut across Tabitha's instructions and pulled Beth from her trance.

'YOU HURT DORIEL!' she screamed, pummelling Steve with her fists. 'I can't believe you would be so brutal. She might be dead because of you. How could you? You'll be arrested.'

Beth blinked as the crowd started muttering. Could Amelia really be this deluded? Had she started believing her own stories? These people were her devoted followers half an hour ago. Would this obvious lie be enough to this snap them out of it?

'Poor Doriel,' a voice came from the crowd. 'I hope she's okay. She's helped me so many times.'

'You didn't say that when you were taking Amelia's freebies,' another woman called out.

'I didn't see why I should choose. But after seeing what Amelia did, I'd be glad to speak to the police.' The woman glared across the crowd, eyes fiery with challenge. The other woman held her gaze for a moment and then her shoulders slumped. 'Me too. Amelia said she was protecting us. That didn't look like protection to me. I don't know who she is anymore.' There was a muttering of agreement.

Beth sat back on the uneven brick paving and dropped her head into her hands, allowing grief to swamp her.

A police car pulled up and a woman climbed out. She looked around and then walked over to Beth and crouched down in front of her. 'You saw what happened?'

Beth wiped tears from her cheeks, but more kept coming. 'Doriel.' She let out a sob. 'The woman who was attacked, she's my friend. She's virtually family.'

The police officer nodded. 'The ambulance is on its way.' She looked over at Doriel and her face darkened. 'She will be looked after. My colleague will take your details so we can arrange to take your statement. Do you have someone you can call?'

Beth put her hand on Jonan's back. 'We're all here already.'

A siren screeched from the hill and an ambulance came around the corner and pulled onto the paving in front of the clock tower. Beth staggered upright and tugged at Jonan's arm. 'We need to get out of their way. Let them get to Doriel. They have to save her.'

Jonan nodded mutely, hauling himself up as though his body were a weight too heavy to bear. He moved backwards as paramedics surrounded Doriel.

After a few minutes she was transferred to a stretcher.

'Can I come with her?' Jonan's voice was hoarse.

'I'm going.' Miranda spoke for the first time. 'Meet us there.'

'But can't we both ...?'

'I'm sorry.' One of the paramedics touched his arm. 'We need space to help your friend. Come to the hospital. We're going to Watford.'

Doriel was carried to the ambulance on a stretcher, followed by a numb-looking Miranda and a police officer. The crowd watched in silence.

Jonan wrapped his arms around his chest. 'I don't know whether I'll ever see her again.' Tears streamed silently down his cheeks. 'We have to go.'

'Beth?' Laura walked over, her hand stretched out, but it dropped to her side as she saw the blood stain on the uneven ground. She cleared her throat.

Beth blinked at the woman who had once been her friend. 'Not now, Laura, please.'

Laura stepped back. 'Would you like a lift to the hospital?'

There was a car in the spot the ambulance had just vacated. The nearside doors were wide open.

'We'll take you straight there.' A tear ran down Laura's cheek.

Beth looked at her friend and then turned to Jonan. He nodded. 'Let's just go.'

58

BETH

Relief flooded Beth as the car pulled into the drop-off bay near A&E. Steve had driven silently and taken lots of back roads to avoid the traffic, leaving Beth wondering whether they were going to the hospital or heading back to the barn where he had imprisoned Doriel and Bill. But he had brought them straight here.

'Please let me know how Doriel is.' Laura's voice was strangled. 'I have the same number.'

Beth nodded. 'Thanks for the lift.'

Miranda was sitting on a bench outside the entrance.

'Mum.' Jonan took her hands and pulled her to her feet, folding her into a tight hug. For once she allowed herself to relax into his arms.

'Miranda?' Dread knifed through Beth as Miranda started to sob. 'What do you know?'

Miranda swallowed, and then stiffened and prised Jonan off her. 'She died in the ambulance. She's gone. I'm sorry.'

'No,' Jonan whispered, and then louder, 'No. She isn't.

There must be something they can do. Something you can do?' You're a powerful healer. Heal Doriel.'

'I can't.' Her voice cracked and she curled in on herself, her body convulsing with sobs. 'I'm sorry. I know she was more mother to you than I ever was.'

'No!' Jonan yelled, and started walking in circles, gasping for breath and pushing his fist into his solar plexus. 'She can't be gone. She can't.'

Beth pulled him close, letting him sob on her shoulder, sending love into him with every cell in her body. She cried with him as grief engulfed them both, threatening to drag them down. 'Jonan, there's nothing she could have done. It's Amelia you should be angry with, not your mother.'

'Don't worry.' Jonan pulled himself up to his full height, eyes blazing. 'I have plenty of anger for Amelia. I will make sure she rots behind bars for the rest of her life. I have CCTV all round the shop. There's no way she can keep her little performance secret.'

Beth nodded. 'Knowing that, you can give yourself time to grieve, to feel it and say goodbye. The rest will take care of itself.'

'But … Doriel …' He choked out the words.

'This was not supposed to happen.' Miranda started pacing. 'I did not want to be left alone. It's not fair.' She was walking faster and faster now, words pouring like water from her mouth. 'I can't believe she abandoned me. First Amelia, and now Doriel. Does the word Triad mean nothing to them?'

'Mum.' Jonan put a hand on her arm, stopping her in her tracks. 'Doriel didn't abandon you, she was murdered. And Amelia didn't walk away all those years ago, you cut her out.

But either way you're not alone. You still have Roland and me. Please don't forget us again.'

Miranda gave a hard laugh. 'Of course. It's always my fault. I know how much I lost when I walked away. Doriel was more mother to you than I was. And Roland had Amelia. I am supposed to be the wise, spiritual one, the powerful one, the one who is all knowing and can channel energy into unbelievable creation. But guess what ... I failed.' She paused and closed her eyes, breathing deeply. 'I am alone.' Her voice broke. 'Doriel was so sure she had finished, that she had changed to the Judgement card and was ascending. She said she was finished with physical life and her path was done. But she didn't think about me, did she? She didn't think about what I would do if she left me behind. I HATE HER FOR LEAVING ME!' she yelled at the stars. 'How do I deal with Amelia without her? Doriel was the glue that held us together. Without her, Amelia and I are a disaster.'

'Would you want to make up with Amelia now?' Beth squeezed her eyes tightly shut as a sob rippled up through her chest. 'She killed Doriel.'

'She did. Doriel made me promise not to hold that against her. Can you believe that? Doriel wanted me to be a paragon of forgiveness! Me! When have I successfully forgiven anyone? I've built a life around fury, and she thinks I can forgive *this* woman for killing *my sister*?'

'Mum.' Jonan's voice cracked. 'Did Doriel speak to you in the ambulance?'

She shook her head. 'She didn't regain consciousness.'

'When did she tell you all of this?'

'She's known for ages. She knew she was going to die, and she knew it would be at Amelia's hand. She was so determined that we had to make up, that her death would accomplish something because we would finally come back together. I told her. I told her it was useless. That if Amelia killed her, I would never forgive her. But she did that infuriating grin that says she knows more than you do, and she told me I would see. What the hell does that mean? I'm an Oracle. I know all about seeing and I really don't see how I am ever going to forgive that woman for destroying my life. Again.'

It was getting dark now, and Jonan's skin was almost translucent in the artificial light from the streetlamp. He swayed and gripped the back of the bench. 'Doriel knew Amelia was going to kill her? Is that why she stopped protecting her head when Amelia was waving that damn brick around?'

Miranda nodded. 'We have been preparing for weeks.'

'That's what you've been doing cloistered up there by yourselves?' Jonan's voice was shrill. 'And you didn't tell me? Doriel was planning her own death, and it didn't occur to you to do something to stop it? Or to tell me?'

'She didn't choose it, Jonan, she saw it. She tried to change things with Amelia, but it didn't work so she accepted it was her time and prepared. She wanted to clear the last of her blockages from this life so she would be free, and to prepare me for what would come next.'

'Free? Free to what? Not incarnate with us again?'

'Don't be like that, Jonan. We're all hurting.' Miranda turned her face to the sky, not caring that the tears flowed down her cheeks.

Jonan shut his eyes and lowered himself to the bench. He bent over, putting his head between his knees. 'She never told me.'

Miranda slumped to the ground, leaning her back against the streetlamp. 'She said you didn't need to know. She trusted you to do your part without instruction. Me, she didn't trust. So she took control.'

Beth crouched down and took Miranda's hands. The older woman stiffened, and then forced herself to relax. Her fingers were freezing cold.

'Miranda, you don't have to forgive Amelia today. I'm sure even Doriel would agree with that. We have suffered a huge loss. You're in shock. Give yourself a chance to process this, to be sad and angry, before you look for the higher ground. I have absolute faith that you'll get there when the time is right. Tonight isn't the night.'

Miranda nodded and then dragged herself up and sat on the bench beside Jonan. She reached out her hand and clasped his. 'I'm sorry I left you, son. It is the biggest regret of my life. I will do everything I can to regain at least a little of what we all lost, if you'll help me.'

Jonan pulled her into a hug. 'I'll always help you, Mum.'

59

ROLAND

ADRENALINE SHOT THROUGH ROLAND WHEN THE DOORBELL rang, followed by a sinking dread as he heard Layla answer the door. An image of Doriel, pale and blood-spattered, flashed into his mind. On her face was the most supreme expression of peace.

A hand on his arm jerked him out of his memories. Jonan was gaunt, his purple eyes haunted. He shook his head and closed his eyes. 'I'm sorry, brother.'

Roland let out a sob, and pulled Jonan into a tight hug, clinging on to the other man as though he were a life raft. They had been abandoned as children and tugged in different directions. They had dealt with grief before, isolated and alone. This time, they would do it together. Doriel would have wanted that.

Jonan's nails dug into his arm, but he didn't care. Doriel had been a mother to Jonan. This would hit him hardest of all.

'Where's Mum? Does she know?' Roland pulled back, wiping his cheek with the back of his hand.

Jonan slumped onto the sofa. 'She was with Doriel when she died.'

'I'm here.' Miranda came through the door followed by Layla. 'Doriel wanted you to know how much she loved you both.' She blinked and then squeezed her eyes tightly shut. 'I can't believe she's gone.'

'Do you feel her?' Roland said, his voice quiet. 'I think I do, but I don't know whether it's real, or I'm making it up.'

'Oh, it's real. She's all around us.' Miranda's voice cracked. 'She knew she was going and she was so damn ready I hated her for it. I do not want her to be gone. I do not want to be alone.'

'Stop it.' Anger surged through Roland. 'I know you love her. We all do. But you're not alone. Don't tell us that Jonan and I don't matter. That only your infernal Triad counts. You came here to be the Mother, not the Oracle. Has it still not occurred to you that maybe *that* is your real lesson?'

Miranda swallowed. She reached out a hand and gripped the side of the table as she sat down slowly. 'I understand. I once ...' She paused and then shook her head. 'I ... You're bringing me a truth. I won't cover it up with an anecdote. I don't have the clarity to answer that question right now. I would prefer to sit with it before I respond.'

Roland let out a long breath as his shoulders slumped. 'Thank you.' He leaned forwards, cradling his head in his hands. 'I can't believe she knew she was going to die and didn't tell us.'

'What would you have done differently if you had known?' Layla crouched in front of him, putting her hands on his knees. 'How would you have lived with that knowledge? I think Doriel gave each of us what she thought we would need. She's taught Abi a lot in the past few weeks.'

'Abi,' Jonan whispered. 'How will we tell her?'

'She knows.' Layla's voice was a hoarse whisper. 'She told me while you were at the hospital. She said she helped Doriel. I don't know what that means.'

'I saw her.' Miranda's voice was rough. 'When Doriel left her body, there was a leopard cub, and a white tiger.'

A sob escaped Layla and she clapped her hand over her mouth.

'I don't know about all of you, but I could do with a drink.' Beth stood up with a shaky laugh.

'Help yourself,' Roland said. 'You can get one for me too.'

There was a general mumbling of assent.

Beth handed out glasses. 'I understand what you said, Layla, but I still agree with Roland. I wish she'd said something. We might have been able to stop it. I keep playing that awful moment over and over in my head. I'm sure we could have done something if we'd known.'

'That's why she didn't tell you.' Miranda's voice was heavy with exhaustion. 'She believed her death would bring us back together. All of us.'

Jonan narrowed his eyes. 'Doriel thought we could reunite with Amelia after this? After Amelia killed her? Surely even Doriel wasn't that deluded.'

Miranda sighed. 'She didn't know how her death would come about, or when, but she knew it was close. She believed her sacrifice would pierce the absurd bubble Amelia is hiding in. She was convinced that either Amelia would give up this doomed ego trip, or her death would allow us to defeat her. Either way, the conflict would end.'

Roland took a deep breath. Did any of them realise how big this was? If Doriel saw her death defeating Amelia, their world was about to change. He hoped it would be a good thing. 'Is that what you see, Miranda?'

Miranda gave a harsh bark of laughter. 'All I see is Doriel's death on repeat. I want to trust her insight and do as she asked me, but I am beyond reconciliation now. I will take Amelia on. And I will win.'

Beth reached over and took Miranda's hand. 'I am as angry as you are, but this isn't about winning. It's not even about Amelia, really. We need to help people see through the manipulation, to help them resist when self-appointed gurus pull them by the neck. People loved Amelia and she wielded them as a weapon. We can teach people to see through that, to become their own heroes.'

Miranda smiled, but it didn't reach her eyes. 'Doriel would have been so proud of you, Beth. Truly, you are taking up her mantel. But that is your path. Amelia is mine. She has always been mine. I just didn't want to see it before. Doriel has left me no choice. I am not letting her get away with it this time.'

Roland held her gaze. 'I'm sorry, Mum. I've been angry with you for so long that I didn't see how I was contributing. I supported and enabled Amelia to become what she is. I have to take responsibility for Doriel's death myself.'

'No. You don't.' Jonan stood up and started pacing. 'We have all made choices and every one of us could argue that we incited Amelia. But nobody is letting her off the hook. Amelia killed Doriel. She has been waging a bizarre war on her for months. The kidnapping, the break-ins, the social media trolling. I thought it was about me, but I know now that was what she wanted me to believe, because she knew it tortured me. Amelia brought that brick down on Doriel's head. She is the one who will carry the weight of that action and I will make damn sure that she carries it alone.'

60

BETH

BETH LURCHED UPRIGHT, DRAWING IN HUGE GASPS OF AIR. Getting out of bed, she walked on unsteady legs to the hall to turn on the light. She pressed her palm into the solidity of the old stone wall, giving her breath time to even out.

'Are you okay?' Jonan's voice was thick with sleep.

'Bad dream. I'm going downstairs to get a drink and wake up a bit. You go back to sleep.'

The house was cold and dark, but it was real, and the dream receded as Beth felt her way down the dark steps to the lounge and then through to the kitchen. She took the milk from the cupboard and poured some into a cup. Decanting it into a saucepan, she added hot chocolate and then put it on the hob to warm. As reality settled, the enormity of the previous day's events hit her, and tears stung her eyes. She had been better off in the nightmare.

'I don't suppose you made enough for two?' Jonan's voice startled her.

She held out her hand for his mug. Dividing the hot

chocolate equally between the two cups, she handed him one then padded through to the living room to sit on the sofa.

'What was the dream?' Jonan slid his hand into hers. 'Something to do with yesterday?'

Beth shrugged. 'I dreamed I was Amelia. I was on *Deep and Dark* talking to Katherine Haversham. I did energy work on Katherine ...'

'What made you think you were Amelia?' Jonan asked when she didn't continue.

Beth frowned. 'Those are all things Amelia has done. I haven't. They refused to have me on. Why would they change their minds now?'

'It was a dream, right? It doesn't have to make sense. But they might change their minds after what Amelia did. Like it or not, we fit the news agenda now.'

Beth shuddered.

'You will never become Amelia. You can trust yourself to adapt her ideas without losing your way.'

'How do you know?' A chill shot down her spine. 'We're both Potential, no? We came with the same blueprint.'

'You came with the same starting point, but you've always been completely different people. You have different destinies and different strengths and weaknesses.'

'Anyway, it's beside the point.' Beth took a sip of hot chocolate. 'I've already tried. They won't talk.'

THE DOOR WAS ALREADY UNLOCKED WHEN THEY ARRIVED AT Lunea the next morning, and the bell rang as they walked in. Roland was behind the desk, a cup of coffee and a newspaper in front of him.

'Have you seen this?' He looked up, one eyebrow raised.

Beth walked over to the desk and read the headline over his shoulder: AMELIA QUESTIONED BY POLICE.

Beth shrugged. 'She's packed the police department full of her friends. You know that better than I do. It won't stick.'

Roland turned the page. There was a picture of Amelia staring directly into the camera. She looked frightened. 'Normally I'd agree with you. But you see that detective? I know him. He used to be one of hers, but that look in his eye is unfamiliar. I think he got out. That makes him a wild card. Even Robson Fall is distancing himself from her now. It's only a matter of time. I'm sure of it.'

'Robson Fall? That is interesting.' Beth skim-read the article. They'd interviewed Fall. He was spouting a load of self-righteous nonsense about how he'd been concerned about Amelia's behaviour for a while, and had taken the decision to walk away to protect his followers and hers. 'He's trying to poach her fans and run the conference without her. We need to do something, or they'll just go from one self-proclaimed guru to another.'

A sense of certainty began in Beth's solar plexus and spread throughout her body. 'I'll try again with *Deep and Dark*. If Laura has turned against Amelia, maybe that will be enough to get me in.'

There was a knock on the door.

'Aren't we open?' Beth frowned and then did a double take. It was Laura and Steve. She walked over to the door and stepped outside. 'Can I help you?'

Laura's eyes were red and puffy. She clutched Steve's hand so tightly her knuckles were white. 'Can we come in? We'd like to apologise. To all of you.'

Beth swallowed. She stepped back and held the door open.

Steve cleared his throat. 'You tried to tell me. You said she was dangerous and wouldn't stand by me. I called you a liar. I honestly didn't believe she would go this far or truly hurt your friends. I don't expect you to forgive me, but thank you for listening.'

'Oh, Beth.' Laura sniffed. 'I don't know what to say. You warned me too and I was horrible to you. I threw you out of your own home. You know you can come back if you want? Of course you don't want to. What was I thinking? I can't believe she killed Doriel. I've been replaying that moment over and over in my mind. The awful sound of it. Seeing her crumple. Seeing Amelia try to blame it all on Steve. We've been to the police and told them everything we know. Absolutely everything. Even the bits that incriminate us. I'm so sorry, Beth. Can you ever forgive me?'

Beth blinked back tears. She swallowed and then lurched forwards and pulled Laura into a hug. The other woman clung to her, shaking with sobs. Beth gave in to the grief and allowed herself to cry.

After a few moments Laura pulled back, sniffed and wiped her eyes. 'I will make as much up to you as I can. I'd like you to come onto *Deep and Dark*. I know you've been trying.'

Beth stepped back. 'You'd sort that for me?'

Laura nodded. 'The spot is yours if you want it. Honestly, you'd be doing us a favour. I'm really worried about Katherine. She hasn't been the same since Amelia inducted her on stage. I'm hoping you can do your thing and help her get back to normal.'

'Could I do it on camera and extend it to everyone watching?'

'You could do that?'

Beth smiled and then turned to Jonan. 'This could be it?'

Laura's phone rang. 'Excuse me.' She slipped out the door as she accepted the call.

Steve coughed, and then looked around sheepishly. He pointed to an amethyst wizard on one of the shelves, and Beth saw Jonan flinch.

'I'm sorry I destroyed your shop.'

'More than once.' Jonan's jaw was tight, but he took a deep breath and his shoulders relaxed. 'But I know how she can get into your head. I won't hold it against you if you walk away from her now.'

'That's fair.' Steve held out his hand. 'Consider us a part of your team. I'm done being her sheep.'

Jonan's hand was dwarfed, but the clouds lifted from his eyes. The scent of incense wafted through the air and Beth heard Doriel's bell-like laughter in her mind. A shiver ran down her spine.

Laura came back into the shop, worrying at her lip with her teeth and picking at the side of one thumbnail. 'That was the studio. There's been a change of plan.'

Beth's heart sank. 'I understand. I appreciate you trying.'

'They're not cancelling you. They've brought the segment forward. It's today. And instead of bringing you into the studio, they want to film on location at the Monk's Inn.'

'The Monk's Inn? But that's Amelia's home.'

Laura nodded. They want to start at the Prison Gateway. They're already setting up a stage. You can do the energy work for Katherine there. She'll interview you and then the show will make a surprise visit to Amelia at the Monk's Inn.'

'She was taken in for questioning this morning,' Jonan said. His voice was flat, but there were flickers of purple in his eyes that told Beth his interest had been piqued.

'She's been released. She arrived at the Inn ten minutes ago. That's why they're moving. They've had an anonymous tip-off that she'll disappear before the police can charge her.'

'The fact that she's been released at all suggests she must still have some sway in the police department.' Roland's voice was oddly clipped and precise. 'I was hoping that detective had switched sides.'

'He has.' Steve's voice was rough. I spoke to him yesterday. 'But he still has to win his boss around. The man is obsessed with her.'

'So she has time to make her move.' Roland cracked his knuckles.

'Unless we act before she does.' Laura shrugged, her voice lighter than Beth had heard it in a long time. 'What do you say, Beth, will you do it?'

'Of course. Give me five minutes.'

Beth grabbed her bag and ran up the stairs. She let herself into Doriel's room and sat on the bed, spreading her palms flat on the duvet, stretching her fingers wide. She closed her eyes and took a deep breath, opening her awareness. *Are you there?*

There were no words, but the light surrounded her, wrapping her in a blanket of warmth. *Am I doing the right thing? Is this what you want?*

You don't need me to tell you that. She could hear Doriel's voice clearly now, the cadence so familiar it made her heart break. *You are wise, Beth, trust yourself. Trust your knowing.*

The presence faded and peace soothed Beth's body for the first time since Doriel collapsed. *I won't let you down.* She sent out the words. She touched up her make-up in the mirror, slung her bag over her shoulder and stood straight, putting her hands on her hips and tilting her chin up, allowing the power pose to give her strength.

'Beth?' Jonan called up the stairs.

Only Beth could take this next step. She took a deep breath, nodded at her reflection, and whispered goodbye to Doriel as she shut the door behind her. Downstairs, the shop had been closed and they were all waiting by the door. Laura held it open as they filed through, and Jonan locked up, nodding to Beth as she slipped her hand into his. This was the moment they had been building towards. Now it was here, Beth wanted nothing more than to turn and run.

61

BETH

The Abbey Gateway was teaming with people. The stone arch that sat between the cathedral and the school had a stage set up in front of it, surrounded by barriers. Katherine Haversham sat on a chair on the stage, with one woman touching up her make-up and another running through points on a clipboard. Behind the barriers, a crowd was growing. A couple in big coats with two small, floppy-eared spaniels, one red and one black and tan, moved towards Beth as she approached the entrance. The woman reached out a gloved hand and touched Beth's arm. Then she pulled back and tucked a strand of grey hair behind her ear. 'Thank you for everything you're doing,' she said. 'You have given people hope. You've given me hope.'

'Thank you.' Beth smiled as adrenaline pounded through her body.

The man held his hands above his head and clapped.

Laura led her through the barriers, waving at the security guards, who nodded and waved back. 'Are you ready?'

Beth nodded. 'Ready as I'll ever be. Does Katherine know I'm coming, or even who I am?'

'Of course! She was very keen on this segment. She's been following you on social media ever since Amelia inducted her.'

Beth stopped. 'She's what?'

Laura stopped and turned round. 'She's been following you.'

'But I called the show and didn't get anywhere.'

Laura shrugged. 'Katherine doesn't answer the phones.'

Beth rolled her eyes. 'Let's get this done.'

She followed Laura onto the stage and over to Katherine Haversham. The other woman looked up, and then did a double take and stood. 'Beth Meyer. It's good to see you again. I remember you from that first day we interviewed Amelia. Even then you were prepared to stand up to her. I admired that. I still do.'

Beth gave a tight smile. 'Thank you. I'm sorry she hurt you. I couldn't believe it when she forced that initiation on you on national TV.'

'Do you know what she did to me?'

Beth nodded. 'She bound you to her using energetic connections. Those connections are like umbilical cords, pumping fear into you and draining you of hope and drive. Plenty of people do this without realising in normal life, but Amelia? She knows exactly what she's doing, and is all the more potent for that. This is how she powers herself. You, and everyone else she's inducted, are acting as her battery.'

'And you can help me?'

'Yes. And everyone watching.' Beth hoped she looked calmer than she felt. She had done this so many times, but doing energy work on national TV was something new entirely.

'How do I know you're not interfering with me for your own purposes?'

Beth frowned. 'It's a good question. Honestly, I have no idea. But I'm not forcing you into anything. If you don't want me to do it, I won't. I can stop at any time, and if you prefer, I can do it privately.'

Katherine held her gaze, eyes narrowed, for an uncomfortably long pause. Then she nodded. 'Good enough. And no need to go private. I want people to see there's a way out of this mess.'

Ten minutes later, Beth was made up, sitting on the stage opposite Katherine. The cameras were getting into position and people were buzzing around them. Beth took deep breaths, trying to calm her nerves. She could see Jonan, Layla and Roland standing at the side, chatting and sending her encouraging looks. But they could have been a million miles away. In every way that mattered, she was alone.

'Welcome to *Deep and Dark*.' Katherine's voice brought her back to the present and she turned to smile at the woman, unsure which camera to look at. 'Today I have a special guest, Beth Meyer, who is here to talk about what happened when Amelia Faustus inducted me into her Haven live on air. She will also show all of us how to throw off the depression and anxiety Amelia is spreading across the airwaves. Welcome, Beth.'

'Thank you, Katherine.'

'I am going to come clean. I haven't been the same since Amelia inducted me into the Haven, and I know I'm not alone in that. I have been experiencing anxiety and a deep sense of powerlessness. I wasn't like this before. Although I have now learned some coping strategies, this isn't something I want to live with long-term. But you tell me you can help?'

Beth nodded. 'Amelia works by triggering your own fears and traumas. I can't put those back in the box, but I can disconnect you from her and make sure she's not pumping fear into you intentionally. That should give you the space to figure out your own stuff at your pace.'

'And you say you can offer this to everyone watching? How does that work?'

Beth took a deep breath. This was the tricky bit. 'Energy isn't bound by time or place. If people want to benefit from the energy work I'm doing for you, they only have to intend it. They can watch this show, and maybe you could put the clip on your website so people can find it later?'

'Absolutely.' Katherine nodded to someone off to the side.

'People can use it whenever and wherever works for them, as many times as they need it. And we will include a link from the Lunea website too. It should be easy to find. You can access the healing by simply watching the clip and deciding you want help. But if you'd like to come to the shop, or speak to me virtually to get individual healing, I can do that too.'

'You've had a lot of dealings with Amelia,' Katherine said, 'we all know that. We've seen much of it play out online. What would you like people to know right now, as they decide where their loyalties lie?'

Beth looked back and forth between the cameras, and a man off to the side pointed to one. Beth turned to face it. 'A lot of you might be feeling lost after seeing the footage from yesterday. You might be wondering whether Amelia was right about the Soul Snatchers, and how you can protect yourself if she's arrested. Please believe me that the Soul Snatchers do not exist. Amelia was the biggest risk to you, and you can be free of her. Simply decide to let her go, and follow this meditation. There's nothing wrong with looking for inspiration and ideas from outside of yourself, but it's time to stop giving your power to gurus. They're people. They make mistakes and push their own agendas like everyone else. Listen to your heart. You know what feels right.' She paused, letting her words sink in.

'Okay.' Katherine shuffled in her seat. 'What are you going to do?'

Beth stood up. 'I'm going to stand behind you.' She walked to the back of Katherine's chair. 'I will put my hands facing you, but I won't touch you. I would ask you, and anyone else who would like help, to imagine yourselves surrounded by a bright golden light.' The light expanded as the people watching focused into the energy. 'Imagine grey cords wrapped around you. Now see yourself taking a pair of scissors and cutting through them.'

Katherine gasped.

'See the cords disintegrating until there is nothing constricting you anymore. On the floor in front of you is the end of the cord that joined you to Amelia. See yourself strike a match. Light the end of the cord and see it burn right up to Amelia, and then flicker out. When you're ready, open your eyes.'

There was a moment of silence, and then Katherine let out a long, slow breath. 'Wow. Did anyone else feel that? An indescribable weight lifted from me. I haven't felt this awake, or positive, since before my initiation. What about all of you?' She turned to the crowd.

'Yes!' A voice called out, and then more and more joined in.

'Come up here,' Katherine waved that first person forward.

A woman pushed her way towards the stage and was ushered through the barriers. Katherine met her at the edge of the platform and reached out a hand to help her up. 'Welcome, sister. Tell us what you experienced.'

'It was like a huge golden wave that washed away the darkness. I still have some of the fear, but nothing like before. For the first time in ages, I want to go and do all the things I normally love. Maybe life will open back up for me now.'

'You've put it so well.' Katherine beamed. 'Don't you agree?' She called out to the crowd and they cheered.

Beth's heart swelled with elation and gratitude. It was happening. Jonan was grinning at her and the air was full of lavender.

Katherine pulled her into a quick hug, and then stepped back. 'So, Beth, will this affect Amelia?'

'She's been drawing energy from everyone she's connected to. We've just cut off part of that power source. Whether or not she will notice that impact, I have no idea.'

'Jonan?' Katherine turned back to the crowd. 'I know you're out there. Will you come up here and talk to us?'

There was another cheer as Jonan stepped through the barrier and up onto the stage. Katherine kissed him on the cheek and then gestured to the third chair.

'Jonan, you've known Amelia for a long time, and the woman who died was your aunt. How do you make sense of what's happened?'

Jonan swallowed. 'Honestly, I haven't found sense in anything yet. Amelia used to be a good person, a person I loved. But she's so caught up in her anger that I don't recognise her anymore. People think gurus are always clear and wise, but they're only people and everyone has good and bad patches, times when they give good advice, and times when they can't tell between their own fear, anger and intuition. This is not a good moment to follow Amelia. I am devastated to have lost Doriel. She was my aunt, but she was also like a mother to me for many years and I will always mourn her. I'm confident Amelia will too, in spite of everything.'

'Shall we go and find out?' Katherine walked to the edge of the stage. The cameras zoomed in on her. 'We are going to pay Amelia a visit to find out what's really going on.'

She stepped off the stage and walked down the hill, flanked by cameras. Beth followed. A hand slid into hers and she turned to see Jonan at her side. She let out a breath. 'Did I do okay?'

'You were amazing. Couldn't have been better.'

She squeezed his hand. 'What about this next bit?'

He let go of her hand and pulled her into his side, wrapping his arm around her shoulders. 'Honestly, I can't see how this is going to go. But we're all here. Roland and Layla are right behind us. Abi is safe with Tabitha. It's time. This is it.'

Beth nodded. She felt it too. The setting sun filled the sky with shining orange and yellow light. Salu and Lunea were by her side, around her, everywhere. She could feel the people she had helped, their energy so much lighter. And up ahead, Amelia: twisted, diminished, desperate and dangerous.

62

BETH

KATHERINE HAVERSHAM SHOVED THE DOOR TO THE MONK'S Inn. It creaked and opened.

Beth followed her in. The Inn had gone from crumbling to stunning and now back to desolate. But today the passage of time was not to blame. It was filthy, covered in cobwebs and broken by violence. There was a hole in the door to Bill's old room. A table had been up-ended and broken into bits in the ballroom, and a patch of tiles in reception was smashed. Beth reached out to touch the desk and then pulled back. It was sticky and smelled strongly of mud and marmite. What had Amelia been doing in here?

'Amelia.' Katherine Haversham stood at the bottom of the stairs, arms stretched wide. '*Deep and Dark* has come to you. Show yourself.'

There was a creak from upstairs. A door slammed, but Amelia did not appear.

Katherine walked to the bottom of the staircase. 'If you don't come down, I will take the cameras and explore every inch of this filthy building. Is this the luxurious Amelia's

Haven you promised us? Is this where the conference was supposed to be held?'

Silence.

'What's in here?' Katherine Haversham reached for the door into Bill's old room.

'No.' Beth grabbed the handle. She had no idea where the instinct to preserve a tiny shred of Amelia's dignity came from. Maybe it was a gesture towards the soul she would be reunited with on the other side. Maybe it was a shove from Doriel. 'But there is a basement this way that's well worth a look.'

'A basement?' Katherine's eyes sparkled. 'That sounds exciting. Let's go and explore.'

'No need.' Amelia's voice came from the top of the stairs. She was paler than Beth had seen her, her hair greasy, dark circles under her eyes. She clutched the banister with so much force her arm muscles stood proud. Fury poured from her as she sent her grey cords snaking towards Beth, grasping for her energy.

Beth strengthened her protections. Amelia's cords fell uselessly at her feet, and then retracted. Amelia gritted her teeth and twisted her face into a smile that looked more like a grimace.

'Welcome to my home. I do wish you had given me notice. I would have tidied up.'

'I bet you would.' Katherine smirked. 'But we are happy to take you as we find you. In fact, we wanted to see the real Amelia, to get an honest vibe from Amelia's Haven and find out what you've actually been offering the people you've inducted into your cult.'

'My cult?' Amelia started walking down the stairs with

exaggerated care. She stumbled, but righted herself and continued closer. 'It's not a cult. It's a sanctuary.'

'A protection racket,' Katherine said through gritted teeth. 'I know. You inducted me.'

'And yet, you have un-inducted yourself. What kind of cult would it be if people were able to extract themselves so easily?'

'Easily?' Katherine's laugh was hard. 'I have struggled and failed to disconnect for a long time. I have Beth to thank for my escape.'

Katherine shot Beth a smile that was so grateful it brought tears to her eyes.

'But not everyone has been so lucky and that's why I'm here. If you're genuinely trying to help people, show us. If this is a haven, let us see it. Tell us how you're going to save us, and without all the silly scare stories. We have seen the darkness you carry. We know you're not protecting us from Soul Snatchers. The only one getting into our souls is you.'

Amelia blanched. 'Katherine darling, I would love to show your viewers around my house, my sanctuary, to show you exactly what Amelia's Haven has to offer you. Unfortunately, though, my house has been interfered with and my staff are not here today so we will need to take a rain check. A fake video on the internet led the police to turn my home over and question me. They have not charged me, but I would like to bring order back to my home before I accept visitors. I invite you to come on a different day.'

'Thank you, but we're here now.' Katherine smiled sweetly at the camera, but Beth could see the clench of her jaw and the force of her hands balled into fists. 'I'm glad you brought up the video. It's showing right now in the top left-hand corner of the screen for our viewers at home. I understand from eyewitnesses that the video was not fake. It was, in fact, a very accurate portrayal of what happened. I have seen numerous other videos that show the same thing from different angles.

'Last night, you killed a woman. She was this man's aunt, I believe. Her friends tell me you previously had her kidnapped but, in spite of everything, she loved you.'

'Lies,' Amelia hissed through gritted teeth. Her eyes flashed, and in that moment her skin appeared grey, her eyes and cheeks sunken. How much weight had she lost? Beth wondered. Beth knew that fury well, but Amelia had never shown it on screen before.

One of the camera operators moved closer, kneeling at the bottom of the stairs and zooming in on her from the most unflattering angle. Amelia's eyes bulged, but she took a deep breath, and then raised an eyebrow at the man. 'I would like to step off the stairs please, if you could just move backwards.'

He held his ground for a moment, and then backed away. He did not stop filming.

Amelia's expression was carefully controlled. 'Doriel was a very dear friend of mine. I am devastated by her death. As the police understood when they released me, I was merely a bystander. She was struck by a man I thought I knew well; a man who has been very loyal to me in the past. I realise now he was out of control. I have given his details to the police, and I believe they are searching for him. The video you saw was a deep fake. I understand you spoke to witnesses, but this man was very clever and covered his actions well. I will be taking this further for the sake of my dear friend, and to clear my own name. I assure you, I am the Amelia you have all grown to know and love. I am the protector you have learned to rely on, and I am the nurturer who will help you through these difficult times.'

Katherine turned to Beth, holding out her microphone. 'Beth, you were there. Did you see this man?'

'You mean Steve?' Beth moved closer to Amelia. 'I heard you were trying to pin it on him, but he was nowhere near Doriel. I saw you hit her. I saw her fall. It's clear in the videos and I promise they are not fakes. That moment will be etched into my memory as long as I live. But you've always blamed things on Steve, haven't you, Amelia? What was it you used to call him? The Sheep? Is that because he followed orders so blindly? He doesn't sound like someone who would murder a woman of his own volition.'

'What was it *you* called him?' Amelia grinned. 'You nicknamed him the Brute as I remember?'

Beth winced. 'We did. But he was your Brute. Your muscle. We always knew that. Doriel knew that even when he kidnapped her and kept her in your prison cell.'

'She's twisting it all.' Amelia's voice cracked. 'I am innocent. The police know it. That's why I'm here.'

'You have stooges in the police.' Beth held her gaze. '*That's* why you're here and not locked in a prison cell. Anyone else would have been locked up by now.'

'I have another witness who would like to be heard.' Katherine grinned as Laura stepped forwards. 'Someone very close to our hearts on *Deep and Dark*. Laura is a trusted member of our team.'

Amelia smiled, her shoulders relaxing as she nodded to Laura.

'I have been faithful to Amelia for a long time.' Laura swallowed. 'As has my boyfriend, Steve. Until yesterday we were the last ones standing. Her personal assistant left days ago. Rose thought we were fools for staying. She told us this was a sinking ship. But we were loyal. You didn't know that did you, Amelia?'

Amelia ground her teeth, but said nothing.

Laura ran a hand through her hair. 'Amelia threw that loyalty back in our faces. Steve was nowhere near Doriel when she died. He was standing with me on the other side of the street. We saw what Amelia did. I'm embarrassed that it had to get to this point for me to see what she was really like, but at least I can now get myself out of this horrible mess. Amelia killed Doriel. If she didn't have such influential followers in the police, she would have been arrested by now. But that isn't going to work anymore. There is a police officer on his way who sees through her. A man she has messed with in the past who has got free of her influence. This is it. This is the end for you, Amelia. It's the end of everything you've created, the end of your bullying, and the end of your lies.'

Amelia gave a nervous laugh. 'Don't be ridiculous. How could I bully someone so much bigger and stronger than me? Have you seen him?' She turned to Katherine and pointed at Steve. 'Look at him. He's built like a brick wall. Now look at me!'

'I think we all know your strength doesn't lie in your muscles.' Katherine looked Amelia up and down. 'What happened to your alliance with Robson Fall? He was there at Doriel's death, filming and briefing the press against you. What did you do to him?'

Amelia looked to the right, and then back to Katherine. She swallowed, licked her lips, and backed away a little. 'Rob and I are friends. We were never a unit. He will do as he chooses, just as he's always done.'

'Weren't you supposed to be running a conference

together any day now? He has stated publicly that he's running it without you. What do you think of that?'

Amelia glanced to the right again and then shifted slightly in that direction. 'Rob can run whatever conference he wants. As can I.'

Amelia's gaze flitted to the right, and then to Jonan and Roland. Finally it landed on Beth. She swallowed. 'My followers know they get my breaking news first. Keep an eye out for my emails if you'd like to know what's coming up.'

Her eyes went blank. A chill ran down Beth's spine. She tuned into her psychic sight and saw the monks drifting into reception.

Salu, Lunea? Beth sent out the thought.

Here, sister.

'Amelia.' Beth's voice was resonant. 'Stop.'

Amelia walked towards her slowly, growing in stature with each step.

Beth met her halfway.

They faced each other. Amelia's energy was shadow, the colours in her aura muddied. Beth could see the grey cords linking her to thousands of people, but as she watched, cord after cord detached. Amelia's face was blank, showing no sign of distress, but her energy was pure fury, a muddy, red pulsing force that beat at Beth's energy field.

As Salu moved into the space between them, anger finally flickered across her face. Her jaw tensed. 'They're here,' she said from between gritted teeth. 'The Soul Snatchers themselves. Can you see them, Katherine?'

Katherine's laugh was high-pitched. Beth sent protective energy her way and when the woman spoke, her voice was steady. 'I don't see anything. You're imagining it.'

'I am not.' Amelia forced out the words. 'And I did not kill Doriel.'

'Let's see, shall we?' A screen off to the side flickered into life. The scene from the day before flooded the surface in uncomfortable clarity. Beth had hoped never to see that awful day again, but energetically open as she was, the images transported her right back into the moment. She saw herself standing with Doriel and Jonan. Saw Amelia come towards them, and then reach down for the brick. Mercifully, the video didn't pick up the sound of the brick hitting Doriel's skull.

Tears pricked Beth's eyes. *I will grieve.* She sent out the words. *But not right now. I cannot hold this process if grief takes over.* A wave of energy flooded her, lifting her, filling her with strength as she fought to hold onto enough of herself to push back Amelia's poison.

The screen went blank and there was complete silence. Katherine's voice had all the stealth of a predator. 'You promised them safety. You promised loyalty. And then you blamed your most faithful follower for the awful crime you committed. How can anyone trust you now?'

'Amelia.' Jonan's voice was soft and warm.

She turned to him and for a moment her eyes were naked, filled with terror and anger. 'Jonan?' She stepped towards him. 'Help me?' Her whisper was barely audible, but it wrapped around Jonan like a chain.

'You can't run away from this.' His face drained of colour, but his voice was firm. 'The only way is through: through the pain and fear of facing the consequences of your actions.'

'No.' She shook her head over and over.

'We are all free, Amelia: free to do and say whatever we

choose. But nothing is without consequence. It's time for you to face up to yours.'

'No.' She shook her head faster now, stumbling towards Jonan and then edging towards the right.

Beth turned to the camera. 'The Soul Snatchers never existed. It's so important you understand that. They were a spectre Amelia conjured to scare you. It is safe to walk away from this. You can release yourself from Amelia's web. Or if you need help, contact Lunea. Either way, let go of Amelia. Live your lives knowing that there are no Soul Snatchers. There are only manipulative people selling harmful stories and gaslighting everyone who speaks up. Stand up for yourself. Stand up for your own choices and reasoning. Reach into your hearts, find your unvarnished truth and let that lead you.'

Pain shot through Beth's scalp and she fell, lurching to the right. Amelia had a fistful of her hair and was dragging her backwards. Beth scrambled to her feet and grabbed Amelia's arm, trying to peel back her fingers and force her to let go. Amelia yanked and Beth yelled, lurching towards the other woman and falling on top of her.

'Keep filming!' Beth heard Katherine's voice as though from a distance.

Amelia let go of her hair, scrambled backwards and then leaned forwards and hooked her arm around Beth's neck. With a violent tug backwards, she pulled Beth close to her chest and then tightened her grip. Beth slid her fingers around Amelia's arm and pulled as hard as she could, but Amelia was stronger than she looked. Beth gasped for air, but Amelia just gripped tighter.

Amelia jerked backwards, dragging Beth with her. 'Let go of her.' Jonan's voice was low and furious.

'What will you do without your little mouse?' Amelia said through gritted teeth. 'If she's gone, you'll have to come back to me.'

'Everyone's watching, Amelia. You're on national television.' Katherine's voice was level.

'I'm untouchable.' She laughed. 'You can't make me let her go.'

'But I can.' Steve's voice was startlingly loud after the whispered conversation. There was a tightening around Beth's neck and then she collapsed forward, gasping for air. Steve had Amelia under the arms and was holding her out while she flailed around.

'Let me go!'

He dropped her, and she landed in a heap on the hard tiled floor. 'I won't let you hurt anyone else.' Steve's voice was rough with emotion. 'I've seen too much. I won't witness any more.' He turned to the cameras. 'I thought Amelia would keep me safe. But she led me into danger, pushed me to harm others, and then tried to frame me in return for my loyalty. She *won't* protect you.'

Beth got to her feet, grabbing hold of the banister at the bottom of the staircase to balance herself.

Amelia looked around, her gaze darting from side to side like a wild animal. Her cheeks were flushed and she was breathing heavily. 'Lies. All of it,' she snarled at the camera. 'It's a conspiracy. They're setting me up.'

'She's in here.' A voice came from outside the Inn. Tabitha.

'It's very creepy.' Abi giggled.

'Thank you. I appreciate your help.' This was a man's voice. Beth recognised it, but she couldn't place it.

Amelia paled. 'No.' She slid her phone out of her pocket

and started fiddling with it. She backed down the hall, one hand on the wall, the other worrying at her phone.

'I don't think so.' Katherine Haversham walked towards her, a smile on her face. 'We haven't finished. And I believe the man outside is a police officer. You wouldn't want to obstruct a murder investigation by running away, would you? It would make you look so guilty.'

The doorknob turned.

The lights went out.

63

BETH

THE MONK'S INN WAS PITCH BLACK.

'For those watching at home,' Katherine's voice rang out through the darkness. 'We're still here, but the lights have gone out.'

The door swung open, letting a sliver of yellow through from the streetlight on the pavement outside.

'What's going on here?' DC Ainsworth's voice cut through the darkness.

A light flickered and then settled on.

'Why are you hiding in the dark?' Abi smirked, her hand in Tabitha's.

'Abi!' Layla lurched towards her. 'Don't come in. Amelia—'

'Has gone.' Katherine's voice was flat, but her eyes flashed and a vein in her jaw throbbed. 'She killed the lights on purpose.'

'Did she know I was coming?' DC Ainsworth walked into the room, looking around and frowning at the camera operator.

'I'm afraid so.' Laura flushed.

DC Ainsworth sighed.

Beth looked at Jonan, started walking down the hall, and then began to run as she realised the back door was swinging on its hinges.

'Beth!' Katherine's voice rang after her, but she didn't stop.

The side gate banged and Beth ducked through. The road outside was empty now apart from one figure running up the hill, before turning right past the TV set and down towards the lake. The few people still dismantling the set watched her, open mouthed, but nobody said a word.

Beth followed Amelia down an unmade track to the lake. Amelia had a good lead, but Beth was gaining on her. At the lake, Amelia turned right and kept running along the path.

Beth was out of breath now, but Amelia was still going so she forced herself forward. She heard a growl and turned her head slightly. Two cats ran beside her, a huge white tiger and a smaller leopard.

Beth gasped as they disappeared and then flickered back into existence. 'Abi, Tabitha,' she whispered and felt a swell of love as the larger cat gave a quiet growl. 'Thank you.'

Amelia had stopped up ahead and was doubled over, breathing hard. When she saw the cats, she froze and then backed away down the path to the edge of the lake.

'Amelia!' Beth called.

Amelia looked at Beth, and then started running around the lake. She got to the bridge and stopped. She leaned on the wall for a moment, and then doubled over and vomited onto the path.

Beth stopped at the foot of the bridge and waited for Amelia to catch her breath. The cats had gone, but Beth could feel their presence and drew strength from it. She wasn't alone.

Amelia was pale. Her eyes were puffy and bloodshot, and her make-up was streaked with tears. 'You got what you wanted.'

'I didn't want any of this. I just wanted you to stop hurting people.'

Amelia gave a brittle laugh. 'You wanted Jonan.'

Beth kept her voice soft. 'I am in love with Jonan. There is nothing wrong with that.'

'Ah yes, the big soulmate destiny. He has convinced you with his stupid stories. But who knows what's real? Is it destiny or delusion? Can you tell the difference?' Amelia spread her arms wide.

Beth sighed. 'I can. Can you? You think you're so powerful, living by different rules to everyone else. But nobody can keep going like that forever.'

'And you want to bring me down?' Amelia let her arms drop.

'No. I want to help people see through your lies so you can't hurt them anymore. I want people to realise they don't need a guru, that their best guide is their own moral compass.'

'Most people want nothing more than someone to trail behind like a lost puppy! They want a sense of belonging. And they want to feel safe. I gave them that.'

Beth shrugged. 'At what cost?'

Amelia wandered over to the side of the bridge. She sagged, sitting down on the cold concrete and leaned her back on the wall. A small flock of Canada geese flew overhead. 'At a cost to my freedom, I expect. The world is not as enamoured with me as it once was.'

'And that isn't even about the lies.' Beth leaned against the bridge wall opposite Amelia. 'Don't you feel any remorse for killing Doriel?'

Amelia's face was impassive for a moment, and then her mask slipped. She dropped her head into her hands and began to sob, her shoulders shaking as she curled in on herself.

Beth watched her but didn't reach out.

The Canada geese still circled overhead. A lone man stood at the edge of the lake, controlling his motorised boat on the water. Beth sighed.

'You have no idea how devastated I am about Doriel.' Amelia's voice was shaky. She sniffed.

'I have an idea.' Jonan stepped onto the bridge, hands shoved in his pockets. Shoulders high around his ears.

Beth looked up, startled. She hadn't heard him approach.

'I know how much you loved Doriel.' He crouched in front of Amelia. 'But I will never understand how you could have allowed yourself to kill her. You've ruined everything, every step of the way.'

'It was an accident, whatever it might look like on that stupid video.' Amelia hiccupped. 'It was a moment of red fury. I didn't plan to do anything with that damn brick. I don't even know why I grabbed it, and I can't remember anything between picking it up and seeing Doriel collapse. I will regret that moment for the rest of my life. And it makes it all so much worse that you hate me now.'

'I hate what you did.' He sighed and leaned back against the wall of the bridge, sitting opposite Amelia. 'I want you to own it and face the consequences.'

'Of course you do.' Tears streamed down her face, but she stood up and stepped back towards the hump of the bridge.

'That would land me in prison, out of your hair.' She walked to the edge of the bridge and looked over the side at the water just below.

Beth stood up, the cold stiffening her bones. She looked across the lake. There were two people walking towards them from the far end. She met Jonan's gaze. He nodded slightly.

Amelia also saw. 'What have you done?' Her voice was croaky. 'Who is that?'

Jonan shrugged. 'Ignore them. It's just the three of us.'

Amelia laughed, but it turned into a sob and a single tear ran down her cheek. 'That's no good to me, Jonan. It never has been. I want you to myself.'

'Let's not go there again.'

'Ah, but you go there all the time. You keep trying to change me, Jonan. If you have no skin in this game, you have no right to try to change me. Love me, or leave me to be who I am.'

Jonan was still for a moment, and then he nodded. 'Done. Be whoever you want to be.' He shrugged. 'But I'm not going to walk away. You made sure of that when you killed Doriel. You tied me to you all over again when you left her to bleed onto the concrete outside Lunea, when you kidnapped her, and when you targeted Beth.' His glaze flickered back to the people approaching fast from the other side of the lake. There was a man and a woman in uniform.

Amelia followed his gaze. 'It's your word against mine when it comes to Doriel. I loved her dearly. She was like a sister to me and I will always miss her. There's no way I would have killed her. In fact, I'm going to offer a high reward to anyone who helps the police catch the real killer. I would watch yourselves if I were you. She died in front of your shop.'

Jonan's eyes flashed with anger, but he said nothing.

Beth slid her hand into Jonan's. 'Nobody will believe you.'

'You've thought that before, haven't you?' She smirked.

A shiver ran down Beth's spine. Amelia's cords were snaking towards her, changing the energy around them. She shivered again. Calling down the light, she blasted herself and Jonan with energy and the intrusion receded. Amelia's grey cords fizzled and dropped away.

Amelia shook her head, and then she backed away.

Beth walked towards her. 'This time is different and you know it. This time we have video evidence and a crowd of witnesses. This time your hold over people is crashing. You are a mess, Amelia. The whole world can see how deluded you are. And you can't get to us anymore. Your power over me, and over Jonan, is finished. Doriel was the only one left to care and you killed her. Do you really think Miranda will save you now?'

Amelia kept shaking her head as she backed towards the lake. 'I am stronger than that. The following I have built will hold.' A swan veered towards her, hissing, and she lurched to the side, stumbled backwards and fell into the lake.

Beth tried not to laugh as Amelia sat in the shallow water, gasping from the cold, her face flame red. 'Stop it,' she hissed, lurching up. She froze as a growl rippled over the water.

A small leopard crouched at the edge of the lake, its long, curved teeth bared. It growled again.

Amelia stumbled, and then turned to look at the island in the middle of the lake as though she was calculating whether she could reach it before the leopard got to her. As she looked away, the leopard flickered for a moment. When she turned back, the image solidified.

Even knowing it was Abi, Beth inched backwards, her

heart hammering. How in control was the girl? Did she know how to hang onto her human consciousness in that form? Beth wished she'd asked Layla more questions.

The scent of lavender drifted over the lake.

'Salu,' Beth whispered.

'Lunea,' Jonan said behind her.

Amelia's face darkened for a moment, and then she turned back to the island. Lunea and Salu stood amongst the trees. 'They will protect me,' Amelia muttered, and started wading out towards the island.

The leopard growled louder this time, and then faded.

Amelia turned back and froze. 'Where is it? Where did it go?' She repeated the question louder and louder. 'Can leopards swim? Could it be underwater? Why aren't you running?' She was yelling now. 'Why aren't you scared?'

Beth looked at Jonan.

He shook his head. 'Don't say anything.'

Amelia was halfway across the lake now. She looked towards the island, her body leaning towards Lunea and Salu. Then she looked back towards Beth and Jonan, and further to where DC Ainsworth stood with a second police officer.

'Please exit the lake.' DC Ainsworth's voice drifted across the water.

Amelia paused, and then turned and went straight for the island.

A growl rippled through the air. Amelia froze. She started wading with exaggerated movements, looked back and then fell forwards, disappearing from sight before rearing up out of the water coughing and spluttering.

'Lunea, Salu, Doriel,' Amelia yelled as she forced her way through the water, slower now. *'Protect me. Don't let it hurt me.'*

'Doriel?' Beth whispered. 'Does she really think Doriel is waiting for her?'

'Come to the side please, Ms Faustus.' DC Ainsworth stepped closer to the edge of the lake.

'Wait.' Amelia waded faster and `then stopped near the island, facing the figures. *'Lunea, help me. Where is Doriel?'* she yelled, her voice just drifting to Beth on the breeze.

The energy pulled at Beth. Jonan reached out and slid his hand into hers, stepping closer. She let out a long breath, and then nodded. Closing her eyes, she imagined roots going into the ground, holding her body steady as her consciousness flew across the water to link with Salu.

His energy flared as their hands met, and his face shone in a smile. *Betalia.*

Beth's energy expanded and Jonan took her other hand.

'No!' Amelia croaked, and then let out a sob. *'You can't do this again. I'm asking for help. I'm desperate. Can't you see? I can't do this anymore.'*

Sister. Lunea floated out over the water, and took Amelia's hands in her own. Amelia was shivering and Lunea cast a circle of warmth around her. *You are desperate because you are resisting. Let go and accept your destiny.*

'And my destiny is what? Prison?' Amelia ended on a screech. *'Is that really the best you can offer me?'*

You chose this for yourself. Lunea let go of Amelia's hands. *That was always your prerogative. It's time to live by those choices. You killed Doriel. You will not see her again.*

'Don't be ridiculous. We know death isn't the end. If she's not here, she's with you. We will be reunited after death. I want to see her. Bring her to me now.'

Salu drifted over the water and put a hand out to cup her

cheek. *You cannot see Doriel. There is no spiritual get-out clause. You live by the rules of your own world.*

'*No.*' Amelia's voice was high-pitched. '*No, no, no, no, no!*' She dropped to her knees in the water, which was up to her chin now. She keened, swaying backwards and forwards.

Salu started to hum, and the sound filled the air around them. Beth's energy lit up from the vibration and Jonan was glowing by her side. The sound resonated within her, and she realised she was also humming, until the hum became a chant and their voices split into a harmony she remembered without ever having heard it. Amelia began to calm until she was quiet, still swaying backwards and forwards, eyes closed, but breathing deeply and evenly.

When she opened her eyes, she looked at Salu, and then at Beth. Finally she stood up, almost falling over in the process, and turned to face Jonan. She swallowed. 'I have truly loved you.' She held his gaze for a moment and then looked down at the water. 'You have always been the light I moved towards.' Shaking her head, she turned and began to wade through the water away from them, and away from DC Ainsworth.

Beth saw DC Ainsworth begin to walk around the lake, and then he started to run.

As Amelia got close to the edge of the lake she pulled up short and stopped. A growl shivered through the air, reverberating through Beth's energy and into her bones. The leopard shimmered in and out of existence on the edge of the lake, teeth bared in a snarl.

Amelia shook her head again, and then turned and ran further around the long, arcing edge of the lake away from them. Beth snapped back into her body. She blinked, reaching out and holding the wooden back of a bench in order to ground, and then she followed, as did DC Ainsworth and Jonan. As Amelia neared the edge, a growl shivered across the water.

She turned and ran again. This time when she approached the edge, the growl was louder. The leopard was solid now.

'Damn, was that ...' DC Ainsworth tailed off as the cat disappeared.

Amelia doubled over, clapped her hands over her ears and screamed. She dropped back to her knees in the freezing water, her hands over her face as she convulsed with sobs.

Salu put a hand on her shoulder.

Beth allowed her consciousness to join them. Amelia's energy was fractured and muddy. Beth could see the cords that powered her continually disconnecting as people used the energy work to separate.

'I'm so tired,' Amelia choked out, sitting back on her heels.

'It's okay to be tired.' Beth put her hand on her other shoulder. 'We all get tired, and you've had such a strange time. You have to learn to manage without drawing energy from other people and I'm sure that will be tough for a while. But it will make things better in the long term. And one day, Amelia, we will all be together again, just like you said. We promised. Do you remember?'

Amelia's eyes were clouded as she frowned at Beth. Then they cleared and Beth could see the soul she had loved. Amelia nodded, and the moment passed. She was once again the woman who had killed Doriel.

Salu reached for Beth's hand. Light flowed over them both and Beth found herself in the throne room, her brother beside her.

You know what you need to do, he said.

Beth frowned. *'Should I remember?'*

Light came from Salu's hands and engulfed her. She expanded into it and then the memories came flooding back. Memories of Amelia, memories of everything they had said before they incarnated.

'You will have to take my powers, sister.' Amelia's voice was softer than Beth was used to. 'I have seen what happens. You have to stand against me with everything you have. Can you do that?'

'I don't know,' the other Beth, Betalia, took Amelia's hands in her own. 'I don't want to harm you.'

'It's the only way.'

Amelia smiled, but she was already fading.

Beth opened her eyes.

Can she rely on you? Salu raised one eyebrow.

Beth wanted to say no. As she looked at the woman in front of her, she saw the sister she had loved before this incarnation, and she didn't want to send her to prison at all, let alone with a fraction of the strength she was used to. *'I have no idea how to do what she asked.'*

Can I rely on you? Amelia's words reverberated through her mind, and certainty settled deep into her gut. She nodded.

Beth stretched out her arms and called down the light. Salu joined her, and then Lunea and Jonan. She reached out further. Abi, Layla, Roland and even Tabitha were there, feeding into the energy. A growl reverberated through the light, and she shivered. A forest of grey cords still stretched out from Amelia into the energy around her. They were dropping continuously, but more kept attaching. Beth could see the flow to Amelia through the cords, and could see the dark, sludgy energy she syphoned off and sent to others.

Beth expanded until she existed across dimensions. She could feel so many versions of herself and Amelia, connected in lifetime after lifetime. Finally she found the versions of them that still stood in the throne room. The Amelia there held her gaze and then nodded as she fed into the energy. Beth went even higher until her edges faded and the distance between herself and the others receded. In the centre of everything was the most profound sense of oneness she had ever experienced.

Surrounding Amelia's energy with light, Beth sent out her intention. *Please remove Amelia's powers ... for now.*

There was a flash, and then the grey cords dropped away, leaving Amelia separate and alone. She keened as her light dimmed and the sadness and fear she had been channelling to others congealed around her in a thick bubble.

Beth felt Amelia's scream as it shivered through the energy. It pulled her out of the oneness and straight back to earth. Amelia was still in the water, soaked and bedraggled, curled in on herself, sobbing.

DC Ainsworth stood on the side of the lake, handcuffs ready. A photographer stood on the other side, snapping photo after photo.

It's time to go, Amelia, Salu's voice was gentle. *It's time to experience the other side of your creation, to experience it as other people do. Your powers are gone.*

'I hate you,' she said from between gritted teeth. 'You told me we were a team, but you have ostracised me and pushed me further and further away. Now you have taken everything. I will never forgive you.'

'Amelia Faustus,' DC Ainsworth called out across the water. 'Please come out of the lake.'

'You can do it.' Beth surrounded Amelia with light.

'Sod off. And stop messing with my energy. Just because I can't block you doesn't mean you should stick your oar in where you're not wanted.'

DC Ainsworth stepped into the lake and waded out, huffing as he waved the ducks away. 'Amelia Faustus, I am arresting you for the murder of Doriel McLaney.' He reached down and clipped the handcuffs around one wrist, before helping her to her feet, turning her around and securing her hands behind her back. 'You do not have to say anything, but it may harm your defence if you do not mention when questioned something that you later rely on in court. Anything you do say may be given in evidence.'

Amelia tilted her chin into the air, but she said nothing. She shivered violently as he led her across the lake. They both paused as a soft growl rippled over the water, and then they stepped onto dry land. The second police officer wrapped her in a silver emergency blanket, and then they walked her back towards the carpark.

Beth allowed herself to ground into her body, taking time to breathe deeply and feel her feet against the hard concrete of the path. She slid her hand into Jonan's. 'Can that really be it?'

'I'm not sure it's ever really it with Amelia, but I don't think she can extricate herself from this one.'

There was a growl, and a small leopard flickered next to Beth. On the other side, a large white tiger was visible for a moment next to Jonan.

Beth smiled. 'Thank you, both of you.'

The cats disappeared as they neared the abbey at the top of the hill. Layla and Roland were sitting on a bench, Abi curled in their laps. Tabitha appeared to be asleep bolt upright.

'Is it done?' Roland slid out from under Abi and stood up as they approached.

Jonan sighed. 'She's been arrested. It's down to the police now.'

Abi sat up, stretched and yawned. 'I heard the police officer talking. He said there's no way she'll get out of it this time.'

'You were spying on the police?' Layla raised her eyebrows and Abi giggled.

Tabitha opened her eyes and smiled. 'You did so well, Abi. You showed a lot of control.'

'I said you could trust me.' Abi grinned and snuggled into Layla's side.

'We couldn't have done it without you.' Beth opened her arms and Abi jumped up and ran into them. Beth held her tight, feeling the little girl breathe in and out. She remembered the moment she saw Abi lying on the concrete, the teachers and pupils at the school staring at her from a distance. And now she thought about this incredible girl who could astral travel as a leopard, and how she had faced off with Amelia by the lake. 'No wonder Doriel thought so highly of you. Wherever she is, she will be very proud of you right now, pumpkin.'

Abi pulled back. 'Wherever she is?' She tilted her head. 'Don't you know?'

'I'm afraid not, sweetie.' Beth took her hands. 'But I know it will be somewhere good.'

'Oh, it is. She told me.' Abi grinned. 'We talk a lot. She's helping me control my leopard. She was with me the whole time by the lake.'

Tabitha gaped. 'That's how you've come on so quickly?'

'I always said Doriel was an excellent lady.' Abi grinned. 'She'll be with me forever. She told me.'

Jonan knelt in front of Abi and took her hand. 'Thank you. I'm so glad Doriel is with you. Maybe one day she'll be with me too.' A tear slid down his cheek.

'She already is!' Abi grinned. 'She says you'll notice her as soon as you can get over being so cross with Amelia.'

Jonan laughed, and then let out a sob. He pulled Abi into a big hug. 'You really are a gift, kitten.'

A growl sent the pigeons fluttering away, and Jonan let go of Abi, lurching back.

She giggled, her eyes sparkling. 'I made you jump.'

'You certainly did.' Jonan high-fived her.

Beth watched them, wonder coursing through her as she saw the timid little girl glowing with fierce joy.

She looked at Jonan, with this big, new family he had pulled around himself. At Roland, who was so relaxed, his hand loosely held in Layla's. At Miranda, chatting comfortably with Roland after so many years of sterile separation. They had all come so far and, in that moment, she could feel her own part in this strange and crazy destiny. They had been locked into straight paths that felt inevitable, but time had forced them to adapt, to change and try out new directions, had brought them to where they needed to be. Even Amelia had her part to play in that.

The Judgement card is about Ascension. Beth heard Doriel's voice clearly in her mind. She looked around, but there was no sign of anyone otherworldly. *It was about my Ascension, moving to the next level, but about yours too. It's time for you to ascend beyond this conflict, and build something new for you, for Jonan, for Layla and Roland, and for Abi. You all deserve this.*

What about Miranda? Beth sent out the thought.

Miranda has her own journey. She knows the way. You and Jonan can focus on yourselves now. You deserve to be happy. I am so proud of you both.

Doriel's voice faded into silence, but her light surrounded them. Abi beamed at Beth, and she couldn't help feeling the girl had heard Doriel's words too.

Jonan stood up and she looped her arm around his waist. 'Doriel was always so proud of you,' she whispered to him. 'You made her happy. You were everything to her.'

'Thank you.' He gave her a squeeze. 'And she knew I'd be alright now I've got you. I think she's been preparing us for this for a long time.'

Beth nodded. 'Did you hear her, a moment ago?'

Jonan turned to face her, taking both her hands in his. 'I didn't. What did she say?'

'She said she wanted us to be happy. I can feel her around us all.'

Jonan beamed. 'Me too. I know she'll always be with us, one way or another.'

What was in their future? Beth wondered. They could choose their own path now, but she had been so caught up in this big destiny she hadn't even thought about what might come next.

EPILOGUE
MIRANDA

MIRANDA BARELY MOVED HER HEAD, BUT SHE TOOK IN THE chaos in the room all the same. The family members sitting at tables, waiting for their own prisoner to arrive. The guards stationed around the edge. Hugs as people were united with loved ones, and then awkward silences as they were divided by ugly, scratched tables.

Amelia slid into the seat opposite her. Miranda had expected her to be embarrassed. Angry maybe. Instead, she stuck her chin in the air and glared down her nose at Miranda.

'I wasn't expecting you. All this noisy, unwashed humanity? It's not really your scene is it, darling?' Amelia's lips quirked up at one corner.

Miranda held her gaze, and then she gave in and smiled. 'We all have to step outside our comfort zones.'

'Seriously, though.' Amelia leaned forwards, putting her elbows on the table and resting her chin on her palm. 'Why did you come?'

Miranda sighed. 'We incarnated together: you, me and

Doriel. Now Doriel has gone and we are the only ones left. We're not the keepers of the path anymore, Amelia. We have only our own journeys to worry about. And if we allow ours to drift further apart, I fear we will lose ourselves as well as each other. This life wasn't supposed to be easy. So here I am, out of my comfort zone, learning what I came to learn and hoping I can help you do the same.'

Amelia frowned at her. She leaned back and crossed her arms over her chest, holding Miranda's gaze for several minutes.

'Is it working?' Miranda raised one eyebrow. 'Can you read me?'

'No. Damn it.' Amelia rolled her eyes. 'They really did a number on me. Can you help me get my powers back.'

Miranda smiled. 'You just have to learn the lessons. As I am doing right here.'

Amelia sighed. 'So it's you and me again? Really? For good this time?'

Miranda gave a single nod. 'You and me. We will make Doriel proud.'

BETH

THE SHOP WAS BUZZING. ROLAND'S WORKSHOP HAD ATTRACTED a huge crowd and they were all browsing and queuing for crystals, oracle cards and sage. Beth still couldn't fathom the way Amelia's followers had adopted Roland when he spoke out about her manipulation. But in the year since she had been arrested, he had helped them build their own autonomy. He joked his goal was to make himself irrelevant but, even though he laughed when he said it, Beth knew he took it extremely seriously.

She left Layla to serve customers and went to join Abi at the coffee table where she was drawing pictures of leopards. 'I like that one.' Beth pointed to a picture of a leopard curled up on the sofa.

'Me too.' The little girl grinned. 'Mummy doesn't like it when I do that with dirty paws, but when I'm a leopard I don't care about things like that.'

Beth grinned. 'Quite right too. Have you seen Jonan?'

'I have.' She carried on drawing.

'Do you want to tell me where he went?'

'Nope.'

Beth raised her eyebrows. 'Please?'

Abi shook her head. 'I promised.'

Beth smiled. It was only a few weeks until the wedding and the surprises were building steadily.

The bells on the door jingled when Jonan came in a few moments later, followed by Laura and Steve. As always, an image of Doriel flitted through Beth's mind. She couldn't believe she'd been gone for a year. Somehow it still felt as though she'd never left.

Jonan kissed her on the cheek. 'Look who I found while I was out.'

Beth hugged Laura, and then Steve. He flushed and shuffled from one foot to the other. She smiled. It had taken her a while, but she'd forgiven him for his part in Doriel and Bill's kidnapping. He had spoken publicly about Amelia's abuse, and had helped a lot of people.

'Would you come on *Deep and Dark* again?' Laura accepted the cup of tea Jonan handed her. 'We've got a panel of Amelia's followers. I was hoping you'd speak to them about where they are a year on, and offer them any help they need. Would you be interested?'

'Of course.' Beth smiled. 'When do you want me?'

'Tomorrow?' I want to do a special edition to honour the anniversary of Doriel's death.'

'Tomorrow it is. And I have a workshop in the evening. Would you two come and talk to people at that? They always love to hear personal stories.'

The last customer went through the door and Beth turned the sign to closed. The sun was setting and the sky was painted in vivid shades of pink and gold. Beth went to the small under-counter fridge and pulled out a bottle of champagne. 'Let's drink to Doriel.' They all gathered around. As Beth handed out glasses, a shiver ran down her spine and she smiled. 'To you, Doriel,' she said, raising her glass. And to Potential.'

LETTER FROM THE AUTHOR

Dear Reader

Thank you for walking by my side.

I started writing The Starfolk Arcana in 2016 with personality cults on the rise. We all know what's happened since then, and I'm sure we can all find Amelias in both the public sphere and our private lives. My hope is that we keep getting better at spotting them, so their power over us reduces.

If you've enjoyed Starfolk Rising and have a moment to put a short review on Amazon, you would make this author very happy. Reviews help a book get picked up by the Amazon algorithm, and they get it in front of potential readers too. So they make an enormous difference.

If you haven't met Tabitha before and would like to know her story, have a look at Wild Shadow. It has tigers, gorgeous musicians, a tiger keeper with a taste for danger and a deadly storm. And if you fancy a freebie, sign up to my mailing list at www.marthadunlop.com for a Starfolk prequel short story where you get to find out what really happened the night Amelia claims to have seen a Soul Snatcher.

I have lots more books in my head waiting to wing their way to you. So do find me on social media, join my mailing list or follow my Amazon page so you hear about new releases. This trilogy may be over, but you will see the characters again and there is a lot more magic on the way!

Lots of love, and happy reading

Martha xxx

ACKNOWLEDGMENTS

Writing is a solitary process and that makes me appreciate the people who have my back and help me get my books out into the world even more.

Thank you to Kathryn Cottam, my structural editor, first reader and all round sounding board and cheer leader. I don't know what I would do without you. Thank you to Eleanor Leese, my fabulous copy editor for your boundless knowledge and encouragement and, of course, the puppy pictures. And thank you to Ravven who designed all the gorgeous covers in this series and was a joy to work with every time.

Thank you to my early readers, and to the bloggers and reviewers. Getting a book noticed is a tough gig and you make it so much easier.

Thank you to everyone who reads my books, and those of you who tell me you've loved them. You keep me writing when it all gets thorny. Every time you tell me you couldn't put my book down, you make my dream come true.

Last but never least, thank you to my family and friends. Thank you for the support, inspiration, time out, dog walks, and for generally having my back. I love you all.

ABOUT THE AUTHOR

Author of The Starfolk Trilogy and Wild Shadow, Martha is a dreamer and a lover of stories. She likes nothing better than spending her days getting to know the characters in her head.

She is a tarot card reader and reiki master, and loves to chat reading, writing and all things mystical on social media, as well as posting pictures of her fellow pack-member, Bertie the Cavalier.

Martha is a fiddle player who fell in love with traditional music, particularly Irish, and is also teaching herself to play the Irish Bouzouki. She played her way through her English degree at York and remembers that time as much for the music as the books.

You can keep up with Martha's news, book releases and extra content at marthadunlop.com. Picture by Gene Genie Photography, www.genegenie.photography

facebook.com/MarthaDunlopStories
instagram.com/marthadunlop
tiktok.com/@marthadunlopwrites

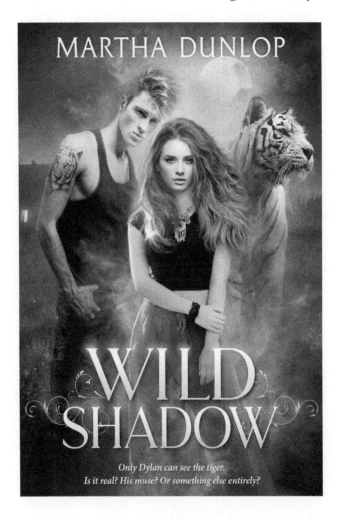

They've spent lifetimes being pulled apart.
This time, they're ready to fight.

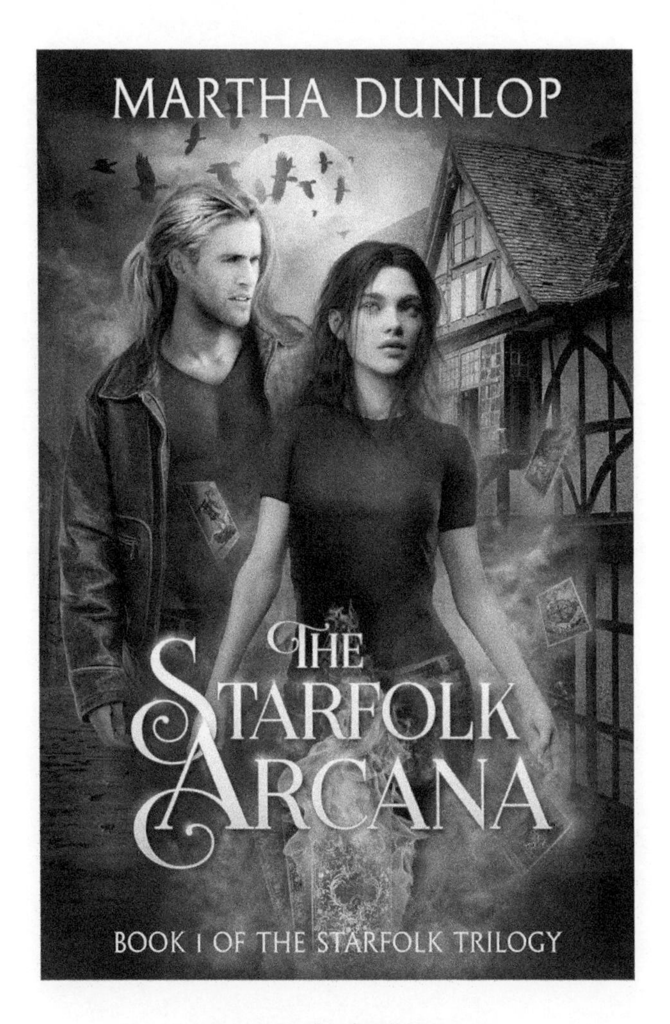

www.marthadunlop.com

A woman destined to change the world.
A timeless adversary determined to stop her.
Only one will win.

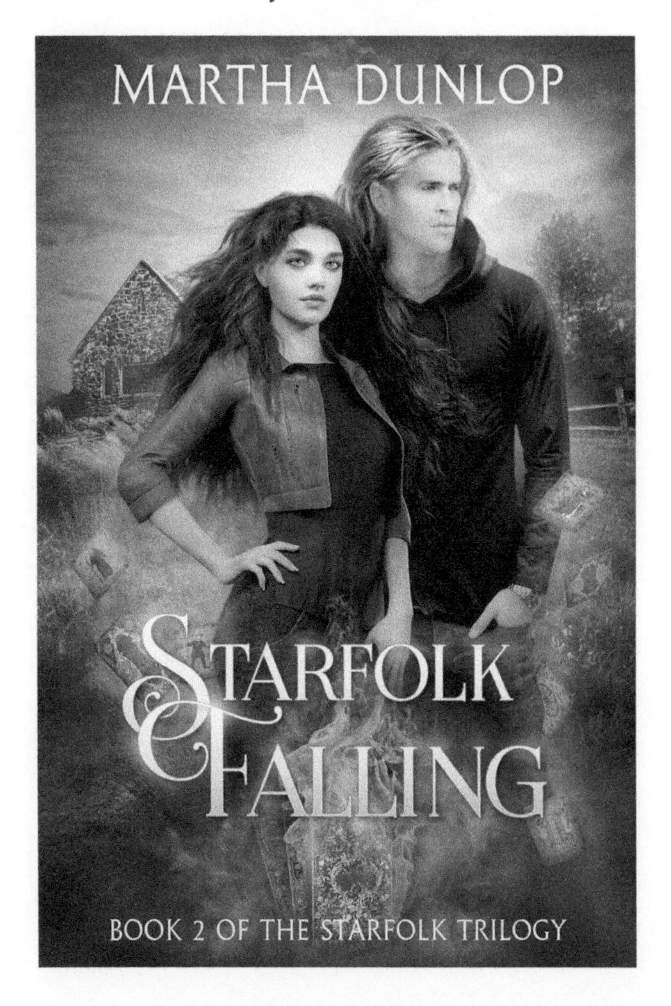

www.marthadunlop.com

Milton Keynes UK
Ingram Content Group UK Ltd.
UKHW010917080324
439029UK00004B/182